W9-CCB-417

PENGUIN CRIME FICTION
NATURAL ENEMY

Jane Langton is the author of seven other Homer Kelly mysteries: *Murder at the Gardner, Good and Dead, Emily Dickinson is Dead, Memorial Hall Murder, Dark Nantucket Noon, The Transcendental Murder,* and *The Dante Game.* She lives with her husband in Lincoln, Massachusetts.

Natural Enemy

Jane Langton

Illustrations by the Author

PENGUIN BOOKS

For Andy

PENGUIN BOOKS
Published by the Penguin Group
Viking Penguin, a division of Penguin Books USA Inc.,
375 Hudson Street, New York, New York 10014, U.S.A.
Penguin Books Ltd, 27 Wrights Lane, London W8 5TZ, England
Penguin Books Australia Ltd, Ringwood, Victoria, Australia
Penguin Books Canada Ltd, 10 Alcorn Avenue, Suite 300,
Toronto, Ontario, Canada M4V 3B2
Penguin Books (N.Z.) Ltd, 182–190 Wairau Road,
Auckland 10, New Zealand

Penguin Books Ltd, Registered Offices:
Harmondsworth, Middlesex, England

First published in the United States of America by
Ticknor & Fields 1982
Published in Penguin Books 1987

3 5 7 9 10 8 6 4

LIBRARY OF CONGRESS CATALOGING IN PUBLICATION DATA
Langton, Jane
Natural enemy.
(Penguin crime fiction)
I. Title.
[PS3562.A515N37 1987] 813'.54 86-17064
ISBN 0 14 01.3393 3

Printed in the United States of America
Set in Electra

Happily there are some to whom nothing in the majestic riddle of the universe is little. They know of what humble materials the bread of thought is kneaded...

Jean Henri Fabre

Natural Enemy

One

THINGS WERE GOING ON AT DIFFERENT LEVELS ON THAT DAY in June.

From ninety-three million miles away, sunshine flooded the uptilted northern hemisphere of the earth. Twenty-four thousand miles over the state of Maryland, some of the sun's light was intercepted by the solar collectors of the communications satellite for the eastern half of the United States, and beamed down to the tracking station at Logan Airport in Boston. This morning the satellite was transmitting an image of Labrador and Greenland, rounding against the dark sky, and a hazy view of a continental landmass nearly obscured by swiftly rushing clouds.

And at four hundred feet above the rocky soil of Massachusetts, the first gusts of wind were buffeting a small helicopter as it droned away from Hanscom Air Force Base and rattled along the border between the suburban towns of Lincoln and Concord.

Lincoln selectman William Warren was surveying his territory. His purpose was prudent and businesslike, but his head was spinning. He had lived in the town nearly all the sixty-five years of his life, but he had never seen it from the air before. Neighborhoods he had known since childhood as linear stretches of road were spreading before him in broad sweeps of landscape.

"Wow," shouted William, straining forward in his seatbelt, "it feels like God up here."

"What's that?" said the pilot.

"You know, looking down at everything from above. Hey, look, you can see everybody on the beach at Walden Pond. Look at the whitecaps on the water. Boy, the wind is really picking up out there." Then William clutched the pilot's arm and pointed at the road streaming below them, dappled in sun and shadow. "You see that kid down there, on the bicycle on Route 126? You know who that is?" Again William was exhilarated by the sense that he was observing the whole world at once, guiding fatalities, prophesying destinies. "That's a young friend of mine, John Hand. I was just talking to him on the phone, half an hour ago."

"What's that you say? Can't hear."

"I said, that kid on the bike, I was just talking to him. Told him he could get a summer job with some friends of mine. See there? He's on his way right now. Hoooeee! What was that?"

The helicopter was lurching and yawing sideways. "Pretty strong wind," said the pilot.

"What did you say?"

"Gusty! If the wind gets any stronger, we better turn back."

"Oh, no, don't do that. This is so terrific. Wow, look at Pine Hill. Looks almost flat from up here. And, my God, look at the size of Buddy Whipple's slate roof! Greenhouse! Tennis court! Say, I didn't realize what a big place he has there. Well, you know, it was an old hunting estate. Rich people named Higginson built it back around the turn of the century. Fox hunting. Horses. You know. Say, maybe I should raise Buddy's tax assessment. That place of his is really colossal. Hey, will you look at that! See those people unloading a lot of stuff from their car?"

"Listen, mister, stop jerking my arm, okay?"

"Oh, sorry. But I mean, it's so amazing. You get this Olympian view of everything from up here. That's a new family moving into Buddy's house. He's renting the place out. Says he can't afford to live there anymore since his father died."

"What's that? I'm kind of deaf in my right ear."

"OH, SORRY. Hey, look at that, you can see Buddy's whole driveway, going down the hill under the trees there, see? And there's the Heron place, that old house at the bottom of the drive. Friends of mine, the Herons. Say, look at that roof of theirs, needs a new roof! Maybe I should lower their property assessment. Hey, there's Edward's girls right there on the lawn. Wish they'd look up. HEY, THERE, VIRGINIA! BARBARA! Nope, they're working at something, not going to look up. You know what? They don't even know young John is coming around the corner on his bike to help them out for the summer. See what I mean? From up here I know their future better than they do themselves. Look, there's the orchard. See those old apple trees? Wow, I haven't been in there in forty years. Used to steal apples in there when I was a kid. All overgrown, just a wilderness now. Hey, hey, did you see that? Cock pheasant! We flushed a cock pheasant!"

"How's that again?"

"Never mind. Bird flew up just now."

The frightened pheasant skimming above the bristling tops of the trees was only thirty feet above the tangled undergrowth of the old apple orchard. Stretching its ringed neck, spreading its wings wide, the pheasant landed awkwardly fifty feet away from the commotion in the bushes and scuttled into the dense cover of low vegetation, still squawking in alarm at the wild tumult in the jungle of honeysuckle and firecherry, the muffled shout, the furious buzzing of angry yellow jackets.

Under the high canopy of leaves Buddy Whipple stood a good six feet four inches above the ground. Staring upward through the high branches, he ignored the pheasant. He was worried about the helicopter. Could it see him? Probably not. The green umbrella of the apple tree was thick over his head, and entangled with wild grape vines. Cautiously Buddy moved farther back into its protective shade. What if the helicopter came back to take a second look? No, the heavy clattering noise was dimmer. Now it was only a faraway vibration in the air. Buddy's heart was beating wildly. Feverish with excitement, he dropped his gaze to the man who lay heaving below him in the trampled undergrowth.

It was a ghastly thing to see. Edward Heron was lying face-up, thrashing from side to side, fighting for air. His head was thrown back, his eyes were bulging. The blue swelling of the wound on his forehead was hardly distinguishable from the cyanotic blue of his face and throat. The sound of his agonized struggle to exhale was long-drawn-out and grating, like dry pebbles rattling over stone. A few yellow jackets had followed the mad scrambling plunge through the overgrown orchard and fastened themselves to Edward's eyelids, his lips, his throat.

Warily Buddy circled the dying man, fascinated in spite of himself. He had never seen an asthmatic attack before. It was Edward's own fault, of course, for getting so mad. Asthmatic people should know better than to let themselves get mad. Everybody knew it was their own emotions that brought on the worst attacks. So it wasn't Buddy's fault. The goddamn man had come along too soon, just a quarter of an hour too soon! A few minutes later and the job would have been done. Edward wouldn't have noticed a damn thing. Buddy's tremendous undertaking would have been completed, and he would have been far away by now. His crowbar, his wheelbarrow, his tools — they would have been gone too. But, no, Edward had to come blundering along, surprising him, grabbing him by the shoulder all of a sudden, asking him what the hell was going on. No wonder Buddy had lost control of himself. No wonder he had picked up that rock. And then, of course, all hell had broken loose. Those yellow jackets, God —

The noise of the chopper had faded away altogether. Edward Heron's breathing was only a hoarse rasping whisper, nearly inaudible, almost nonexistent. How long would it take him to die?

6

Patiently Buddy folded his arms, determined to wait it out. Then to his surprise he found himself grinning. A tense high giggle was welling up in his throat. Lucky again! He'd been lucky again! Well, to do himself justice, he shouldn't say lucky exactly. It wasn't just luck. It was his own prompt action, his own quick response to a crisis, his own gift for knowing what to do that had made things work out so well. Then Buddy told himself again, as he had told himself so many times before, how strange it was, how really strange, that most people had no feeling for opportunity. Among all the people he knew, only Buddy himself seemed to have been born with a quick foresight that was like a sixth sense, an instantaneous grasp of what needed to be done, a willingness to work his head off to get what he wanted, an eagerness to knock on doors no one else had ever tried to open, to hammer at them until the rusted locks and hinges busted off at last. It was too bad other people were so simpleminded and slow. But Buddy was proud and glad. He felt lucky, really lucky, to have been born the kind of person that he was.

It was all over. Edward Heron had stopped struggling. There was no motion in the broad shoulders, no lifting and falling of the denim jacket, no terrible wheezing struggle for breath.

Buddy rolled the body over with his foot and saw the empty ground beneath it. Nothing was growing on that strip of dirt. It was part of the line of bare soil running along the edge of the tangled orchard. He couldn't leave the body there. Bending down, Buddy picked it up easily and slung it over his shoulder. A yellow jacket stung him on the back of the neck, but Buddy hardly felt it. Shoving his way through the head-high thicket, he dropped his burden for a moment on the stone wall, leaped over the wall in one bound, picked up the body again and carried it to the farthest apple tree in the jungle of honeysuckle and firecherry. There he let it fall. Then, lowering himself to the ground, Buddy leaned his back against the tree and closed his eyes, waiting for his excited heart to quiet down. He was thinking hard.

*

Beyond the orchard a wilderness of blackberry canes and low briers filled an acre that had once been part of a tilled field. Above the wilderness the sloping lawn rose to the house. East of the house stretched a long two-story shed.

On the frame of one of the shed doors a spider was sleeping.

Once upon a time the shed had sheltered a summer kitchen, three buggies, a hired man, and many cords of wood. Now it enclosed a laundry, a workshop, a toolroom, and a loft for the storage of miscellaneous objects. As the helicopter buzzed over

Pine Hill its whirling blades sent an expanding globe of turbulence through the air, setting up strong vibrations in the framework of the shed. Storm windows clicked against each other in their deep leaning rows in the loft, clay pots shifted in their brittle stacks, saws and hammers rattled against the pegboard in the workshop, the dryer knocked against the washing machine in the laundry, and all through the shed the sheathing boards trembled, loosening by another fraction of an inch the old square nails that held them together.

And in a crack between the shivering lintel and the frame of the workshop door, the dormant spider was shaken awake. Crawling slowly out of the crevice where she had spent the winter, she paused in the sunlight, her eight dim eyes nearly blinded by the glare, then dropped on a silken line into the shadow behind the door. Halfway to the sill she stopped paying out thread from her spinnerets and rested, hanging upside down.

Two

THE WIND SWEEPING ACROSS WALDEN POND KNOCKED AGAINST
the light frame of John Hand's ten-speed bike as he leaned over
the handlebars and raced along Route 126 in the direction of
Edward Heron's house. Of course it wouldn't be Edward Heron
who would be hiring him, if all went well. It would be Mr.
Heron's two daughters, Barbara and Virginia. Barbara was a
nurse — she had been in college with John's Aunt Mary — and
Virginia was much younger. John had met Virginia. A long time
ago there had been that spelling competition, way back in grammar school. Well, naturally it was only John who had been in
grammar school. Virginia must have been in high school by that
time. There had been a picture of the winners in the *Concord
Journal*, Virginia long and lank in a shapeless dress; John, the
runner-up, just a fragile-looking little kid. Virginia hadn't seemed
excited by her victory, just patient and kind. Looking back now
from the point of view of an older person — almost a college
freshman — John thought he knew how she had felt. You had
to do things like that sometimes — you had to enter spelling
competitions and science fairs and try out for the school play —
but you didn't have to care about it. Virginia Heron would have
been just as glad if she had lost and John had won.

Hugging the side of the road, leaning into the sharp curve

11

beyond the last Walden Pond parking lot, John blamed himself for waiting this long to get a summer job. After all, he had promised his parents he would earn money this summer. They had gone away, halfway around the world, and left him to help his Aunt Mary and Uncle Homer take care of his little brother Benny, and of course they had just assumed he'd get a job with the Lincoln Public Works Department to help pay the huge college fees that were coming up next fall. Here he was, all accepted at the University of New Hampshire, the college of his choice — what if he couldn't afford to go there after all? Not many other places had a whole big department in entomology. Usually there was just a course or two in the catalogue. And that big famous spider specialist was there too, Dr. Underhill. So John couldn't just give it up and go to someplace cheaper, like Middlesex Community College.

The sandy verges of the sharp S-curve were slippery and dangerous under John's speeding wheels. He shifted gears and slowed down, wondering why the Public Works Department hadn't swept up the sand earlier in the spring. A year ago last April John had stirred up the sand on this very road himself, and brushed it to one side in the big town sweeper. He had enjoyed it, churning slowly along the narrow streets of Lincoln in the big machine during his spring vacation. And then all summer he had worked on the road crew, putting in a bicycle path on the north side of town. It had been good hard outdoor work. John's pale shoulders and narrow rib cage had turned a raw and fiery red, and his thin arms had gained muscle.

So this morning it had been a blow to be told that the Lincoln road crew had no use for him this summer. "I'm sorry, John," Mr. Warren had said on the phone, "but this recession has hit the town as hard as it's hit everybody else. Town Meeting wouldn't even vote us a new cruiser to replace the old Pontiac. Remember the old Pontiac? Now, listen here, John, I've got an idea."

And then Mr. Warren had told him about the job notice posted at the drugstore. "You know the Herons there on Route 126? Where those big brick gateposts are?"

"You mean those rich people who live near Walden Pond?"

"That's right. Well, I don't know about rich. They had to sell that big house to the Whipples, a long time ago. They're living in the farmhouse now, at the bottom of the hill. I guess Edward isn't much of a businessman. Had to give up breeding queer kinds of plants in that greenhouse up there, and sell out. Anyway, Barbara and Virginia want somebody to help around the place. Free board and room thrown in. I don't know how much they'll pay. You could see if the job's still open."

So then John had changed his shirt and combed his hair and started right out for the Herons' house, feverish with curiosity, eager to see the place and be hired by the girl who could spell *iridescent*.

Now there was a lightness of anxiety in his chest as he swooped between the brick gateposts and started up the hill. The driveway had been tarred fifty years back, when the big house was still a fancy hunting lodge. But now only a few chunks of asphalt stood high among the gulleys and trenches and wallowing tire tracks. At the fork in the driveway John paused for a second, then turned to the right in the direction of the farmhouse. The house was shabby, but it had a nice shape, decided John, and it fitted into the gently sloping hillside. He remembered something his father had said once — that the first settlers always got the best sites. His father had been talking about their own house in Concord on the level meadows beside the Assabet River. But this eighteenth-century house was like that too. To the north it was protected by the rise of Pine Hill, and to the south it faced a broad sunny slope.

Dismounting, John trundled his bike through an opening in the hedge and across a round lawn surrounded by flowerbeds. Leaning the bike against a tall arching yew, he walked up a set of shallow stone steps into a small courtyard. His eyes took in everything at once — the big window, the peeling clapboards, the seedling tomatoes sprawled on a tray on the low stone wall. Those tomatoes should have been planted out by this time, thought John gratefully. These people really need me. I can take care of things like that.

There was no doorbell, only a brass knocker like an ear of corn. John rapped it loudly, and waited, feeling a flush rise around his ears.

No one came to the door.

He knocked again.

Still no answer. Slowly the fascinating structure so full of exciting life became a cavernous house of hollow rooms, empty and unoccupied.

Disappointed, John turned away. Instantly he saw Barbara and Virginia Heron at the bottom of the front yard.

Three

THEY WERE KNEELING WITH THEIR BACKS TO HIM AT THE LOWER edge of the lawn, absorbed in something. John could see a number of things beside them on the ground. Swiftly he itemized them in his mind: the pile of lopped branches, the old bedspread heaped with sandy dirt and rocks, the basket of gardening tools, the big power lawnmower.

John was pleased to see the lawnmower and the acres of uncut grass. That was something else he could do for them. In the last ten years John had cut about a thousand square miles of lawn. He ran eagerly down the hill, buffeted by the warm wind, then stopped short, afraid of startling the two women, they seemed so completely engrossed in what they were doing.

"Here's one," murmured the dark-haired woman who must be Barbara. "Let me have those long-handled clippers."

John cleared his throat, stepped forward, and picked up the clippers. The two women looked up at him in surprise.

"I've come about the job," said John, holding out the clippers, handle end first. "My name's John Hand."

The woman in the absurd squashed hat smiled at him — Virginia! The other one — Barbara — said a crisp "Thank you," and bent once again to the task. "There," she said, "that does it, I think."

Now John could see what they were up to. They had cut off all the branches of a honeysuckle bush and were groping underneath the bristling stump, cutting the roots one by one. They were fighting back against the weedy wilderness of honeysuckle that was tossing its wiry branches in the wind just beyond the edge of the lawn.

They stood up. At once John was abashed by their height, by their slightness in their loose shirts and blue jeans, by the length of the dirty hands taking a firm hold on the stump. He reached down too with his clean hands, and together they jerked at the stubborn spiny mass. It wouldn't budge.

"There must be a tap root or something," said John. Dropping to his knees, he felt around in the sandy dirt, aware of their keen eyes on his back. "Yes, here it is." He pawed for the clippers, and felt them being put into his hand. Reaching under the stump, he wrestled with the thick root, cut halfway through it, grasped it again in the metal jaws, braced himself with one outflung leg, heaved hard with both arms on the handles, and snapped through the last inch. "There," he said, getting up again, breathing hard. "It ought to come now."

16

Again the three of them laid hands on the honeysuckle stump. But before they could pull at it together, they were interrupted.

"Here, you people. Just let go and let the old master give it the heave-ho."

The task was taken away from them. They were being brushed aside. Someone was grasping the stump with big sunburned hands, tussling it left and right, jerking it from its socket with a shout, brandishing the great bristling chunk of chopped stubs and sandy roots over his head, then hurling it high into the air and far away into the honeysuckle jungle.

John followed its crazy arc with his eyes, hardly believing what he saw. Then he stumbled out of the way as the man with the brown beard snatched up the clippers and pushed past him to begin jabbing at another sprawling bush. Plucking out a snaky branch, reaching for another, he shouted cheerfully over his shoulder, "I've come for that job of yours. Why didn't you tell your own next-door neighbor you needed help? What are friends for, anyway? Here's old Buddy Whipple, at your service. And a room in your house is just what the doctor ordered. Did I tell you I'm renting my place to somebody else? People just moved in. So I haven't got any place to stay myself. Promised them I'd get out right away. So if it's okay with you kids, I'll just move in this afternoon, right?" Whisk, whisk. Wiry branches flew out of the honeysuckle bush and flopped on the ground. The entire bush was decapitated. Buddy turned around, grinning. "How about it?"

John's heart sank. He had heard of Buddy Whipple. Buddy Whipple was the owner of the big old hunting lodge at the top of the hill. An old friend of the family. Well, so much for John's chance at a job around here.

But Barbara Heron was glancing at him shrewdly. She turned to Buddy. "I'm sorry," she said, "you're too late. The job's gone. We've hired young John here."

"John?" For the first time Buddy Whipple looked at John. Then he laughed, throwing back his head. "Listen here, Barbara, you don't need to hire anybody. I'll work for you girls for nothing in my spare time. Pay for my room and board too. Glad to do it.

So you'll be ahead of the game. What do you say, Virginia?"

Virginia turned away and began picking up the stones they had clawed out from the roots of the honeysuckle. "Well, I really think we're committed already," she said, dropping the stones back in the hole.

"Oh, come on, Virginia, John's just a kid. John won't mind." Buddy grinned and winked at John. "There's lots of jobs in town for John. I'll speak to William Warren at the town hall. William will find him something."

But Barbara was firm. "A promise is a promise."

Ducking his head to hide his grin, John helped Virginia pick up the corners of the old bedspread and dump the dirt back where it had come from. But Buddy wasn't giving up.

"Listen here, you kids, let me talk to your father. Where's Edward? I'll just have a word with Edward."

Barbara picked up her basket of tools and said nothing. Virginia seemed not to have heard. Dreamily she flapped the bedspread in the stiff breeze. Idly a startled crow tipped off a branch of an oak tree and eased himself, cawing, into the air.

There was an uncomfortable pause.

"Well, come on," insisted Buddy, "where is he? Is he up at the house? He must be around here someplace."

Relenting, Barbara pointed at the trees that mounded high above the surrounding jungle of honeysuckle and firethorn and blackberry bramble. "Well, go ahead, ask him. He's over there somewhere. The idiot. Over there in the old orchard, if you can find a way in. It's an awful tangle. Dad thinks he's working out lot lines for some big real-estate boondoggle or other. Of course he's got another think coming. He'll have to reckon with us first. With me, anyhow. I'd commit murder before I'd sell a single square foot of this place."

"Can I tell him that from you?" said Buddy. Turning quickly, he began bounding through the sea of honeysuckle, leaping over entanglements of catbrier and wild grapevine.

"Tell him anything you please," said Barbara angrily. Then she looked at John, and her face cleared. "You came along in the nick of time. Good for you."

Virginia was smiling at him too. "I know who you are. You were four or five years younger, but you could spell better than I could."

The sun came out between two towering masses of rushing cloud. "No, I couldn't," said John, feeling warm with pleasure. "You won, remember? But on the whole," — he cleared his throat, making a joke — "it was an iridescent occasion." Then he turned sober. "But maybe your father will want to hire Mr. —"

"No, no," said Barbara. "You'll be working for us. And you're the one we want." Putting down her basket, she dusted her hand on her pants and reached it to John. "I'm Barbara Heron. I went to college with your Aunt Mary Kelly."

"Well, say, Aunt Mary and Uncle Homer are living in my house right now, there on Barretts Mill Road in Concord. They're taking care of my kid brother Benny while my parents are away." John picked up the clippers and looked around eagerly, ready to rip out all the honeysuckle bushes in Middlesex County.

"Here he comes again." Virginia turned away from the sight of Buddy Whipple, and began folding her dusty bedspread. Leaning toward Barbara she whispered fiercely, "He can't stay, right? He doesn't get the guest room. Never, never. Don't you agree?"

"Of course," murmured Barbara.

Buddy had been running, lurching through the underbrush, panting in sobbing breaths. Now he stopped running, put one arm around Virginia and reached with the other for Barbara.

"I found your father," he said. "I'm terribly sorry, Virginia, Barbara. I'm very much afraid your father is dead."

Four

TRAILING AT THE REAR OF THE HURRYING PROCESSION, JOHN SAW the last of the yellow jackets. Beyond the upthrown arms of Virginia there was a glint of gold on striped abdomens as the last outriders lifted from the body of Edward Heron and hung motionless for a moment, trembling in the sunshine.

"Vespis diabolica," he murmured to himself. "Yellow jackets," John said aloud, speaking up in warning. "Watch out."

But they were gone. John watched as Barbara and Virginia threw themselves down beside the heavy man on the ground. Barbara was listening for his breath, feeling for his pulse. She was breathing into his mouth, pressing down with her hands on his chest, giving curt instructions to Virginia. Now Virginia was helping, blowing air into her father's lungs while Barbara continued to bend over the blue denim jacket, her shoulders rising and falling, her arms thrusting, her hands locked together. She was accusing herself bitterly. "Another attack! I never should have let him out of my sight, not when he was so mad at me." Barbara was looking around wildly. "His asthma medicine, where is it? He swore he'd carry it all the time. He promised me." Leaning forward and back, forward and back, Barbara looked up accusingly at Buddy. "What happened to it? Where in God's name is it?"

Buddy merely looked sad and shrugged his shoulders.

"Epinephrin," insisted Barbara. "There was a syringe of epinephrin and some antihistamine tablets. It was in a little red box, a little cardboard box. He promised me he'd carry it all the time. It was in his pocket this morning. *I saw it* in his pocket."

"Maybe he tried to use it," suggested John gently, "and he couldn't manage it, and then, you know, maybe he dropped it." Embarrassed, feeling like an intruder, John turned away and began looking in the trampled undergrowth for a red box, a glint of glass, a scattering of pills. He found nothing. He came back and watched as Barbara stopped pushing on her father's chest and leaned back despairingly. Touching her sister's shoulder, she shook her head.

They were giving up. Barbara helped Virginia to her feet. Virginia began to cry as Buddy stooped to pick up the body of her father. John made a gesture, offering to help, but then he stood back, astonished at the ease with which Buddy slung the dead weight over his shoulder like a light sack and carried it through the tangled scrub of brier and honeysuckle. Virginia and Barbara stumbled after him, emerging from the vine-clad canopy of the orchard into the sunshine and the blowing wind.

John brought up the rear. Even in his shocked confusion he couldn't help noticing how many honeysuckle bushes remained to be rooted out — there were hundreds of them, thousands! At the edge of the lawn he saw Barbara pause to pick up her basket of tools. Virginia was making a vague dab at the bedspread. The wind was tugging it out of her hands. John ran after it and plucked it out of a dogwood tree. Folding the bedspread clumsily, he hurried up the sloping lawn, trying not to look at the dark grey-purple face lolling over Buddy's shoulder.

Ahead of them loomed the house. Its grey paint darkened as the sun disappeared again behind the racing clouds, and John saw how badly the place needed paint. It looked long and gloomy and ramshackle. Walking up the steps into the small courtyard, he felt his head throbbing with excitement and uncertainty. He hung back. What should he do now? Should he murmur something polite and just slip away? Would it be all right to come back again later on? But when? Tomorrow? Did he have a job or not? Now that Buddy Whipple was helping them out in this family disaster, Virginia and Barbara might feel they owed the job to him. John stood hesitantly beside the low stone wall. Oh, God, how could he think of anything so selfish at a time like this?

"I'll get the door," said Barbara, moving quickly ahead of Buddy, holding the screen open so that he could shuffle indoors with his heavy burden, then following him in.

Well, decided John, he'd better just go home. Reluctantly he began to back away. But at the last minute Virginia turned and glanced at him. Her face was a mute appeal, and the motion of her arm in the air was so bereft that John was bound by it.

Mounting the stone step, he entered the house.

Five

THE SPIDER WAS MOLTING. BRACING HERSELF AGAINST THE FRAME of the shed door, she pulled the last of her eight legs from its dried sheath and began crawling upward. In the angle between the end of the horizontal lintel and the vertical board at the side of the door, there was a crack where the two pieces of wood had rotted apart. Here the spider made herself a resting place of crisscrossing threads. As Buddy Whipple entered the kitchen at the other end of the house and lowered the body of Edward Heron to a long bench against the wall, the spider hooked her claws into the threads and hung there suspended, her body expanding in the breezy warmth of the afternoon, every jointed leg freshly supple and newly coated with delicate hairs.

Buddy was taking charge. John stood back and watched him moving around the kitchen with calm confidence, pushing Barbara and Virginia gently into chairs, pouring out small glasses of whiskey, urging it on them, taking some himself. Buddy flourished the bottle at John, but John shook his head. He liked whiskey all right, but it went to his head, and he didn't want to look like a fool right now. He felt foolish enough, as it was, and envious of Buddy. Well, after all, Buddy belonged here. He was an old friend of the family. He'd be here to help them out all summer. They wouldn't need John. They would thank him and say they were sorry, but he could see how it was, couldn't he, now that things had changed? Instantly John chastised himself for being selfish again, for thinking only about what he wanted for himself. As Buddy hurried into the next room and began making phone calls, John went to the sink and washed a stack of dirty dishes, anxious to show he could be useful too.

And then his hopes rose. Buddy was leaving. He was running past the window, waving at them gallantly. A gusty wind was tossing the lilacs and moving in a soft bluster through the maple trees beside the driveway. The wind blew back Buddy's hair and beard as he ran down the steps. Was he gone for good? Looking possessively around the room, John felt his hankering for the job increase. The kitchen of the Herons' house was the best room he had ever seen. It was a large room with a broad window on the south side. Trays of leggy seedlings lay on a board in front of the window. John wanted to get his hands on them. He yearned to dig up a patch of ground and plant the seedlings. He wanted to move in and be part of this place, this kitchen. He had never seen a house he liked so much. Well, of course it was easy to like the places where rich people lived. Their houses were just naturally better than other people's houses.

Barbara was standing with her face against the window, muttering to herself, staring after Buddy as he ran up the hill.

"What did you say?" said Virginia, getting up to take her hand.

"I said, it was my fault."

"Now, Barbara, you mustn't let yourself be so —"

"I shouldn't have let father go down there by himself. He was in my care. I always felt he was in my care. But it isn't just that. It's more than that."

Barbara shook her head violently. Waves of chagrin flooded her as she remembered the rancor of the last encounter in the kitchen, and the fury with which she had shrilled at her father, refusing him the pond, the upper and lower fields, even the wooded borders of the driveway. And then, enraged at her, he had shouted back, "Well, for Christ's sake, how about the orchard? Is there something sacred about the orchard? You haven't even been in the orchard in twenty years."

"Well, go ahead," she had said. "Go ahead, damn you. I don't give a damn what you do." And he had rushed away to look at the orchard, to pace it off, to tell himself he was going to divide it up into expensive parcels of real estate and regain the family fortune. She had sworn at him. Her last words to her father had been, "Damn you." And now he was gone. Gone with all his crazy schemes, his nervous chatter, his eager, impossible solutions. Barbara closed her eyes, picturing him gasping, struggling for breath.

John was exploring the refrigerator. "There's some ham in here," he said softly. "I could slice up this piece of cheese. Ham and cheese sandwiches okay with you people?" Without waiting for an answer, John laid out slices of bread on the counter and began slathering them with mayonnaise. Behind his back he heard Virginia going to the door. Someone was outside on the doorstep. It was the doctor. Buddy was coming in too, right behind the doctor.

The doctor was angry. Without a word of greeting, he crossed the room to the bench where Edward Heron lay, drew back the coat Buddy had thrown over him, and grimaced painfully. "Where the hell was he?" he said bitterly, turning to Barbara. "Where was his medicine? I told him it was a case of life and death. That last attack nearly killed him. I told him. And I trusted you, Barbara. I mean, with a registered nurse in the house to keep after him, I thought he would be all right. Oh, what the hell, I'm sorry. It was his fault, not yours."

Barbara at last began to cry. She wept silently, her shoulders heaving, her arms loose at her sides, watching the doctor listen to her father's silent chest. The doctor stood up, threw the coat back over Edward Heron's face, crossed the room and embraced her awkwardly. "Ah, well," he said, patting Virginia's arm, "he was an old friend. Look here, I'll call the funeral people, if you like. Mr. Bailey is pretty straightforward. Would you like me to give him a ring?"

"I've already attended to it," said Buddy.

"Buddy's already attended to it," said Virginia dryly.

"Oh, well, then. Good. I'll be on my way."

"Don't forget your bag," said John quickly, picking up the small black suitcase.

"Bag?" said the doctor. "That's not my bag." Nodding his head gravely, he opened the door. Then he looked back over his shoulder. "See here, Barbara, I wish you'd come back to Emerson Hospital and work on my floor. Seriously. We're shorthanded up there. And even if we weren't, a good nurse like you would be a blessing. How about it? What did you stop working for anyway?"

Barbara shook her head at him, unable to speak. The doctor left.

Buddy picked up the bag. "It's mine," he said. "I went back home and picked up a pair of pajamas. I mean, I'm staying here tonight. I just think you people should have a man in the house. Okay, Virginia? Okay, Barbara? I'll just be here tonight in case you need me."

Barbara and Virginia looked at each other with red eyes and said nothing. John felt resentful. *A man in the house,* as if he, John, weren't man enough to take care of things. But he looked at the red splotches on Buddy's bare arms and spoke up amiably. "Boy, you really got zapped by those yellow jackets. What happened anyway? What kind of nest was it?"

Buddy held up his arms and looked at them too. "Oh, you know, it was one of those — you know the kind, a big paper one. It was right there in a tree. You know, sort of a big bush, I guess, with this nest in it, a great big round —" Buddy made a shape in the air.

"In a bush? But that's not —" John stopped, and held his tongue. Later on he would go down there and take a look for himself. Yellow jackets didn't build paper nests in bushes. They'd have one in a hole in the ground, or under a rock someplace. But Buddy wouldn't know that. It was only the white-faced hornets, *Vespula maculata,* that made those big paper nests in bushes and trees. If Buddy had seen a big one, it would have been left over from last year. And there wouldn't have been any live hornets in it to sting him. John opened his mouth to ask more questions, but Virginia was speaking to Buddy, her eyes dangerously bright.

"Listen, Buddy, you don't need to stay here. Really. After all, we've got somebody else. John's going to be here from now on."

"Oh, well, John." Buddy laughed. "Good old John. John's just a baby. What you girls need is an old greyhead like me. I'll just stay here tonight to make you girls feel safe and sound."

Once again John flinched. Old greyhead. Buddy wasn't old and grey any more than he, John, was too young to be any help. But John kept still. Virginia had stuck up for him, and that was enough. His chest filled with an excited push of breath. Of course it was sad, really sad and terrible, that Mr. Heron was dead, but there was something thrilling about it at the same time.

"I'll just take the guest room," said Buddy, waving his suitcase, then letting it sag on the floor. "I think I'll go upstairs right now, if you kids don't mind, and lie down for a minute. Okay with you?" For a moment the red face with its curly brown beard looked sallow under the sunburn. Buddy's shoulders were drooping with exhaustion.

Relenting, Barbara stood aside and said nothing as Buddy left the room. Virginia merely turned away and looked out the window.

"Look," she said, "the wind is rising."

John looked out, too, at the landscape spread wide beyond the window. The racing clouds had closed in, eliminating the patches of sunshine. Over the house there was a squealing rush of starlings. The branches of a big oak tree were lunging up and down. Then, with a crack, one dropped and fell slowly through the tree, striking the ground with an audible thump and bounding down the hill.

It was a queer kind of wind, thought John. Unnatural, the way it was picking up those little twigs and leaves and whirling them high in the air. Too much force exerted in an unexpected direction. Then John was reminded of something else. Closing his eyes he saw a thick red neck, swollen with yellow jacket stings, bent for an instant over the stump of the honeysuckle bush, and then the arms and shoulders rearing up as Buddy hurled the bristling stump far away — too far, impossibly far — into the thicket. John opened his eyes and shook his head. Nobody could throw that far, not even those guys with sixteen-pound iron balls at track meets. He must have been mistaken.

Six

THE WIND GREW STRONGER. IN CONCORD A MINIATURE TORNADO whistled across the summer fields, tearing shingles from the roof of John Hand's house on Barretts Mill Road, picking up a plastic trash bin from the backyard, scattering its contents all over the orchard behind the house.

Mary and Homer Kelly heard the roar of the wind, and the bump and clatter. They ran outside and began dashing after fluttering pieces of bread wrapper and wadded fragments of Kleenex, while five-year-old Benny, John's little brother, brought out another wastebasket just for fun and let its contents blow away too.

Homer rushed Benny indoors again, and spanked him out of sight of the neighbors. But Benny's howling was worse than his naughtiness, and his recovery was worse than his howling, because he promptly began reciting the capital cities of South America at the top of his lungs. When the telephone rang, it was the last straw. The shrill ring mounted above the piercing whine of Benny's recitation and catapulted Homer out of his chair. He lunged at the telephone, intending to snatch it up and crash it down. But Mary got there first.

"Oh, John, dear," she said into the phone, smiling broadly at Homer, "we were just beginning to worry about you."

"Montevideo, Uruguay!" bawled Benny.

"I've got a letter for you from your mother," said Mary. "How did it go today, dear? Did Mr. Warren give you your job back? He didn't? Oh, hush, Benny, dear, I can't hear."

"Caracas, Venezuela! Lima, Peru!"

"You've got another job instead? Oh, good for you, John. What? Oh, no, how terrible. Mr. Heron? Oh, that's just terrible. I mean, I used to know his family when I was in school with Barbara. Benny, dear, please."

"Santiago, Chile!"

Homer hurled himself at Benny and wrestled him to the floor. Benny screamed with joy. Frantic with rage, Homer clapped his hands over Benny's mouth and hung on.

It was no joke. A whole week in the company of his remarkable five-year-old nephew was wearing Homer down. He was sick and tired of the high-pitched precocity of Benny's perpetual chatter, exhausted by Benny's fantastic feats of memory. The bright sparkle in the boy's baby eyes made Homer feel over the hill. His stomach was sagging; his brain was decayed. Every day he was losing thirty thousand brain cells to old age, or was it thirty million? Whatever it was, it was certainly a fact that he was growing stupider with every passing day. What if his students should discover the passing of his genius, those young men and women who had signed up in such numbers for the Thoreau seminar he was teaching with Mary at the local college on Walden Street? What if they began whispering among themselves that one of their professors was losing his grip, that he was turning prematurely senile, that he couldn't remember a single utterance of the great man of Walden Pond?

Benny bit him, and rolled over with shrieks of laughter.

"Ouch!" yelped Homer. Shaking his wounded fingers he turned to his wife as she put down the phone, and whimpered, "What was that all about? Didn't John get the job?"

"Oh, Homer, something awful happened," said Mary. But then, detecting in herself a morbid pleasure in disaster, she flattened her voice and related calmly the news of Edward Heron's death.

"Good God," said Homer. "The poor bastard. You say our John's going to be working for his daughters?"

"La Paz, Bolivia!" shrieked Benny, and then, having rounded off the South American continent, he began on the large cities of the Japanese archipelago. "Tokyo! Osaka! Kobe! Yokohama!"

Oh, God, it was hopeless. Groaning aloud, Homer picked up his tiny nephew and hoisted him to his shoulder. "You know, Mary," he shouted, "I wondered why Gwen and Tom took Freddy and Miranda along to that summer conference on the culture of fruit trees in New Delhi, and left poor little Benny behind with John. Of course, John had to be here to earn money for school, but Benny? Why didn't they take Benny? Did you notice the way they nipped out of the house with all their luggage the minute we came in the door? They were afraid we'd change our minds."

Mary laughed. "Well, thank heaven, he still needs a nap every day. Gwen told me his daily naptime was all that kept her sane." Mary reached up for Benny and took him in her arms. "Come on, dear. Time for bed."

Instantly Benny's eyelids drooped. Leaning his head on Mary's shoulder he stuck his thumb in his mouth and allowed himself to be carried upstairs.

Left alone in the pulsing silence, Homer breathed a sigh of relief. Taking a can of beer out of the refrigerator, he settled down gratefully at the kitchen table with his card file. As Mary came downstairs again he shook his head at her mournfully. "Three whole months of this. I don't know if I can take it. When I married you, I didn't know you were going to give birth to a frightful little nephew like Benny. Say, listen, do you think we could leak some kind of brain-damaging gas through the keyhole of his nursery? Just to lower his IQ a hundred points or so, and make him human like other people? And now, my God, we're going to be stuck here without John. I'm really going to miss that boy. He was kind of a buffer between us and Benny, and he was going to babysit for us once in a while. Now it's just us and the infant monster, all by ourselves."

"Well, I'm glad for John, all the same," said Mary. "He's all excited. And he's promised to take his spider collection with him. We can be grateful for that. I wonder what it's like at the Herons' now. You know, Homer, I used to know Barbara Heron in college. That was when they lived in the big house, with all the gardens."

"The big house?"

"There in Lincoln. Near Walden Pond. Right across the Concord town line. It was a big hunting estate in the old days. Alexander Higginson built it. One of the Boston Higginsons. Of course, that was before big income taxes and the collapse of the stock market. There was a kennel and a stable and a piggery and a huge imitation-Tudor house at the top of the hill, with a great hall and a vast fireplace and a lot of stuffed moose heads hanging from the balcony. Barbara's grandfather bought it from Higginson in the nineteen-thirties. But by the time I knew the Herons, the whole place was going to seed."

"Where did old grandfather Heron get his money?" said Homer.

"Well, I don't know exactly. Copper mines or something. There wasn't much left by the time Edward came along. And he didn't do much to help the family fortune. He was an amateur horticulturalist, playing around in the greenhouse, breeding black peonies and green roses and things like that, and clipping his sprawling bushes into fancy shapes." Mary gazed dreamily at Homer, seeing instead the mossy path around the dark secret pond, the forest of pines and hemlocks, the ponies grazing on the open field. "We used to pick snails off the peonies, and in the winter we slid down the front yard on hideous plated tea trays. I'm sorry the Herons aren't in the big house any more. Barbara's father sold it a while back to old Mr. Whipple, and they divided the land up between them, and the Herons went down the driveway to live in the old farmhouse, where their help had lived before." Mary began poking in the refrigerator. "Homer, you pig, did you take the last can of beer?"

"Whoops, sorry." Regretfully Homer turned his empty can upside down.

Mary picked up the kettle to make coffee, then paused with the kettle in her hand. "Mrs. Whipple died — everybody said it was an excess of good works — and then Mr. Whipple fell ill with some nasty kind of cancer, and Barbara Heron went back up the hill and nursed him until he died. So now there's only Buddy left." Mary gazed dreamily at the faucet as she filled the kettle. "Virginia Heron — I wonder what she's doing now? The fabled Virginia. I mean, Barbara's the one I used to know. Virginia was just a little girl then."

"Fabled?" said Homer. "Why? Is she some sort of goddess, beautiful as the dawn?"

"Oh, no, not really." Mary thought it over. "I mean, she's not like a movie star. Not that kind of beautiful. But beautiful as the dawn? That's more what she's like. Yes, that's just about right."

"Oh, come on," scoffed Homer. "Beautiful as the dawn. When one woman says another woman is beautiful, you know she's overlooking a flat chest, a cross-eyed squint, and a nose like a brussels sprout. But of course," — Homer looked pious and rolled his eyes at the ceiling — "she has this *spiritual* expression. She's just so terribly *nice*."

"Well, all right, Homer, you wait. Why don't you come with me to her father's memorial service and see for yourself? It's going to be on Saturday, John says." Mary leaned across Homer and turned on the television set. "Time for the news. I wonder if they'll say anything about Mr. Heron's death."

"And the weather," said Homer. "Maybe they'll say something about that freak wind."

"... freak wind at Logan Airport," said the newsman, talking rapidly, obviously excited, "has resulted in the crash on takeoff of a chartered turbojet and the death of the governor of Massachusetts with a party of seven."

"My God," said Homer.

"Lieutenant Governor Michael J. Brumble is at this moment taking the oath of office in the west wing of the Massachusetts State House on Beacon Hill. From now on, Lieutenant Governor Mike Brumble will be performing the duties of the governor of the Commonwealth of Massachusetts." The newsman's voice darkened, as he slipped easily from simple reporting to the pronouncement of his own political opinions. "It has already been rumored that the state Democratic leadership will insist on a party caucus in the fall to determine whether or not Brumble will in fact become the Democratic candidate for the gubernatorial election in November. Sources predict that this appalling tragedy will provide a golden opportunity for the political comeback of Democratic ex-Governor Howard Croney, whose twelve years in office resulted in the construction of two thousand miles of highway connecting every village, hamlet, and crossroads in the state of Massachusetts. Thus do the political fortunes of —"

"Oh, shut up, you son of a bitch." Homer switched off the TV savagely. "Damned vulture. What a ghastly turn of events. Poor old Brumble. He hasn't got a chance of winning the nomination next fall, not with that bastard Croney piling in against him with all his cement mixers grinding and his blacktop boiling and glopping down over every green meadow in Massachusetts. Not a chance in holy hell."

Seven

HOWARD CRONEY HAD BEEN DRIVING HIS WIFE CRAZY FOR FOUR years, ever since his defeat in the last election. After his twelve-year occupation of the State House had come to an end, he had done nothing but lean back in his rocking lounge chair and watch television — baseball games, football games, hockey games, basketball games, soap operas, game shows, and situation come-dies. But now, staring in rapture at the burning wreckage of his successor's chartered plane, he sprang to his feet, slopping his vodka and tonic on the floor, spraying potato chips all over the rug, and shouted the happy news to his wife, who was passing through the living room with a basket of laundry.

"Oh, the poor soul," said Madeline Croney, dropping the basket in dismay.

"Pour soul?" cried the ex-governor. "Poor soul? Madeline, don't you understand? Don't you see what this means?"

The phone rang, and Croney was soon in excited conversation with a colleague from days gone by. Phone call followed eager phone call. "Contractors," reported Croney happily, rush-ing to the kitchen for a refill, rattling the ice cubes out of the tray. "You'd think every building contractor in the state and the president of every highway construction firm was urging me to run for office, and trying to pour money into my campaign."

"Well, naturally," said Madeline Croney testily, "your well-known propensity for building eight-lane loop-the-loops through every cow pasture in Massachusetts might have something to do with that." The ex-governor's wife was a sensible woman with a sharp tongue, who was occasionally able to control her husband's excesses and farfetched vainglories, and keep him loosely within the bounds of legality. "What about Lieutenant Governor Brumble? Don't you think he might get a lot of votes in the party caucus? I mean, now he'll have two or three months in office to show people what he can do."

"Who, old Brumblepuss?" Howard Croney whooped with derisive laughter. "Look, Madeline, the man can't even campaign outside the city of Boston. He's scared of cows. He won't even look out the window of the State House at the green grass on Boston Common. How do you think he's going to get votes in Fitchburg? Springfield? Great Barrington? Honestly, my pet, you can't really believe the man would have a chance, running for the nomination against a person of my experience, a man of my—"

"Well, I don't know. You never can tell. I always kind of liked the man myself."

"Good Christ, woman, whose side are you on?"

"You know, I sometimes wonder," said Madeline Croney with some asperity, snatching up the bottle of vodka and slamming it back in the cupboard.

The phone rang again, and immediately Howard Croney's frown of irritation was transformed. He chatted gaily for a while, and chuckled, and listened, then said good-bye. "Delighted to hear from a new supporter. Welcome aboard!"

"Who was that?" said Madeline. "Another gravel-pit baron, I'll bet."

"No, indeed," said Croney huffily. "It was a young man out there in one of those snobbish suburbs. He simply wanted to wish me well. Says he'd like to help out in any way he possibly can. I've got his name here. Clarence Whipple. Sounds like one of those old Yankee families that came over on the

Mayflower. Real class. Harvard or Yale man, I shouldn't wonder. Princeton, maybe. Nice upstanding sort of chap, not like some of the trash that's growing up nowadays. You know, real friendly. Wants me to call him Buddy. That's his nickname, Buddy."

"Hmmmmm," murmured Madeline Croney sagely. "I wonder what *he* wants?"

Eight

IN THE EARLY HOURS OF THE DAY OF EDWARD HERON'S FUNERAL, the weather satellite hung high over the Atlantic seaboard in the eternal sunlight of outer space. From the house at the foot of Pine Hill in Lincoln, Massachusetts, it was only a fixed speck in the night sky. Virginia Heron lay awake in her bedroom at the east end of the house, gazing at the window. She was not thinking of the day to come and her father's funeral. She was wondering whether rabbits were eating the peas in the vegetable garden. How many rabbits were there, anyway, on an acre of New England rural soil? How many woodchucks, racoons, squirrels? There had been a deer in the woods a year or two ago. Were they all gone now? And once she had seen a fox in the wilderness at the bottom of the lawn. It had been standing still, looking around curiously like a small dog. Alexander Higginson would have been pleased to see the fox. He would have put on his scarlet coat with the white collar and the green piping, the dark scarlet coat of the master of the Middlesex Foxhounds, and ridden after it with a hue and cry. Virginia stared at the rectangle of limpid sky, and imagined the out-of-doors alive with four-legged creatures. This hour of the night belonged to them. Only when the occupants of the house woke up, and yawned and dressed themselves, only when everybody was going about the day's work, only then did the wild owners withdraw and the

two-legged ones take over. It seemed fair enough to Virginia, sharing the place, owning it in the daytime, giving it up by night.

Below Virginia's window the spider was at work, building the first web of her second year of life. Dropping a line to the sill of the shed door, she secured her thread, then quickly ascended again. Soon she had constructed a framework and spread across it a set of evenly spaced radial filaments. Without pausing to rest she began circling outward from the center, adjusting the distance between one circle and another by the length of one of her hind legs, moving swiftly, as if she had not spent the last six months in a state of suspended animation. Around and around she sped, pausing at each radius to secure her line, hurrying on to a final circumferential thread, then working her way in again, laying down a new system of spiraling silk, more delicate than the first, more deadly, coated with sticky beads. Around she went, around and around, declaring this corner of the dim universe her own territory and hunting ground.

Above the shed door and a little to the west was the window of John's room. As the night sky turned grey, John, too, woke up. It was only the second waking in his new room. Getting up on one elbow, looking around possessively at the small space, he felt glad to be there, even though the ceiling was half fallen down and the window frames were rotten and the elegant cast-iron radiator wasn't connected to anything at all. Virginia and Barbara had given him the choice of their father's old bedroom and the guest room, even though Buddy Whipple's gear was littering the guest room. But John had already attached himself to this room out in the shed. Some hired man had lived in it once, hanging his clothes on the iron hooks in the narrow closet under the eaves, coming and going through the laundry by his own pitch-black twisting stairway.

Barbara had laughed. "Well, all right. Help yourself. You can wash in the set tubs downstairs, I guess." And later she had handed him a white porcelain vessel with a matching lid decorated with violets. John had never seen one before, but he recognized its charm and usefulness at once and put it on the floor of his closet.

And then he had moved in. He had piled all his possessions in Aunt Mary's car, and on the top he had roped his mattress, a long piece of plywood, a pair of sawhorses and his bicycle, and Aunt Mary had driven him over. "Say good-bye to Uncle Homer for me," said John, feeling guilty. "I'm really sorry to be leaving you people in the lurch." He had spent a happy afternoon arranging everything. The sawhorses and the plywood made a table for his spider collection, his web frames, his screen-topped jars and plastic vegetable containers. John's collection was mostly common spiders. He had a pair of cellar spiders, the female with her egg sac in her mouth, half a dozen house spiders with hundreds of nearly invisible young, a couple of sheet-web spiders with littered webs, and a little jumping spider with beady eyes that always seemed to be looking right back at him. John's big brown tarantula was an old friend, the only spider with a name — Fred — living comfortably in one of the screen-topped vegetable containers. The prize of his collection was a trapdoor spider from Georgia, her shiny black face hidden under a mossy door. Behind the jars stood his web frames. John loved these spiders best. Every evening at dusk he could watch one or the other of his *Nuctenea sclopetarias* build a perfect orb, just as it had done on the covered bridge over the Nashua River where he had found it. Beside the web frames lay his tools: his flashlight, his tweezers for inserting bugs, his cup for trapping mosquitoes against the window, and his chart for recording what each spider had consumed, and how many wrapped carcasses turned up at the bottom of his frames and jars, and which spiders had spun egg sacs, and how many spiderlings had been hatched.

At the end of the table John arranged his natural history notebook and his collection of spider books — his Emerton and Levi and Gertsch, and his precious old copies of Fabre's *The Life of the Spider* and *The Life of the Fly*. John worshipped the memory of Jean Henri Fabre, just the way his Aunt Mary and Uncle Homer put their feet down reverently wherever Henry Thoreau had taken a walk in the woods, or tramped along the Milldam. Old Fabre had spent half a lifetime sitting under an umbrella in the burning sunlight of southern France, watching his beloved creatures, preferring to study them alive rather than dead under a microscope. Part of John's mental furniture — along with the rules for the German prepositions that take the dative, and the anatomy of a dissected frog, and how to integrate from zero to infinity, and the feel of the long brown hair of a certain girl in his high school chemistry class — were bright pictures of Fabre's experiments. John would never forget the Pine Processionary caterpillars traveling forever around the rim of Fabre's pot, nor his tiny spiderlings floating to the ceiling on the warm column of air over a patch of sunlight on the floor, nor the eight bright eyes of the wolf spider in its hole, nor the luminous eggs of the glowworm shining under the ground. Maybe someday John would be another Fabre. Well, of course, probably nobody else could be as good an observer and experimenter as that. But there were a lot of things about common

41

bugs and spiders that people didn't know yet. Maybe by being patient, by just watching and watching, by just keeping an eye on things that were around all the time, maybe John too would discover things that nobody had ever known before — just by being patient, like Jean Henri Fabre.

John punched his pillow upright, put his hands behind his head, and beamed around at his room. He liked being all by himself in the shed. He liked the windows that reached from the floor to the low slanting ceiling. In the morning the sunlight poured in from the southeast and in the afternoon from the southwest and at night he could see Scorpio hanging near the southern horizon, with Antares gleaming in the middle like the diamond eye of the wolf spider in its hole. Scorpio was John's favorite constellation, because it was an arthropod, like a spider.

John could see something else from his front window. Virginia Heron's window was at right angles to his own. Most of the time he couldn't see inside her room, because the light merely glanced off the glass, giving back only the color of the sky. It was a perfect example of something John had learned in physics class last spring: *the angle of incidence equals the angle of reflection.* If you are looking at a reflecting surface at an angle, you can't see in, because the light entering your eye has just bounced off the glass at the same angle. It's only if you're looking from the front, more or less, that you can really see inside a room through a pane of glass. So Virginia's privacy was safe. It was different, of course, at night, when the room was lighted. Then John could see the edge of a dresser through the transparent curtain. Modestly then he would turn his eyes away. But now it was morning, and John had no compunction about gazing at the crystalline light of early dawn in the wobbly glass of Virginia's window. He imagined that she, too, was lying awake, looking out at the faraway line of trees, the white pines standing up above the rest, their irregular branches silhouetted against the sky.

He had better get up soon. There were an awful lot of

things to do today. After the church service there was going to be a sort of party for old friends of the family. The house had to be cleaned up. And they were going to serve some kind of fancy food, and coffee and tea. "Tea," Barbara had groaned. "It's so darned complicated. The hot water and the milk and the sugar and the little lemon slices."

So John would be running errands, vacuuming rugs, borrowing a coffeepot from the Star Market. Yesterday he had confessed to Virginia in the presence of Buddy Whipple that he wasn't old enough yet to buy a bottle of sherry, so somebody else would have to get it, and then he had felt dumb, really dumb. Buddy had guffawed, and John had wanted to kill him. How old was Buddy anyway? Not much older than Virginia. And Virginia was only five years older than John. But in a funny way she seemed much older than that, as old as Barbara, as old as his mother. Not old and grey, but old and knowing. Not that she acted as if she knew everything. She kept it all to herself. She just looked amused as the world went past her, and didn't say anything at all.

Nine

THE MORNING HAD BEEN COOL, BUT BY THE TIME BUDDY DROVE
off to the Second Parish Church with Barbara and Virginia,
there was a promise of midday heat.

Left at home, John had a list of things to do. At the top
of the list was flowers. He was supposed to pick some flowers
and put them here and there. John picked a big bunch of peonies in the backyard, brought them into the kitchen and stuck
them in a pitcher.

"Oh, thank God, I got here just in time."

John jumped with surprise. A woman was standing at his
elbow with a large carton in her arms.

"Amelia Farhang," said the woman. "I just happen to be
the chairperson of the Middlesex County Society of Flower Arrangers. What are you doing to those *wretched* peonies? Move
over."

John moved over and helped Mrs. Farhang heave her carton up on the counter.

"I thought the least I could do for Edward was arrange the
flowers for the service. But I got the time wrong. I mean, I
peeked in just now, but the minister was talking, and they had
this nearly invisible arrangement of wild flowers. You'd think
they would have had the grace to display some of Edward's own

emerald roses or those remarkable cadmium-orange canna lilies of his, you know, the ones he bred himself. But all I could see was a jack-in-the-pulpit! Some kind of joke, I guess, because of being in the church, you see. Not in very good taste, do you think? Anyway, I rushed over here to see what I could do about the house. Something for the mantle, right? And the dining room table? Here. Stand back. What I need is elbow room. First of all, we've got to do something about these peonies of yours." Mrs. Farhang picked up a peony and narrowed her eyes. "The problem of the peony. Only one, I think." Swiftly she tore the leaves from the stalk and stuffed the bare stem into a piece of plastic foam. "What does the peony say? That is the question. The language of the flowers, you see. What, after all, does the peony say?"

She was frowning at John, holding the peony and the plastic foam up in the air. He jerked to attention. The woman expected an answer. "What does it say?" John looked at the peony and shrugged his shoulders. "Well, it's sort of shaggy. You know, full. Sort of rich and full?"

"Not bad." Mrs. Farhang pulled a long strand of dried kelp out of her carton. "*Success and prosperity,* that's what the peony stands for. Not exactly suitable for this occasion. Wait till you see what I do with the collection of materials in this box. *Regret,* that's what these flowers are going to say. *Gentle regret and sympathy. Consolation in time of sorrow.* Here, take all the rest of these foolish posies and toss them out."

"Well, okay, if you say so." John picked up his dazzling pitcher of peonies, cumulus cloudheads of feathery blossoms blood-flecked with random splotches of scarlet, and carried it upstairs. In the second floor hallway he hesitated between Virginia's bedroom and Barbara's. But then, feeling shy of Virginia's, he opened the door of Barbara's room and went inside.

He had already visited Barbara's room that morning. Barbara had sent him upstairs with her gardening basket, which was to be put away out of sight. Now he put the pitcher of peonies on the dresser next to the basket, with its clippers and trowel and green garden string, its small containers of lime and bonemeal, its new pair of gardening gloves. "Gloves," Barbara had said scornfully, handing him the basket, "what good do they do? I put them on so carefully, and the next thing I know, I've taken them off and there's dirt ground into my fingernails again. Look at these hands. How am I ever going to get them clean enough for church?"

Buddy's room was just across the hall from Barbara's. John looked at the closed door, then turned the knob and looked in. Buddy's suitcase lay open on the unmade bed. Was Buddy packing up, getting ready to leave? John stared around the room at the heap of heavy winter clothing piled on a chair, the pair of skis leaning in the corner, the big stereo speakers in the middle of the floor. Buddy wasn't planning to go anywhere in a hurry. He was moving in, making himself at home. "Shit," said John softly. Oh, the hell with Buddy. Slamming the door, John ran downstairs. He must get back to work. There were some trays in a cupboard somewhere. He was supposed to put a lot of crackers and some cheese on the trays.

In the downstairs hall Mrs. Farhang was in his way. She was standing beside the hall table with her peony arrangement in a tall piece of sewer pipe. Fastening the end of a long strand of kelp to the wall with a piece of tape, she stepped back to take a look. "There," she said proudly. "How do you like that?"

John shook his head, and said "Well," and wondered what the peony would say in the language of the flowers if it could talk. "I'm so embarrassed," or something like that. He was relieved to hear a car in the driveway. Squeezing past Mrs. Farhang, he ran to the kitchen door.

And on the doorstep he was thankful once again. The old red Volvo belonging to his Uncle Homer was pulling to a stop beside the stone wall.

"What did you do with Benny?" said John, running up to the car.

"Oh, we had to hire a kid around the corner, thanks to you and your new job," said Uncle Homer gruffly. "Wasn't in the contract. There we are, pinned down with that scary little kid, morning, noon and night."

"I'm really sorry, Uncle Homer," said John, grinning. "He is a menace, isn't he?"

"You're darn right. His brain ought to be pickled and put on display in some medical museum, not allowed to grow up and take over the world, the way it threatens to do now."

John laughed. He was fond of his Uncle Homer, although he sometimes wondered how the man had succeeded in becoming what he was in life. For one thing he was quite famous as a kind of detective, although John found it hard to imagine him running down criminals as an assistant district attorney in the old days, when, after all — just look at him — look at the way the poor guy was always tripping over his own feet. And he was supposed to be this big expert on Emerson and Thoreau, and that was strange too, because Thoreau had been a naturalist, like Fabre, and Uncle Homer couldn't even tell a robin from a blue-jay. He couldn't even see things when you pointed right at them, for God's sake. "Look, Uncle Homer," John would say, "there's an *Apis mellifera*, you know, a honeybee," and Uncle Homer would wave his hands around and shout, "Where, where?" and not be able to focus on the thing at all, even when it was right there under his nose. Uncle Homer was nice, all right, and funny, all right, but he was really stupid about some things.

"Come on in, you people," said John, holding open the screen door.

But Uncle Homer was looking back down the driveway, and plucking Aunt Mary's sleeve. "My dear, look who's here. A vision from the past. Isn't that —?"

"Mrs. Bewley," said Mary. Smiling warmly, she went to meet the woman who was straggling up the road, her crazed old face alight, her hands reaching out to take Mary's, and to help herself to any trailing ends of scarf or glove or pocketbook that might be unattached, or dangling, or otherwise not firmly chained or glued.

"A famous kleptomaniac, Mrs. Bewley," Homer murmured

to John. "Nobody seems to mind. When something turns up missing, you just make a visit to Mrs. Bewley and ask her if she knows where you might be able to find a pair of size fourteen jogging sneakers, and she pulls them out of her closet and thrusts them at you with gleeful shouts, all thrilled and excited to be helping you out. She's hard of hearing, so you have to speak up. You know, John, that knitted hat of hers looks awfully familiar. I've been missing it for some time, ever since that day at the library last month. WELL, HELLO THERE, MRS. BEWLEY. WHAT A NICE CAP YOU HAVE THERE. JUST THE KIND I LIKE MYSELF."

"OH, IS IT?" Mrs. Bewley snatched it off and forced it on Homer. "TAKE IT, TAKE IT! NO, NO, YOU JUST KEEP IT. ISN'T THAT NICE?"

"WELL, THANK YOU. THAT'S VERY GENEROUS OF YOU."

Mary took Mrs. Bewley's arm. "YOU'RE LIVING RIGHT NEXT DOOR NOW?"

"YES, I MOVED IN WITH BROTHER WHEN I RE-TIRED. HE'S PASSED ON NOW, BUT I'VE STILL GOT MICKEY AND MINNIE AND MARGIE AND MOLLY AND MILLIE AND MURIEL AND MAXIE AND MI-CHELLE."

Baffled, Homer glanced at Mary. "Grandchildren?"

"Chickens, I think," murmured Mary. "Remember her little chickens?"

"Come on in, why don't you?" said John. "Make yourselves at home. I have to tell these other people where to park."

Homer was curious to see the house that had been nearest to Walden Pond when Henry Thoreau lived there. Homer had looked up the history of the house in the library, and he knew that some part of it had occupied this hillside a long time before Henry was born, way back when Walden was only a pond in the middle of a woodlot. A man named Billing had lived here when Lincoln was only an outlying part of Concord, and he was supposed to have made the rope for the meeting house bell.

In Thoreau's day Jacob Baker had lived here, and Henry had thought him an improvident farmer because he had raised as fair corn as anybody and had given it all to his stock. And then at the turn of the century along had come Alexander Higginson, who had been not merely improvident but extravagant. He had pursued his expensive horsey passion untroubled by the high cultural principles of his father, Henry Lee Higginson, who was busily founding the Boston Symphony, or of his second cousin Thomas Wentworth Higginson, who had corresponded with Emily Dickinson. He had bought the whole farm. He had built a great imitation-Tudor hunting lodge and kennel and stable up the hill and housed his servants in Jacob Baker's house and his Ayershire cattle in the now-vanished barn.

Well, thought Homer, looking around the small entry hall and peering into the living room, it takes a heap o' livin' to make a house a home, and this one has certainly had a heap o' somethin'. It's certainly done a heap o' saggin'. The floor of the living room drifted downhill to the east, accompanied by the ceiling. Homer told himself to hug the west wall if he didn't want his hair to graze the plaster overhead.

As the small rooms filled with the friends and relatives of Edward Heron, Homer was soon separated from his wife. He stood at one side sipping sherry, studying the public observance of Edward's departure from the land of the living. None of the guests seemed deeply grieved. Coffee and tea and sherry were warming digestive systems, going to heads. Subdued expressions of sympathy were giving way to a noisy babble, as men and women who hadn't seen each other for weeks or years forgot the reason they were gathered together. Time was closing smoothly over Edward Heron, leaving no seam.

Then in a gap between grey heads and lifted coffee cups, Homer caught a glimpse of the pink cheeks and bright eyes of an old friend, Jane Plankton, the famous Miss Jane Plankton of Eliot and Janeway, a prosperous Cambridge investment firm. Homer was enchanted to see that Miss Plankton had been tossed into a corner with old Mrs. Bewley by the tide that was slowly sweeping the funeral party from the bereaved daughters at the door to the table of food and drink in the dining room to the larger gathering place of the living room and out again to the hallway and the door and the open air. Slowly Homer began to press in the direction of Miss Plankton, trying not to trample feet or destroy inherited crockery.

"Isn't it sad?" Miss Plankton was saying to Mrs. Bewley, coming to the point at once, as was her way.

"WHAT'S THAT?"

"I said, ISN'T IT SAD. I WILL MISS EDWARD. HE WAS A CHILDHOOD FRIEND."

Mrs. Bewley seemed to have forgotten the nature of the occasion. Her eyes were fixed on the pair of old-fashioned spectacles hanging on Miss Plankton's polyester breast.

"THEM LITTLE GLASSES. AIN'T THEY NICE?"

"What?" Miss Plankton looked down in surprise. "OH, MY LORGNETTE. OH, YES, ISN'T IT AMUSING? A LITTLE AFFECTATION." Then Miss Plankton gave a squeal of pain as Mrs. Bewley grasped the chain of the lorgnette and dragged it ruthlessly upward.

Homer Kelly was near enough to behold this act of thievery. Squeezing clumsily past Mrs. Amelia Farhang with outstretched protesting hand, he surged forward. But Mrs. Bewley was jerking the chain loose from Miss Plankton's hair ribbon and lowering it joyfully over her own frowsy head. As Homer drew alongside, she lifted the lorgnette and peered at him, adopting at once an air of majesty. Dropping his hand, Homer watched her stalk away with Miss Plankton's stolen property — a ragged duchess, a threadbare aristocrat, the queen of a madhouse — and tried to control his mirth.

Miss Plankton was charmed. "Oh, Homer," she gasped, "what a *darling* woman."

"Don't worry," said Homer. "I'll get it back. No problem. It's just a matter of tactful reborrowing. Something like the economics of a capitalist country. As the director of a vast financial empire, you must know all about it. Leave it to me."

"Oh, no!" Miss Plankton was horrified. "Not on any account! I am simply hugely amused! It was a treat! She's welcome to it! See how she simply adores it! I am truly pleased!"

But this act of brigandage was only the beginning. The melancholy reception that had begun as a sympathetic grazing of lips against cheeks, a soft clucking of solace and consolation, an enclosing circle of friendship, ended — as Virginia said later — like a descending invasion of turkey vultures: beaks tearing, claws ripping, red wattles inflamed.

Ten

HOMER WAS ADRIFT AGAIN. HE STOOD ON THE SIDELINES IN DOUR
reflection on the paradox of rustic suburban wealth. Look at this
place, all old-fashioned antiquity and inherited furniture, a room-
ful of polite folks who had all been to Harvard. Homer was a
little sore on the subject of Harvard, because the closest he himself had been to Harvard as a young man was the teeming cross-
ing of Boylston and Brattle Streets and Massachusetts Avenue,
where he had directed traffic while Harvard students surged across
the street into the Yard. Later on he had acquired a cheap city-
college education somehow or other, and a law degree at night
school. And then he had picked up a mass of miscellaneous information by himself and written a lot of books. Christ, he had
even taught at Harvard. But he still felt a faint grudge against
the easy self-assurance of the kids who had flooded the intersec-
tion of Harvard Square in days gone by. Here they were, the
same crowd. Grouchily Homer imagined their comfortable domestic establishments. They all lived in picture-book farmhouses,
only every blade of grass was like a dollar bill, and the weathered
fence rails were so much beaten silver. Homer saw them posing
as old farmers too, on weekends, in their L. L. Bean Maine hunting gumboots and field coats and wood-chopping vests, but every
January and February they were off to Switzerland to ski, or

basking on the beach in the Virgin Islands. It was too bad the IRS didn't require everybody to make a full public confession of family income. Homer smiled at this pleasant fancy. Suppose you had to post it beside your mailbox:

Annual Earned Income — Wife   ————————
Husband   ————————
Annual Income from Investments   ————————

What a revelation! Because nobody ever told. It was the most carefully guarded of all secrets, the one hushed fact that never came to light.

What about these Heron women, for example, wondered Homer, how rich were they? Mary said Edward didn't have much money. Well, how much was not very much? His daughters were probably well off. They stayed at home. They didn't work. They probably just clipped coupons like heiresses in days of yore.

John Hand was passing a plate of little cakes. He too had thought of Virginia and Barbara as a pair of wealthy women. But now he was disabused. They weren't rich after all. Holding out his plate to a couple of Edward Heron's old friends, he was shocked to hear a brutal summary of Mr. Heron's financial misfortunes.

"Wouldn't you know Edward would end up poor as a churchmouse," said the man in the bow tie, helping himself from the plate, not looking at John. "Those flowers he invented never amounted to anything. Did you know he put a second mortgage on this property?"

Poor as a churchmouse — that wasn't fair to *Mus musculus*, who probably had better sense than to hole up in a church anyway, thought John scornfully. Smiling to himself, he presented his plate to the man in the conservative three-piece suit, Putnam Farhang. Mr. Farhang was the husband of the flower-arranging lady and the president of some big insurance company.

Mr. Farhang waved John's plate away. "Then I'm afraid those girls don't have anything left," he said, "beyond this mortgaged tumbledown house and forty acres of land. I understand Barbara hasn't been using her RN degree lately. Maybe she'll go back to work now. And as for Virginia, listen to this. I dropped in a month ago to see Edward, and there was that young woman, dirty from head to foot, dragging a huge uprooted tree on a toboggan. Must have weighed three hundred pounds. Said she'd dug it up; she was transplanting it someplace else. Why doesn't a handsome girl like Virginia just get married? I'd take a flyer at her myself, if I weren't hogtied already." Mr. Farhang glanced furtively at his wife across the room, then shook his head. "Queer ducks, these Heron women."

John was enraged, but he merely turned his back, pretending to rearrange the cakes on his plate, and kept his ears open.

The man in the bow tie chuckled. "Of course there's only one way out," he said. "They'll have to sell off some of this property. That's what Edward was working on when he died. Knowing Edward, I suppose he would have made a mess of it. Maybe his daughters will be able to do it right. Of course I'll offer my services. Development mortgages, that sort of thing. Our firm —"

John wandered away, wondering how two big important business men could gossip so freely about Mr. Heron's affairs in front of a third party like himself. But then he caught sight of a child across the room, a kid with a familiar pale face and big moony glasses. It was his own reflection in the mirror. They had thought him too young to matter.

As luck would have it, John's next customer was the real-estate developer who had been working with Edward Heron. The man was introducing himself to Barbara. He was blundering and floundering and putting his foot in his mouth. "Deeply sorry," he said. "Such a loss ... shocked ... feel for you at this time ... your father and I ... about to undertake ... forty parcels ... cluster development."

"Oh, so it was you, was it?" said Barbara sharply. "It was for your sake he was prowling around that wilderness on the day he died?"

The developer didn't seem to recognize this question as an accusation of murder. He bungled on. "Mr. Heron was making a preliminary survey, a rough plan, suggesting some of the best house sites, recommending places to be cleared for the most efficient clustering of the individual units. We were going to prepare a contract just as soon as — I hope you ladies will be able — after an interval, of course, a chance for you to recover from this sad — sit down with us in order to revitalize —"

"No," said Barbara. "Never. Impossible. You can just forget the whole thing. Here, why don't you have something to eat? John, give this man some cake."

Obediently the man took the last piece of cake, lifted it to the gaping hole of his mouth, and gazed vacantly at Barbara's retreating back.

"Excuse me," murmured John, hurrying after Barbara. In the kitchen he found her leaning against the wall of the pantry with her back to him. She turned her ravaged face to John, blew her nose, and said loudly, "It was my fault, you see. That's the whole trouble."

John couldn't think of anything to say. He picked up cakes and refilled his plate, as Barbara strode past him into the dining room and reached out her hands to an old friend.

"William," said Barbara.

Selectman William Warren clasped Barbara's hands and squeezed her fingers. He said nothing, but his eyes filled. Then he began telling her about the good times he had enjoyed with Edward when they were young men together, the trip to the Rockies in the early forties. He would show her the pictures.

"Oh, William, I'd love to see them."

"I'll bring them over one of these days. And pretty soon you can see the new aerial photographs we're taking of the whole town. I was out the other day in a helicopter, taking a look. Fascinating, your place from the air. Oh, and listen here, Barbara, I've got to sit down with you girls and talk about the change in the law."

"What change in the law?"

'It's the evaluation of open land, you see. From now on it's all going to be assessed as marketable real estate. One hundred percent evaluation. You can't just have a house and ten acres any more, and keep the land as low-taxed property. Everybody's going to have to put their nice fields and woods on the market, that's what I'm afraid of. It's no joke. Your taxes will go way up. That's why your father was so eager to sell out."

"Listen, William, I don't want any part of that. Selling out, I mean. Neither does Virginia."

"Good girl, Now, look here. There are a couple of things you can do. You can try to sell some of it to the town for conservation. Has to be passed by Town Meeting. That way it would never be built on. It would still be there to look at. Just some nice trails for people to walk on. Or you could make a real effort to use it as farmland. Then it can be taxed at a lower rate. You can sell hay. You can raise corn. You can — "

"That's where I come in," said Buddy Whipple, looming up at Barbara's elbow. "I can manage the whole thing. I know exactly what Barbara should do. Now, look here, Barbara, you don't want to be pressured into handing over anything to the Conservation Commission. The whole city of Boston would be parking their cars on the road, leaving trash all over the place, trampling everything flat. Motorcycles and trail bikes all over the place. Bonfires. Don't be a fool, Barbara."

William Warren glanced at Buddy, then turned back to Barbara. "If you decide to use it as farmland, then you have to make a profit of at least five hundred dollars a year, to call it real agricultural use. Come see me at the town hall, and we can work it all out."

"But I've got it all in my head," said Buddy. "I can show them on paper in black and white. I mean, I'd enjoy it. What are friends for?"

Barbara too seemed not to notice Buddy. "I'll come, William. Thank you. That would be a real act of kindness."

Buddy grinned at their two averted faces and turned away, shrugging his shoulders. He could wait. Sooner or later he would win Barbara over. It was a trick he had discovered in childhood, how to make people like him. Now it was second nature — the big grin, the jolly disarming laughter, the bear hug, the easy arm around the shoulder. Slowly now Buddy moved through the crowded rooms, amiable, complete in himself, famous for being himself, for saying bluff hearty things. His was the largest presence in the house. Whatever empty space had been left by Edward Heron was now occupied. Buddy was everywhere — in the dining room, the kitchen, the living room, the hallway — shaking hands, embracing elderly women who had seen him grow up, talking cheerfully about "the girls" and his determination to see that they were looked after, that they wouldn't be alone. He would be staying on in the house, looking after the practical side of things, helping out, taking care of Barbara and Virginia.

"Well, it doesn't surprise me at all," said Dolores Leech, the town nurse, standing on tiptoe to give Buddy a peck on the cheek. "You sound just like your dear father." Dolores lowered her voice. "Honestly, Buddy, I don't know how to thank you for your generosity. If it hadn't been for that loan of yours, I don't know what I would have done. Since Carl died I've barely been able to pay my property taxes. Do you know, I've actually been thinking seriously of lowering my property assessment by getting in a carpenter and a plumber and tearing down the garage and ripping out the downstairs bath? I must say, Buddy, I'd certainly rather be in debt to you than to the town treasurer. Are you sure you can really spare it?"

"Oh, go on, Dolores," said Buddy, "of course I can. Look at me, a single guy, no family. And I've got some people renting out the big house now. And there are some other things in the works. Irons in the fire — you know. Say, listen here, Dolores, what do you think of the race for governor?"

"Oh, dear, wasn't that plane crash the most tragic thing? I must say, I don't know what I think about Lieutenant Governor Brumble. He's not exactly — I mean, I just don't know if I want to vote for him in the fall or not. I'm going to wait and see who the Republicans put up. At least they're honest. You know what I mean."

"Look, Dolores, the lieutenant governor may not even get the Democratic nomination. Suppose, just suppose, the nominee were ex-Governor Croney? What would you think of that?"

"Croney? *Howard Croney?* Oh, come on, Buddy, everybody knows he's a crook."

"No, no, I think you're doing him an injustice. Listen here, I think he may be exactly what the state of Massachusetts needs right now. You know, somebody aggressive like that, starting big projects, building, bringing in lots of public-works jobs. Think it over. Don't make up your mind too soon."

"Well, if you say so, Buddy. I certainly do respect your opinion."

On the other side of the room Virginia had turned away from her visitors. She was looking out the window, trying to collect her wits. Her face ached with smiling. There was a mosquito on the window, and Virginia rested her mind on it, welcoming its remote disinterest. It wanted nothing from her but a drop or two of blood. She watched as the mosquito lifted from the glass and settled its delicate legs on her arm. Only an hour ago she had been standing beside the rectangular spade-cut in the grass of the cemetery, and therefore she was feeling particularly mortal at the moment, transitory and passing like her father. Whereas the mosquito was eternal. All mosquitoes were the same mosquito. This mosquito was a million years old, a billion. In her foolish insistence on being distinct, one person and no other, Virginia Heron was here for a day, gone tomorrow. One smack of a giant hand and she would be extinguished.

"Look at the poor thing," whispered Muffy Weatherbee to her friend Peggy Glover, gazing at Virginia's back. "Those two girls will be all alone now."

"So tragic," said Peggy politely. But Peggy was gazing with fascination at the mantelpiece, the wainscoting, the furniture. "Have you ever been in this house before? The whole place must be really quite historic."

"Oh, Peggy," giggled Muffy, "I'll have to confess I'm being really pushy, coming here today. I didn't even know Mr. Heron at all. I was just curious to see his house. Of course, I knew Virginia. I mean, we grew up together. I mean, we went to the first few grades together, before I went to Concord Academy. I remember her in fifth grade, kind of tall for her age and gangly. She sort of hung back and never put her hand up, but she always knew the answer. Everybody was sort of in awe of her, you know? Even then. I remember," mused Muffy, gazing into the past, "she had this funny sweater. Well, anyway, what I meant to say was —," Muffy waved her hand at the ceiling, the floor, the wall. "I was wondering if the SOS Committee should take this place on."

"SOS? Oh, you mean the Save Our Sites Committee?"

"Isn't that a clever abbreviation? And of course sometimes it really is a matter of life and death. Take this place here, for instance. I don't think the Herons have done all they could with the house, do you? It's a little shabby, don't you think? If it were mine, I'd paint the outside white and the shutters black and — oh, you know the kind of thing. Wouldn't it be fun? And I'd have a polished brass knocker on the door and a picket fence and a pretty glass lantern on a pole."

"Who lived here anyway?" said Peggy Glover. "I mean, during the American Revolution?"

"Why don't we find out? Somebody must have! Some minuteman! There should be a sign beside the door. You know, a plaque, a brass plaque, so everybody would know. And an effort at restoration. But I hear the poor girls don't have a dime. Oh, Virginia, dear, how I have felt for you in your great loss!"

Muffy threw out her arms and enclosed Virginia in a vacant embrace. Virginia endured it, standing upright like a loose board.

"I've just been wondering, Virginia," said Muffy eagerly, "if we couldn't recommend your house to the Save Our Sites Committee. I mean, we could all help out. We could have a weekend, just for the house. We could paint it up. I mean, all it needs is a little — a little —"

"Elbow grease?" suggested Virginia.

"Exactly! And we could all rush over with our paintbrushes, the whole membership, you know, with buckets of white paint and, you know, ladders, and have a working picnic. And we girls could bring casseroles, and pies. What about some day this summer?" Muffy's eyes were focused on a vision of checkered tablecloths on the grass and pie baskets and cheery husbands and jolly children frolicking on the lawn.

"I'm sorry," said Virginia amiably, "but I don't think—"

"And the inside," said Peggy Glover. "I know someone who could help you out. An expert on old interiors. You know, like wallpaper. Pretty Williamsburg patterns with drapes to match. Canopy beds. Dust ruffles. Of course all in the best of taste."

Virginia looked dreamily at her shoes. "Raspberries," she said.

"What did you say?" said Peggy, thinking she had been insulted.

"Raspberries and cream. Good taste always makes me think of fresh raspberries and cream." Then Virginia looked up eagerly at Muffy. "You know, I often wonder whether or not there is some absolute standard of aesthetic perfection out there somewhere." She gestured at the window.

"Where?" said Muffy, glancing blankly at the window.

Virginia laughed and waved her hand at the ceiling. "Oh, you know, in the stars. I wonder about it all the time. I wish there were. I wish I knew."

Muffy glanced at Peggy, then turned back to Virginia tactfully. "What Peggy was talking about, I think, Virginia, was simply a true feeling for the past. Authenticity. You know. Keeping everything sort of old, in keeping with the house."

"I think about that too," said Virginia, "all the time. I wonder what it must have been like here a long time ago."

"Yes, yes, what it must have been like!" echoed Muffy.

"I expect it was pretty savage, don't you think so?"

Muffy's smile faded. "Savage?" she said.

"Stark. Bleak. No trees, only stumps. Cowpats. Horse dung. Pig manure. Smoke-blackened rooms. Unwashed illiterate people huddled against the cold. Trampled dirt around the house. A muddy cart track to Concord. Do you know, wherever we dig around here we find pieces of broken china and glass and scraps of old iron, as if they just hurled everything in all directions out the window."

Muffy looked at Peggy, shocked by this perversion of their common vision of the past, with its butter-churning, candle-making, musket-seizing forefathers — those large comfortable families beaming around their jolly hearthsides where great black pots were bubbling over blazing logs; the women bustling around the kitchen in aprons and ruffled mobcaps, baking bread in their beehive ovens; the men smoking long clay pipes; and then at bed-time everyone picking up those little pewter candlesticks — that nice gift shop in Concord had some just like them — and climb-ing the stairs to their plump featherbeds. Muffy stroked Virginia's arm affectionately, and scuttled away with Peggy Glover.

The minister of the Second Parish moved in quickly to take Muffy's place. "You'll call on me, won't you, Virginia, if you ever feel the slightest need?" He too squeezed her arm. Arthur Potter was a balding young man with the beginnings of a cozy tummy. He was new to the Second Parish. He had started his ministry with eager enthusiasm, but recently he had begun to find funerals a trial. At first it had been challenging, trying to put into practice the techniques he had learned in divinity school for handling death and dying. "Death and dying" — it had been all the rage at school — not dying yourself, naturally, but getting together in groups and discussing it. Reverend Potter had never personally known anyone who had actually passed away, but the talk sessions had been exciting, just so fabulous, all about the emotional needs of the bereaved, and so on. So his first actual funeral had been doubly disappointing. The family had been so grief-stricken they had cursed his kindly mini-sermon and his tender handclasps, and had screamed at him to get out of the house. The next woman, with her dying husband, had been even worse. The widow-to-be had been positively gleeful, if not down-right flirtatious.

But now Edward Heron's death provided Mr. Potter with another opportunity. He was eager to exercise his talents for creative consolation on two women as interesting as Virginia and Barbara Heron. Did he dare stand on tiptoe and give Virginia an avuncular kiss? Something in the way Virginia was gazing at the floor told him it wouldn't be quite — not yet. He took her hand instead and gave it a couple of extra-firm double squeezes.

His director of teenage religious education was less cautious. Cherry Peaches Schermerhorn was new to the congregation too. This morning she had begged for a part in the memorial service in order to get into the heart of the spiritual community at once, to plunge to the very center of the suburban tragedy right away, to see human beings with their artificial surfaces torn away, their naked selves stripped bare. But then, right here in the home of the deceased, Cherry Peaches had been struck by an idea so exciting, so really fantastic, that she had decided to just barge right in, to be *open* and *honest*. When Cherry Peaches Schermerhorn got on the ball, there was no holding her back. "Cherry Peaches Schermerhorn here," she said. "I mean, my name is really Cynthia Pauline, but everybody calls me Cherry Peaches. Could we use it?" she said, beaming at Virginia. "Your place, I mean? The kids? Could we come here sometime for a retreat?"

"A retreat?" said Virginia warily. "A retreat from what?"

"A retreat from what!" Cherry Peaches laughed merrily. She was a radiantly healthy girl with orange hair fizzing out of her scalp and a good deal of spherical geometry bursting out of her clothing. "It is a funny word, isn't it? It's just the kids, you see, in the church. They need to get away from their parents. You know. To retreat, if you will, from the nuclear family, the happy hour, the two-hundred-thousand-dollar home, the TV. They need to get away from divorce and the cutthroat competition of the executive marketplace and the feverish success-orientation of their mothers and fathers. They need to sort things out, to sum things up, to get their heads together, to remember where they came from. You know."

"Where they came from?" said Virginia slowly. "But I thought you just said they need to get away from where they came from?"

"No, no, I mean where they originally came from. The bassinet. The mother's breast. The safety of the womb."

"Cherry's been really so successful with our teenagers," said Arthur Potter enthusiastically. "She knows how to get them to come to grips with their own infant traumas. It's really just fabulous, what she's doing. So exciting, all the latest discoveries in adolescent therapy. Encountering the dark side of the self, all that sort of thing. Sometimes all they need is a good scream. You know. It's all really just so fantastic."

"All we want, you see, is a rural setting. Nature, the source and mother of us all." Cherry Peaches put her hand on Virginia's arm. Touching was so important. "Some place like this. I mean, it would be like going deep into the country, the primitive experience of the farm, without the trouble and expense of going to Maine or Vermont, you see?"

"Well, I don't know," mumbled Virginia, wanting to scream herself. A picture came unbidden into her mind, a memory of a clumsy Palestinian village she had manufactured long ago in Sunday school out of flour and salt. Turning away, looking for help, she reached for her sister.

Barbara was there. Barbara inserted herself between Virginia and Arthur Potter. She was shaking hands, expressing gratitude for official ministerial services. She was seeing them to the door. She was coming back to introduce Virginia to an old friend.

"You remember Mary Morgan, don't you, Virginia? She's Mrs. Homer Kelly now. That's a name that means something around here. Have you met Homer? Homer, my sister Virginia."

Virginia remembered Barbara's friend Mary. She remembered the three of them down on their knees at the muddy edge of the pond in the heady sunshine of springtime, collecting pollywogs in jars of cloudy pond water, and thrilling rides down the snowy hillside in the winter, and the bumping scrape of the dented tea tray on the driveway at the bottom of the hill. Virginia shook hands with Homer Kelly and smiled at Mary, who looked the same as ever — large-boned, dark-haired, and calm. "What you two are famous for around here," said Virginia, "is having John for a nephew. We're so grateful for having him here right now. We're really glad he came along."

"That boy," said Homer, grinning proudly. "Of course, you know he betrayed our sacred trust. We thought he'd help us take care of his little brother this summer. But, no, he's deserted his post, abandoned ship." Homer looked curiously at the young woman who was supposed to be as beautiful as the dawn. Well, she wasn't. Mary should have her head examined. The girl was lank and thin, her clothes drooping as if she had never taken them off the clothes hanger. Her colorless hair was hooked back behind her ears. The two sisters looked alike. The older one was gaunt, not bothering to be good-looking, the younger woman spare in the same way, not bothering to be beautiful. The difference between bothering and not bothering was a subtle carelessness and inattention to detail. You had to care somehow, if you were going to be beautiful as the dawn. Homer stood aside and observed the keen glances of Barbara's deeply lidded eyes and the way Virginia rushed in with a warble of absurd loquacity, her eyes alight with amusement, her long fingers waving in the air, her dazzling metaphor left hanging, her ponderous question unanswered, set aside, given its due place in the mysterious scheme by which life in this house ran its course. Smart. The woman was probably terribly clever. A passage from *Walden* came into Homer's head — "Humility like darkness reveals the heavenly lights." An idiotic piety, implying absolutely zilch. Homer put his arm around his wife and began urging her toward the door.

Everyone else was leaving too. People were hovering in the doorway, bestowing dry kisses and feathery embraces. In the hall Mary caught sight of Mrs. Bewley bending over the mound of jackets and scarves and pocketbooks. "Oh, Mrs. Bewley," said Mary, pulling her gently toward the door, "MAY WE DROP YOU OFF?"

But Buddy was reaching for Mrs. Bewley too, taking her gallantly by the arm. "I'll see her home," he said. "It's right around the corner. OKAY, MRS. BEWLEY? ALL RIGHT WITH YOU IF I COME IN AND PAY YOU A CALL?"

65

Mrs. Bewley snatched up Miss Plankton's lorgnette from her bosom and gazed at him regally. "WELL, SURE," she said, "YOU BET."

John stood in the door and watched Buddy shout gaily in the old woman's ear as they negotiated the stone step and moved across the courtyard. He envied Buddy his comfortable way with women, the ease with which he could put his arms around an elderly lady or kiss a girl as if he were their uncle. How old was he, anyway? Twenty-four, maybe? Twenty-five? Six or seven years older than me. *That's all*. It's funny the way it feels like about thirty or forty. I'll never catch up, if I live to be a hundred. I'll always just be a stupid little kid whenever he's around. "So long, Aunt Mary," said John. "Uncle Homer."

But Aunt Mary was looking back at Dolores Leech, the town nurse, who was just settling herself down for a good heart-to-heart talk with a grey-faced Barbara. "Are you coming, Dolores?" said Mary. "We go right past your house."

"Oh," said Dolores Leech, getting up reluctantly. "Well, all right, in that case."

The door closed on Homer and Mary Kelly and Dolores Leech.

Barbara's shoulders drooped with relief. She picked up a tea-cup from the floor and put it on the mantel. For the first time she caught sight of Mrs. Farhang's flower arrangement, a spare work of art consisting of a cabbage rose and a stalk of rhubarb. "Good God," said Barbara, "what's that?"

"It was some lady who came early," said John. "Mrs. Farhang. She's this big flower arranger. She just wanted to help you out."

"Well, thank God, she's gone now," said Virginia. Plucking the rhubarb out of the jar she put it rakishly behind one ear. "If one more person had come up to me with another *Dear Virginia*, I would have run outside and hidden myself in the woods."

"Oh, Virginia! Virginia, *dear!*"

A woman was standing at the foot of the front hall stairs. "Oh, you don't know me, but we did meet. I mean, we did once.

Dotty Gardenside. I think it was at the church, perhaps, or was it — ? Oh, I've heard so much about you both, and I'm sorry the occasion is so inauspicious. I just want to say how dreadfully sorry I am about the untimely — I mean, I've just been upstairs having the teeniest peek at your darling home. What a lovely place you have here! No bath on the first floor? No lav in the master bedroom? And what a pity there's no garage! Virginia — may I call you Virginia? I mean, I've heard so much about you. I mean, I feel I've known you all my life. Are you girls going to be staying on? I just happen to be a professional realtor. Gardenside Associates. Or would a simpler home in a condo or an apartment seem more attractive now?"

Barbara stared at Dotty Gardenside. The woman had studied the obituaries in the paper, looking for sudden changes of address, hoping for further sad transferrals by the bereaved survivors. A hearse follower. "You're an old friend of my father's?" said Barbara, moving forward menacingly.

"Oh, no, I didn't have that pleasure." Mrs. Gardenside backed nervously to the door and poked under a bench in the hall. "My bag. It isn't here. It's missing."

"I expect it's in your car," said Barbara coldly.

"It was here, I tell you. Right here, with a hundred and fifty dollars in cash and all my credit cards. I put it right here."

"Well, I'm sure none of our *friends* would have taken it."

"I'll have to notify the police."

"Well, yes, I suppose that's the right thing to do. Good-bye, Mrs. Gardenside."

The door closed with a bang behind Dotty Gardenside, and Barbara threw back her head and laughed. "Mrs. Bewley swiped it. Oh, God bless Mrs. Bewley. Oh, thank God, that's the last of them."

But there was one more. Muffy Weatherbee, bright-eyed, her face flushed pink, was bursting in the door again. "Oh, Barbara dear, Virginia. Forgive me, but I was just driving out onto the road. You know, that nasty curve where your driveway comes out on Route 126, and I had such an exciting notion, I just thought

I would rush back and tell you. It's 126, you know. They're going to reroute 126."

Barbara was stupefied. "They're going to what?"

"Haven't you heard? They're going to straighten out the curve. They're going to come right up your driveway with a big new road. That's what I heard. Oh, wouldn't it be just terrible? So I had this terrific idea. The Save Our Sites Committee will make it a historic site. A museum. We'll fix it up, you know, the way I said, with all the Williamsburg —" Muffy was breathless with visions. "Oh, I'm so excited. You'd have to open your house, of course, once or twice a week, but it would mean we could all share in the heritage. I mean, because it's part of local history!"

Virginia towered in the doorway, monumental, barring the way. "I'll walk you to your car," she said.

"And then the road people wouldn't be able to budge, do you see?" Muffy trotted excitedly after Virginia across the grass of the round garden. "They'd have to build the new road on the other side. You know, they couldn't invade the sacred premises of a historic site."

"No," said Virginia, shaking her head. "I'm sorry, but we wouldn't want to do that."

"Because I'll bet a minuteman lived here. We'll have a brass plaque on the house and a sign out on the road, and — what did you say?"

"I said no. We couldn't. We just couldn't. We like our house the way it is now."

Muffy opened the door of her car and got in. "But that attitude is so shortsighted, so — don't you think you're being very selfish? You people are only *stewards*, after all, of this priceless — I mean, doesn't it really belong to everyone? And what about 126? Did you hear what I said? They'll come right up the driveway!" Muffy looked up at Virginia, at the small head far away against the sky, dark against the sun, refusing.

Virginia felt sorry for Muffy Weatherbee. How could she stop the buzzing, the little drilling whine? Leaning down into the car window, she gestured with her stalk of rhubarb. "It's all right. The house, I mean. We'll take good care of it."

Her kindness was more intimidating than her refusal. Muffy gaped at her, then at the boy who had appeared from nowhere. Cowed, she started her car, stalled it, started it again, backed up, turned it around and fled at last down the driveway, disappearing among the new green thickets of maple saplings beyond the curve of the stone wall.

"I'm afraid she's just a skirmish-rider," said Virginia to John. "She'll come back. Or rather, she'll send in big guns next time. Important people. You'll see. Old friends of my father's."

Then the ground opened up in front of Virginia. A long dark box was descending in fits and starts as the ropes jerked through the handles. A thud of dirt struck the top.

Virginia ran ahead of John. He followed her awkwardly into the house, saying nothing, not daring even to touch her sleeve.

Eleven

JOHN WAS SITTING AT HIS PLYWOOD DESK, WRITING IN HIS NATURAL
history notebook.

I found a barn spider last night. They're kind of rare around here.
It's the first one I ever saw. Mostly they're farther north, like in
Maine, like the spider called Charlotte in *Charlotte's Web*, because
E. B. White lives in Maine. I was outdoors with my flashlight and
my butterfly net looking for moths to feed my spiders, when I
noticed something in the corner of the shed door. I wouldn't have
seen it at all, if it weren't for my stereoscopic vision. My eyes
could sense an almost invisible plane between me and the door. It
was a good-sized orb web, a little lopsided, and the spider was up
at the top in a little nest of loose threads, upside down about a
quarter of an inch from the top of the door. She's a female, really
pretty. Sort of grey with blue markings, a little bit furry.

I'm going to keep an eye on her and see what she does. Maybe I'll
get an umbrella and sit under it like Fabre by the hour. (And a
hat. He had this flat black hat.)

It was Sunday morning, the day after the funeral. John lifted
his head from his notebook. What was that noise? He hadn't
paid any attention to the distant drone, but now it had become
a faraway clattering, an almost inaudible sort of — what? — a

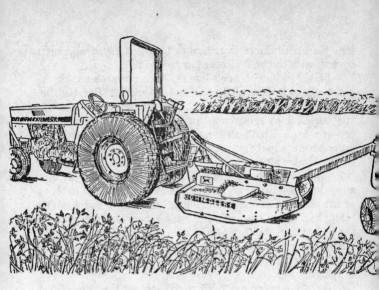

ripping noise. What the heck was it? John closed his notebook and went to the window.

The International diesel tractor was old, but the John Deere apparatus trailing behind it was new, a five-foot rotary mower that would slice through stands of inch-thick brush. Buddy was driving the tractor. He squinted in the morning sun and grinned to himself as he lurched through the head-high jungle of aspen, buckthorn, honeysuckle and firecherry, listening to the tearing snap of a thousand wiry stems, bent and trampled by the tractor, then whipped off at ground level by the great blade of the mower. He couldn't help laughing. It was really so funny, the quick way his mind worked. Most of the time he wasn't even conscious of figuring things out. He just knew what to do. One swift action followed another, almost as if his body didn't need direction from his head. By the time Barbara and Virginia woke up this morning and looked out the window, it would be too late. He'd have the really critical part of the tangled wilderness covered with scattered pieces of mangled brush.

Buddy pictured himself leaning down from the tractor, explaining it to Barbara, all friendly and reasonable: "But, Barbara, you heard what William Warren said yesterday. We've got to put our land to agricultural use if we're going to lower our property taxes. That's all I'm doing. I mean, look at this. It's no good the way it is now. Just a jungle of weeds." And then he would play his trump card . . .

". . . just a jungle of weeds, Barbara." Buddy put his arm around the roll bar of the tractor and lowered his head to shout at her above the noise of his idling engine. She was standing below him in her bathrobe, her green rubber boots planted on the bed of torn mulch that had been a forest of honeysuckle a moment ago. She was looking up at him angrily. John Hand stood beside her, fully dressed, looking up too with his blank baby face.

Barbara was furious. "Where did you get this damn thing anyway?"

"The town barn. Nobody uses it on Sunday. Harvey Cunningham, you know, the superintendent of public works, he lets me use the machinery on Sundays sometimes. And anyway, Barbara, you seem to forget." Buddy raised his voice. "It's my own land I'm working on here."

"Your own land? What do you mean, your own land? The hell it is. This is ours, right here. You know it's ours."

"No, no. I'm sorry, Barbara, you're wrong. The bound is over that way. The stone wall. You're all mixed up."

"The stone wall?" Barbara swung around. "It's over that way? Are you sure? I could have sworn —"

"Of course I'm sure. Go look. It's over in that big mess of honeysuckle beyond that line of apple trees. Go ahead. You'll find it right over there."

Barbara looked at the apple trees, her mouth open. Then she shrugged her shoulders. "Oh, well, the hell with it. Go ahead. Do your worst." She backed away from the tractor, lifting her bathrobe. The hem was wet from the dew-laden grass, plucked and draggled by the fierce thorny canes of the blackberry patch.

John backed up too, and together they watched Buddy adjust the throttle and put the tractor in gear. Grinning at them, he drove away, swaying gently from side to side on the high seat. Behind him the great invisible blade of the mower gnashed at the low forest of bushes. Ripping and chopping, it threw out in a wide arc a thick cover of ground honeysuckle and firecherry. Where there had once been dappled shade there was now only a raw new surface exposed to the morning sun.

"He makes me so damn mad," said Barbara.

"I guess he means well," said John slowly. John didn't think he had the family standing to say anything critical about Buddy Whipple, although there certainly were a lot of strong feelings he would have enjoyed putting into words.

"Means well!" said Barbara. "In a pig's eye, he means well."

John was entranced. He had never heard anybody say "in a pig's eye" before. And he was glad to know that Barbara didn't trust Buddy, because it was really awful the way the guy had moved right in on the two of them. Why didn't they make him leave? Well, Barbara had tried to. Last night after all those people went home, she had hinted around that he should go too. She had practically put her hands on Buddy's chest and shoved him. But Virginia hadn't said anything. She hadn't helped her sister at all. Why not? Walking slowly up the sloping lawn, John gazed at the weedy grass under his feet and wondered what kind of hold Buddy had on Virginia. He was afraid he knew what kind of hold it was. Goddamn him anyway. John drew a deep shaky breath.

"What would you like me to do around here today?" he said to Barbara.

"Oh, John, it's Sunday. You're not supposed to work on Sunday. Nor on Saturday, either, only yesterday we certainly couldn't have done without you. I'm not even sure we said thank-you yesterday, John, we were all so exhausted." Barbara clumped along more slowly in her rubber boots and turned on

John a smile of friendly interest. "Tell me, how are your spiders doing?"

"Oh, they're fine. They didn't seem to mind being moved. I'm keeping track of their behavior in a journal. You know, like Jean Henri Fabre. Did you ever hear of Fabre?"

"Fabre? The insect man? Yes, of course."

John was charmed. "Well, I think he was just great. I've got some of his books. Aunt Mary keeps looking for them in second-hand bookstores. *The Sacred Beetle*, *The Hunting Wasps*. There are a lot of books like that."

Barbara stopped and looked at him. "Tell me, John, what were those wasps around my father the other day?"

"Yellow jackets. They're very ordinary, but they've got a terrible sting."

Barbara began climbing up the hill again. "Well, I just wondered. Listen, would you see if you can find my father's asthma medicine, back there in the apple orchard? It's got to be there someplace. A small box, about so big. Bright red. There was a little hypodermic needle in it, and some pills. I've looked all over the house for it. I've ransacked his things. It just isn't to be found."

"Well, okay. Yes, of course I will." John turned around and began to run down the hill.

"There's a stone wall down there someplace," Barbara shouted after him. "The edge of the property. From there it goes all the way to the road. Listen, I shouldn't be doing this to you. After today you're not supposed to work until Wednesday. You hear me?"

Twelve

THE TRACTOR AND THE ROTARY MOWER WERE STILL RATTLING AND whining far away as John stepped high-footed over the acre of catbrier and honeysuckle that was a kind of front yard to the wilderness of the old apple orchard. The wilderness itself was not a pleasant forest but a nearly impenetrable jungle, thorny with blackberry, itchy with poison ivy, entangled with wild grapevine. Oak stumps sprouted huge watersuckers with ugly enormous leaves. The bark of the firecherry was shiny like cheap purple dress goods. The apple trees were buried deep. Only their cloudy tops were visible.

Above the clash and clatter of Buddy's tractor, John could hear the shredding snap of small stems and twigs that had once been a brushy cover for all kinds of wildlife. He grimaced at the thought of the small creatures now being destroyed with every dip and wallow of the big machine. Maybe a few of them might escape to this side of the stone wall and survive, at least until Buddy found a way to come after them over here as well.

John had a new feeling of uneasiness about Buddy. In the last day or two Buddy's body seemed to have grown bigger, huger. Like a spider, he had molted into a larger instar. For a moment John had a picture of Buddy picking up a limp Virginia in his pedipalps and sucking all the life out of her.

Angrily John shook himself. Why was he standing here, staring at a white blob of bird droppings on a leaf? Where was the stone wall? It must be somewhere to the left. If he kept pushing that way he would have to stumble on it sooner or later. And then it would be something solid to get his bearings by.

Yes, there it was, running between two lines of apple trees. Maybe those yellow jackets had made their nest in a low crevice among the stones of the wall. Slowly John made his way beside it, bending double to peer under the lowest boulders and examine chinks under protruding cobblestones. At the very end of the wall he found what he was looking for, the remains of a small nest. Fragments of grey paper were clinging to several of the stones at the lowest level. They seemed to have been torn apart.

Getting down on hands and knees, John studied the ruins. Breaking off a fragment, he saw dried grubs curled in the open cells. They were dead. There was no longer any healthy coming and going of worker females, providing the grubs with food. Something violent had happened to the community just as it was beginning to get its little world organized. Maybe Edward Heron had smashed into it by mistake. Maybe the nasty encounter with the yellow jackets had brought on his asthma attack.

John stood up and backed away, and looked at the stone wall.

It wasn't the kind that had been built with care. It wasn't a handsome piece of carefully constructed useful architecture like some of the stone walls he had seen in Concord. No great boulders had been dragged out of the ground by oxen and hauled into line and eased into place with crowbars until they fitted snugly against one another. Nor had the top of this wall been cleverly assembled from flat stones along a stretched piece of string. This old wall was little more than a running rockpile of stones hastily cleared from a field. They had been dug up and dumped on a stoneboat and dragged to the edge of the clearing and dropped in a clumsy row. And yet the careless diligence of that old farmer had achieved this eternal consequence, this casual monument marking the borderline between one man's land and the next. The wall was a legal property boundary, listed in the Middlesex County Registry of Deeds. "Bounded to the southeast by a stone wall running westerly three-hundred-and-fifty feet to an oak tree." That was the way the old deeds went.

John looked at the heaped cobblestones and imagined some eighteenth-century farmer's fingers spread around two of them, left hand and right hand, holding them over the rockpile, then dropping them and going back for more. The wall must have been an ugly accumulation at first, with raw orange boulders and glaring white ones piled together higglety-pigglety. Now time had softened the colors to a uniform grey. The exposed surfaces were green with moss, grey-blue with rings and patches of lichen.

Reverently John stroked one of the uppermost stones, feeling the lichen rough on the palm of his hand. The racketing noise of Buddy's machinery had stopped. John could hear a crow cawing in the cornfield. A pair of Canada geese flew over his head, then a small flight of starlings. For a moment, with the stone under his hand, John lost himself.

It could be any time. There was nothing man-made here but the stone wall. Maybe it was June, 1775, and the Revolutionary War had only just begun, just last April, down the road in Concord. Farmers and storekeepers, carpenters and wheelrights, old men and young men from Lincoln and Sudbury — they had shouldered their muskets and walked past this very farm on their way to meet the British Regulars. Maybe John Hand was a minuteman himself. Maybe he too had been at the fight on the nineteenth of April.

Or maybe this instant of time was really a moment in the eighteen-fifties, and he was Henry Thoreau, measuring the accuracy of this farmer's boundaries, standing here beside the stone wall with his surveying instruments over his shoulder, his little telescope and his iron measuring chains. Henry would have liked the Canada geese. The geese were carrying the mail of the seasons, Henry would have said. And he would have been sorry to see the wilderness cleared on the other side of the wall, because wildness, he had said, was the preservation of the world. Wildness — bushy tangles, trackless wastes in Maine, where immense trees toppled over in the virgin forest and there was nobody there to hear them fall, old orchards reclaimed from the farmer's care by rabbits and snakes, pheasants and woodchucks, field mice and yellow jackets —

The noisy machine began again, faltered, then steadied to a rattling roar. John swept forward one hundred and thirty-five years, took his hand from the stone and moved away from the wall.

"I didn't find anything," said John apologetically, spreading his empty hands.

"Well, too bad," said Barbara. "Where can that damned stuff be? I could have sworn he had that little red box with him. I saw it sticking out of his pocket that morning, I know I did."

"Have you got some yellow soap?" said John. "There was a lot of poison ivy down there."

Barbara found him some yellow soap. She stood in the kitchen and watched him scrub his hands and arms. "I'm going to talk to your Uncle Homer," she said.

"My Uncle Homer? What for?"

Barbara paused. Then she spoke slowly. "Because he appreciates the significance of little things. Like the absence of that little hypodermic syringe of epinephrin. He'll be interested in that."

"Oh, you mean, because he was a detective once in the district attorney's office. That's right, I keep forgetting about that. Only I don't see what he can tell you," said John honestly. "I mean, he's not really very practical. I don't see how he solved any of those crimes. I mean, my Aunt Mary is the one who knows what's wrong with the car and how to put a new plug on a lamp cord." John remembered an occasion a few years ago that had rankled in his heart, when his Uncle Homer had tried to help him finish a plastic airplane model and had managed to smash the whole thing. Of course Uncle Homer had gone right out and

78

bought him a new one, but John had been forced to begin the whole tricky project all over again.

Barbara was amused. "A prophet without honor among his own nephews, I see," she said. "Never mind. You wait till you hear what your Uncle Homer says about that missing little red box of medicine."

Thirteen

JOHN SET ASIDE THE NEXT MORNING TO KEEP AN EYE ON HIS BARN spider and take notes. At first in the glare of sunlight on the shed he couldn't find her web. And then he was startled by a blue jay, flying out of the neighboring hemlock tree with a rush of wings and a raucous cry. Looking in among the close network of lacy branches, John saw the blue jay's coarsely built nest. It was high in the tree, way up over his head. He wondered if the eggs had hatched. A nestful of hungry baby birds would be bad news for a tasty spider. This was a dangerous neighborhood. And what if the blue jay had found the spider already? John gazed once again at the top of the shed door, and then the tissue of silk displayed itself, trembling in a breeze so light that it shook no leaf of the lilac bush beside the porch. There it was, the same orb web. There were holes in it now, battlegrounds, places where the fabric had been destroyed. If he were to stand right here and watch all morning, would he see the spider catch anything?

Dreamily John stood in front of the shed door, staring up-ward, leaning back with his arms folded, until a meandering gnat, gyrating mindlessly in the air in a cloud of other gnats, dashed itself against the silken threads. Almost before John had registered the fact that something was heaving in one corner of the web, the spider was rushing from her lair at the top of the door frame.

She was pulling out silk from her spinnerets with her hind legs, wrapping the gnat up swiftly like a butcher tying a piece of meat.

John was delighted. That was neat, really neat! Patiently he watched the drama to its end, when the spider paused in her wrapping motions, turned herself rightside up, held the package in her palps close to her mouth, and sank her paralyzing fangs into a juicy gnat-portion. Would she carry the package away to gobble later on? No. She had settled down. She had begun to suck.

In the guest room upstairs, Buddy Whipple was writing a letter. Buddy enjoyed writing letters. A letter was different from a conversation. In a face-to-face encounter you couldn't ever be in total control of the situation, but in a letter you could get down on paper exactly what you wanted to say in the best possible language, and leave out whatever didn't fit in. It was like addressing a jury without the presence of opposing counsel, in some courtroom where you had a free hand with the judge.

Dolores Leech, RN
Lincoln Town Nurse
Beulah Terrace
Lincoln, Mass.

Dear Dolores,

The other day after Mr. Heron's funeral, I visited Mrs. Alice Bewley in her home on Route 126. I was really shocked to see the way she lives. It was really unsanitary in there. I think you would be doing the old lady a kindness if you would pay her a visit. I have a strong suspicion her living conditions are way below acceptable health standards. I wonder if she wouldn't be better off in a good nursing home? I understand the poor old girl doesn't have any living relatives to take responsibility for her, so it's up to friends and neighbors like you and me. And the sooner the better.

So much for business matters. It was good to see you. Not tearing out any bathrooms yet, I hope? Not going after the garage with a sledgehammer?

Yours,
Buddy Whipple

Buddy read his letter over and smiled to himself. The final paragraph pleased him. In a jocular way it would remind Dolores of his personal loan. Just a little reminder, that was all it was. Just the lightest of light touches. Now it was her turn to do him a favor.

Of course getting old lady Bewley off the property and into

a nursing home was only the first step. The place would still belong to her. Idly Buddy wondered whether or not Mrs. Bewley had been keeping up with her taxes. Did she have a pension? She had been a domestic servant all her life. Shrewdly Buddy suspected that no arrangements had been made for social security payments. It was an interesting line of thought. Well, he would look into it. But right now — Buddy looked at his watch and jumped up from his chair. There was just time to take a shower and get dressed for that big luncheon with ex-Governor Croney at the Ramada Inn. There would be a lot of people, there, all kinds of potential backers and supporters, but maybe he'd get a chance to put a word or two in Croney's ear. Just a bee in his bonnet. No harm in grinding his own axe before everybody else came along with their own demands and expectations.

As it turned out, the place was packed. Buddy was disappointed to find himself in a crowded corner of the big function room, far from the head table, with harassed waiters squeezing around his chair, slapping down plates of cold tunafish salad. But after the Neapolitan ice cream and the tepid coffee, after Croney's hearty little speech and his campaign manager's pep talk, Buddy distinguished himself by getting to his feet and making several superb suggestions for the handling of conservative voters in the western suburbs of Boston.

After lunch, as everybody began crowding toward the door, the campaign manager plucked Buddy's sleeve and invited him to stay for a private drink in the cocktail lounge.

And there in the dim light of the bar, Buddy really enjoyed himself. He had eaten very little of the colorless lunch, so the drinks went down smoothly, and soon he was light-headed, confidential, and palsy-walsy. After his third Scotch he made the campaign manager an impulsive, magnificent offer.

"My house," he said. "I've got this big old house out there in Lincoln. Oh, I don't live in it myself. Can't afford to. I rent it out for a king's ransom. But those people don't have any lease. I can get them out of there any time I want. And the place would be just great for a suburban campaign headquarters. Naturally

I'd lower the rent for a good cause like this. We could put in a switchboard. Keep our fingers on the pulse of the whole state. Great place to have parties, fund raisers."

"Well, that's very kind of you," breathed the campaign manager.

Fourteen

WHEN BARBARA HERON KNOCKED ON THE DOOR OF THE HOUSE on Barretts Mill Road, she found Homer Kelly at home alone.

"Where's John's little brother?" said Barbara.

Homer waved her into the living room. "Be grateful that I have a heroic wife. She's taken the little weirdo to the zoo. I don't know what all those nice sensible four-legged animals will think of our little two-legged monster. But who cares? We are alone. We can breathe free. We can hear ourselves think. Sit down. I'll just move Benny's reading matter out of the way, these little books about kitties and bunnies." Homer picked up the *World Almanac* and dropped the one-volume *Columbia Encyclopedia* on the floor, breaking the spine.

Barbara sat down. "It's just this thing I wanted to ask you, that's all. And see what you thought. It's my father's medicine. It's missing — the little kit he carried around with him all the time in case of an asthma attack. There was a syringe of epinephrin and a bottle of antihistamine tablets. They were in a little red box about so big — ," Barbara held up her fingers. "He always had it with him. I saw to that. And I can swear I saw it in the pocket of his jacket that morning."

"But he could have dropped it anywhere in that wilderness down there, couldn't he?" said Homer. "Maybe he was in such a panic he couldn't handle the needle, and he dropped it. And then he tried to run to the house for help, only he couldn't get that far."

"But John crawled all over that orchard," said Barbara. "He looked really carefully. You know, he went over it with a fine-tooth —"

"A fine-tooth comb," said Homer, with a trace of bitterness in his voice — Homer had been mixed up with fine-tooth combs before. "Pretty hard to find a little thing like that. Needle in a haystack, right?"

"But the box was red. You couldn't miss it," insisted Barbara. "It has to be somewhere. I looked through his stuff in the house, and under the seat of his car. I tell you it isn't anywhere. How could it be missing? Tell me! Under what circumstances could my father's asthma medicine be absolutely gone?"

She was staring at him accusingly. Homer blinked uncomfortably and looked down at the chess game on the coffee table, where Benny's pawn had Homer's king in check. Groaning under his breath, he dropped his gaze to the Scrabble board on the floor, where Benny, with an impossible collection of letters — two Ls, two Es, two Us and a K — had come up with the word *ukulele*. "Well, I don't know," grumbled Homer. "Maybe those yellow jackets stole it. Now, come on, Barbara, don't torture yourself with afterthoughts."

Barbara picked up Homer's fallen queen and turned it over and over in her hand. "Well, never mind, Homer. I just wanted to get it off my chest. I think somebody had it in for my father. And then —," Barbara dropped the queen on the floor and reached down to pick it up — "then I went and made it worse." Hastily she dropped the queen back on the table and put into words at last what she had really come to say. "Listen, Homer, it's Buddy. I'm worried about Buddy Whipple. He's moved right in. He won't leave."

"Buddy Whipple?" Homer was surprised. "Well, tell him to get out."

"I have. I tell him all the time. But he just grins and shrugs his shoulders, and says, 'Virginia, what do you think?' And then Virginia —" Barbara paused, biting her lip.

"Virginia what?"

"She lets him stay."

"Why?"

"I haven't the faintest idea. She won't talk about it."

"Well, I don't see what I can do. I should think it was up to you girls. I suppose he's paying rent?"

"Oh, yes, and of course he says he's going to do a lot of work. He wants to turn both our places into farms in order to reduce our property taxes. You know, he's going to raise hay on most of it, and lease some of it for horse pasturage, so he says he'll put up fences, and then he's going to rent out some more of it to that dairy that grows cattle corn. At least he claims that's what he's going to do. And he's promised to do something about Route 126. They're threatening to change the route and take it up our driveway. Buddy thinks he can throw his weight around and get them to change their minds." Barbara made a wry face. "That's our Buddy. And he's promised to take on the Save Our Sites Committee, who want to — oh, I know he thinks he's going to be a big help. But I just don't like it. He's just so damned —" Barbara slapped the coffee table with the flat of her hand. The chessmen jumped. "I want him out!"

Homer stroked his chin. "You didn't happen to — ah — look in his room for the medicine?"

"As a matter of fact, I did. It wasn't there."

"Well, I'll admit it's peculiar that the stuff has turned up missing. But it's not what you'd call evidence, for or against anybody."

"It's Virginia, you see," said Barbara, sounding desperate. "Somehow he's got her on his side. I tell you, Homer, he's a monster."

There was a bright chatter at the door.

"Oh, no," said Homer, "talk about monsters, here comes Benny. They're back." Homer's voice turned sepulchral. "Well, hello there, Benny, old boy. Welcome home."

"Oh, Barbara, hello," said Mary. "I'm glad you're still here. Did Homer tell you it's his birthday? Well, it is. Look, Homer, I bought you a present. I decided we should send Gwen and Tom a complete record of Benny's whole life while they're away. You know, lots of really cute snapshots. So here it is, your new camera for taking pictures of Benny."

Homer was aghast. "Listen, woman, you know I can't handle one of those damn things. I'm too dumb. Focal length, aperture, all that stuff, I can't get it through my head. I appreciate the thought, and all, but you wasted your money."

"No, no, I'll teach you how. It's perfectly simple. Oh, Barbara, you've got to hear what Benny's been learning in the car. I've been teaching him nursery rhymes. That's right, Homer, nursery rhymes. I mean, if he's going to go around memorizing things, he might as well be learning five-year-old things instead of the contents of the Columbia Encyclopedia, right? Now, come on, Benny, say a nursery rhyme for Barbara."

Benny struck a pose in his small red overalls and recited at the top of his lungs:

> LITTLE MISS MUFFET!
> SAT ON A TUFFET!
> EATING HER CURDS AND WHEY!
> ALONG CAME A SPIDER!
> AND SAT DOWN BESIDE HER!
> AND FRIGHTENED MISS MUFFET AWAY!

Then Benny made a sudden lunge, and sank his teeth in Barbara's knee.

"Oh, no, Benny! No, no! Not like that!" Mary snatched him up and gave him a good whack. Homer shouted with rage. Benny bawled loudly.

Barbara, laughing like the good sport she was, rubbed her knee hard and went home.

Fifteen

"TONIGHT LOOK FOR STRONG BREEZES," SAID THE CHANNEL 4 meteorologist, pointing to the streak of cloud running from Maine to the Gulf of Mexico on his satellite picture. "Nothing like the freak tornados of last month, of course. Just a weather front moving rapidly out to sea."

In Lincoln the wind began to rise about midnight. It whipped the forgotten laundry on the line with sharp reports and tumbled the trees in the front yard with soft rushing sounds and made the old floorboards creak. It blew the barn spider right out of her silken nest at the top of the shed door. Away she went, blowing on a threadline, landing unhurt on a tossing sheet. From that uneasy resting place she mounted to the laundry rope, and from there to the porch column. There, as the wind died down, she built a new web, suspending it from the pillar and the porch ceiling, with stabilizing lines running to the floor and to the handlebars of John's bicycle. Next morning a mosquito blundered into the spiral thread and sent a wild message quivering up the woven strands to the spider poised on the ceiling. Swiftly she rushed at the mosquito, wrapped it, paralyzed it, then cut the carcass out of the web. Moving heavily with a full belly, she was unprepared for disaster. When the shadow of the blue jay fell across the wooden pillar, the spider had time only to

hook the claws of her forelegs into her silken shroud-lines and hang on.

Away flew the jay. It landed in the hemlock tree, hopped deeper into the interior and poised itself above the five small birds in its nest. Stuffing the contents of its beak into one of the yawning mouths, the jay was disappointed to discover only a single jointed leg. Squawking angrily, she rushed up into the sunlight again and swooped once more around the porch at the east end of the house.

But now the angle of pillar and porch roof was empty. Only the shell of a swaddled mosquito swayed in the vacant threads of the spiderweb. The spider itself had fled, scuttling away to a crack in the ceiling, moving rapidly on only seven legs.

John spent the day hard at work in the yard. He began with the sunken garden. It had once been Edward Heron's pride. But Mr. Heron must have been neglecting it lately. His green roses were a jungle of thorns and mildew and black spot. Witchgrass and thistle choked his evil-looking canna lilies, the color of dried blood. John spent the morning on his hands and knees, his back bare to the sun, digging up dandelions and purslane from between the paving stones. After lunch he went down on his knees again in the vegetable garden, pulling up lamb's quarters and quack grass. The vegetable garden was forty feet square. John's back and shoulders turned an angry red.

After supper he was back out-of-doors. This time he was avoiding Buddy, who was lording it over the kitchen, talking loudly about his new political connections, about all the VIPs he would be running around with now, and all the big important stuff they were planning to do. John filled the lawnmower with gasoline, set the blade high, jerked on the starter rope, and guided the lumbering machine down the hill to the tall grass around the vegetable garden.

The grass was too high for the mower. The engine kept balking, buzzing at too high-pitched a whine, and then John would have to pull it back and push it in again, careful to cut only a narrow swath at a time.

He was pleased with the result. The small field was covered with soft heaps of long grass. In the twilight he raked them up, carried them in armfuls to the garden, and spread them around the freshly weeded tomatoes and cucumbers, the zucchini, the summer squash, the green peppers, the eggplant, the pole beans. Sooner or later the weeds would come right back up again, but the heaped grass would dampen their enthusiasm for a while. And the fresh grassy carpet looked really nice along the rows.

Then in the grey gloom John stretched a length of string along the four sides of the bed. Its white line stood out sharply in the gathering darkness, and he had no trouble using the edging tool to make a clean border all the way around, defining which part of the world was orderly garden, which the chaos of the field. Mosquitoes moved around him in a feathery cloud, brushing vaguely against his face and arms. But mosquitoes never bit him much — he tasted bad or something — and John didn't even bother to wave them away.

He was just finishing when Barbara looked out the door, silhouetted against the light of the lamp in the hall, and called to him, "Hey, you crazy kid, come on inside."

John hadn't been feeling tired at all, but as he put away his tools in the shed, his bones ached. His shoulders were sore with sunburn. Feeling a little feverish, he groped his way up the narrow stairs to his room and put on his pajama pants. Then he remembered his barn spider. He picked up his flashlight and went back downstairs.

Opening the laundry door to the porch, John gazed two hundred million miles westward straight into the glossy eye of the planet Venus, sinking toward the horizon in the neighborhood of the crescent moon. For a second John remembered a sentence of Fabre's about the great geometrician whose divine compass measures all things, but then he set the ringing words aside. It sounded nice, but you couldn't talk like that any more — unless you were like Mrs. Farhang. John snickered softly to himself, "What does the planet Venus actually say?" Then he moved across the grass in his bare feet and aimed his flashlight at the top of the shed door.

That was funny. Only the tattered remains of a web were left in the corner of the door frame. There was no spider poised in a nest of threads at the top of the door. Had she been gobbled up by something? Maybe she had simply moved someplace else. John poked his flashlight around the window of the laundry, the corners of the porch. Soon he was relieved to see a new web in the angle between the ceiling and one of the porch pillars. Brushing past the clean laundry, smelling the sunshine trapped in the hanging shirts, John put a spotlight on the spider as she moved slowly across the top of the web.

"Good old girl," he said. "There you are again. Hey, oh, wow, what happened to you?"

Something was missing. John counted the legs twice. There were only seven. The third leg on the right side of the cephalothorax was gone. "Autotomy," whispered John to himself. "Something tried to grab you and you saved yourself by losing a leg. Good for you, old girl. Now, the question is, will the leg grow back? I'll keep an eye on you. Take care."

Sixteen

Next day John showed the web to Virginia. The morning was cool and cloudy. Beads of mist clung to the silken strands.

"Oh, isn't that pretty," said Virginia. "Where's the spider?"

"She's hiding up there at the top. In the daytime she only comes out if something lands on the web."

"What if you poked it with a little stick?"

"No, it wouldn't have the right frequency of vibration. You have to use a tuning fork. Have you got a tuning fork?"

"No."

"Well, then, you have to put in a fly or something." John made a sudden motion, snatching something out of the air. Lifting his fist he held it under the web, then opened his hand. A speck blundered upward.

"Oh, look at that," said Virginia. "It's stuck. It can't get away."

"Here she comes," whispered John. "See? She's really fast. Now she's paying out line and throwing it over. She's wrapping up her breakfast."

"Horrible," said Virginia, shuddering. "Horrible, horrible. What's she doing now? She's just sitting there."

"She's poisoning it. Then she'll suck it dry."

Virginia moaned and turned away. "Why couldn't everything in the world have been vegetarian? I mean, since the beginning of time?"

"Wasps are worse than that," said John. "Some of them catch spiders and paralyze them and lay their eggs on them, and then when the wasp grubs hatch out, they eat the parts of the spiders in just the right order, so the guts get saved till last, so the spiders won't die too soon. They'll still be fresh and delicious."

Virginia grimaced with horror. "Oh, that's terrible. It's so appalling that the world should have been made that way." She clenched her fists. "But if it's as rotten as that, you have to know it. I mean, some of it is so beautiful — ," Virginia waved her hand at the maple tree in front of the house, a towering volume of ten thousand fresh green leaves, " — you forget that life on earth is founded on this rapacity, this nightmare."

She was really upset. John was astonished. "But don't you think they're amazing?" he said. "Spiders, I mean? They do such amazing things. They're so complicated, and the things they do by instinct are so — well, just so fascinating."

"Listen," said Virginia, frowning, staring fiercely at a ragged dishcloth hanging beside her on the laundry line, "I've thought about this before, and there's a way out. You can believe in progress."

"Progress? I thought nobody believed in progress any more. Just — you know — in the old days. People like Ralph Waldo Emerson maybe, but nobody anymore, right?"

"No, no." Virginia shook her head. "I don't mean scientific and industrial progress. I mean, people can be better than animals. Or they could learn to be, someday. Little by little. At least they're not all cannibals, like your spider. Oh, I know what you're going to say. We still have wars, worse than ever before, and nuclear bombs and mass murderers. We're not even as good as Socrates, twenty-five hundred years ago. Well, I'm not saying I agree with my idea of progress. But at least it's a logical way out."

"After all," said John cheerfully, "everybody isn't a mass murderer, right? Some people are okay."

Virginia's solemnity collapsed. She laughed. "Some people

are okay! Oh, that's right. You, for instance. You, standing there looking at your spider, you almost balance out its horribleness. Really, I mean it, you really do."

"Well, but spiders aren't all bad. Look, there's something really interesting about this one." John pointed out the place where the barn spider had lost a leg. "It will grow back. If people could replace lost limbs like that, it would be really useful."

"What are you two staring at?"

It was Buddy, coming out on the porch, carrying his Winchester shotgun jauntily under one arm.

Virginia looked at the shotgun. "What are you going to do with that thing?"

"Oh, I'm an old sharpshooter from way back. There's a lot of things running around in the woods, good to eat, just going to waste."

"Oh, you wouldn't." Virginia was scandalized.

"Sure I would. And besides, every household needs some kind of protection. You know, some kind of old musket hanging on the wall. A shotgun in the closet. You never know when some madman might show up, some nut from Walden Pond." Buddy slapped the barrel of his gun. "Say," he said, looking up at the spiderweb, "isn't that cute? A nice little cobweb all covered with dew." With a casual sweep of his gun barrel, Buddy brushed it away.

Virginia was shocked. She dropped to her knees, looking for the spider. "Buddy, you clumsy ox, what did you do that for?"

"Well, what the hell?" said Buddy. "I'm sorry."

"The spider's all right." John pointed upward. "She's okay. See? She's still there."

Virginia stood up and looked at the spider crawling across the ceiling. "Can she make another web?"

"Oh, sure. Every day, if she wants to. It only takes her an hour or so. I've watched them lots of times. I've got some web frames in my room. My Nuctenea sclopetarias make new webs every couple of days. Say — ," John looked eagerly at Virginia, " — would you like to see my collection?"

"Oh, yes," said Virginia, "I would."

Buddy hadn't been invited, but he followed them up the narrow stairway. He had no intention of leaving them alone in John's room by themselves. In spite of himself, Buddy was irritated at the way John kept winning brownie points with Virginia. And wouldn't you know, in John's room she was just *fascinated* with everything. She oohed and aahed at the spiderwebs in the wooden boxes and watched John dump a couple of spiders out of his jars and hold them in his hand. Now she was watching reverently as he pulled a box out from under his bed and opened the top.

"What's that smell?" said Buddy, wrinkling his nose.

"Bran," said John. "I raise mealworms in this box of bran. Spider fodder. The spiders like them and they're easy to keep. Mealworms take care of themselves. They eat the bran, grow up into beetles, mate and lay eggs, and the eggs hatch and produce more mealworms, and then they pupate and change into beetles. They just go on and on, without any help from me."

"I see." Virginia smiled. "To the mealworms that box is the whole universe, right? Do they think it's a miracle when light floods in and one of them gets snatched to glory?"

"Well, what would you think," babbled John, "if there was a big crack in the sky right now and a gigantic beetle reached out his colossal claw —"

Buddy felt pushed aside, ignored. He could feel Virginia's respect for John mounting, filling the small room, pressing against the cracked ceiling and the rickety windows — all for a bunch of spiders, a creepy hobby for a stupid kid. It wasn't fair. Buddy himself was really doing big things for Virginia, knocking himself out, solving every problem as it reared its head, setting great forces into motion, big things, really big. And yet they didn't count for anything, next to a bunch of fucking bugs in this little bastard's room.

Angrily Buddy picked up a catalogue and looked through it, not seeing the pages as they flipped past his thumb. The trouble was, John wasn't really such a little kid. He might look like one, but he was — what? — sixteen, seventeen? Old enough to be gone on Virginia. You could smell it, sickly sweet in the room, like the stink of that filthy stuff in the box. But the real question was what Virginia thought of John. Was he just a cute little kid, or was he a budding entomologist and fucking big future Ph.D.? Oh God, how could you tell with Virginia?

Sullenly Buddy stared at the pamphlet in his hand. It was a catalogue of insects you could order from some place in Georgia.

Terrestrial isopods. Wood lice,

said the catalogue.

L624: pr sow bugs. Field-collected.
Per 12 . . . $2.50; 100 . . . $17.50.

Imagine paying seventeen-fifty for a bunch of wood lice! Buddy's eyes drifted down the page.

Latrodectus mactans. Black widow spider. Poisonous.
Females only. Live delivery not guaranteed.
Each . . . $7.50.

Seven-fifty for a black widow spider? Now that was more like it. Cheap at twice the price.

Seventeen

THE RABBITS HAD EATEN MOST OF BARBARA'S BEANS. BARBARA and Virginia and John looked at the devastation. "You know what I could do," said John, "I could build a chicken-wire fence. Bury it deep against woodchucks. Did you know there's a woodchuck hole over there? Huge, really enormous."

"Oh, I don't care about the woodchucks, or the rabbits either," said Barbara. "What really bothers me is the birds. They're just waiting to come down and grab all the raspberries."

"I can fix that too," said John. "I'll just mow the lawn first. Then I'll show you."

With the little electric lawnmower John buzzed around the perimeter of the sunken garden and whizzed back and forth across the flat lawn in front of the house. Then he gathered up a basket of grass clippings and emptied it on the floor of his room. He took a shirt and a pair of old pants out of his closet and stuffed them with the clippings. There was a dusty tennis racquet cover in a box in the loft and a beekeeper's veiled hat hanging on a hook in the laundry. John stuffed the tennis racquet cover with newspapers, fastened the whole thing together with safety pins, crowned it with the beekeeper's hat, hung it on a stick, and brought it down to the vegetable garden. Virginia clapped her hands and ran off to the attic for a lacy shawl and some plastic roses.

"It's a transvestite scarecrow," she said, laughing, pinning the roses to the hat, standing back to watch the shawl lift and billow in the breeze.

"I could give it some motorized arms," suggested John brightly. "They'd really whirl around."

"Never mind," said Barbara, who didn't believe in the scarecrow. "Let it alone. At least it looks nice." She turned her head. "What's that? All that shouting?"

The three of them ran up the hill to find Buddy's tenant at the door of the house, yelling at Buddy. Buddy turned to them with a smile of amused innocence and shrugged his shoulders helplessly. John looked with sympathy at the tenant. The poor man was out of luck. He had signed no legal documents. He had no lease, no way of fighting back against the arrogant whim of his landlord. He was stalking away in a rage.

A few days later John saw the tenant's car bumping down the driveway. It was packed with wife, children, baby, au pair girl, dogs, cats, suitcases, bassinet, playpen, and a large green parrot in a cage. The evicted father of the family leaned out of the driver's seat and shook his fist at John. The dogs barked. The parrot squawked.

"Don't look at me," murmured John. "It's not my fault."

No sooner were the old occupants out of Buddy's house than the new ones were in. Up the driveway lurched the cars of the friends and supporters of ex-Governor Howard Croney, and Croney's own Lincoln Continental, hired for the duration, and the big red-white-and-blue campaign vans with loudspeakers and huge signs mounted on top — RE-ELECT CRONEY, EXPERIENCE COUNTS.

One day a small yellow car pulled into the driveway and stopped behind Virginia as she was filling a watering can at the faucet under the kitchen window. Virginia didn't hear the car.

She was paying close attention to the change in pitch of the pouring water. As the echoing chamber in the watering can grew smaller, the musical splash tinkled higher and higher. When the driver of the car got out and slammed the door, Virginia looked up in surprise.

"Would you be so good as to tell me where those idiots are swarming?" said Madeline Croney. "I know it's around here somewhere."

Virginia recognized the ex-Governor's wife. Feeling a gush of sympathy, she smiled and directed her up the hill.

Croney himself stopped at the house the next day and beamed at John. "Hello, son. Isn't this a lovely home you've got here! I've come for Mr. Whipple. And of course I'd be pleased to meet your parents, shake their hand."

So Buddy was busier than ever. He was away and up the hill, then down again, brimming at the supper table with political savvy and inside talk. Croney had made him campaign coordinator for the western suburbs of Boston. "He wants me to call him Howie," said Buddy proudly.

"Listen here, Buddy," said Barbara, "why don't you live up there now? I should think you'd be a lot more comfortable in your own bed."

"Oh, no," said Buddy. "I wouldn't want to leave you people alone. And, say, that reminds me. I've got to go to the town hall and talk to William Warren about the things we're planning to do down here. You know, for our new agricultural status. Hey, something occurred to me the other day. We could call your trees a woodlot."

"The trees?" said Barbara. "The copper beech trees? The white pines?"

"Well, you know, you just call it timber, and you get a different assessment. It doesn't mean you have to cut them down. And there's the orchard down there. Sooner or later you could clear out the jungle and prune the trees."

"I like that jungle the way it is now," said Virginia stubbornly.

"How about the pond?" said Barbara dryly. "Why don't you stock it with fish and have a fish farm?"

"Not a bad idea," said Buddy, grinning.

"Now, look here, Buddy," said Barbara. "I won't have you lying to William on our behalf."

"Of course not," said Buddy. "Tell you what. Why don't we go see him together? You tell him about your place. I'll tell him about mine."

"Good," said Barbara grimly.

Buddy went to bed, pleased with his progress on all fronts. It was just a matter of knowing how to do things, of reaching forward to arrange the shape of things. You had to think ahead. Not like most people, who just lay flat on their backs and let the future roll right over them. His own mind was always darting in front of him, exploring his options, examining possible actions, comparing them with each other, thinking about it and thinking about it, until the right one seemed to shine in a shaft of light. And then there were always a lot of steps to be taken first, and sometimes sudden opportunities opened up in front of you when you least expected them, and you could always tell when you were on the right track, because the rewards would begin to pour in, and the congratulations. But sometimes there was only the secret knowledge that things were working out. Like that letter this morning, from Dolores Leech. Without even knowing it, Dolores was playing her part in the unrolling of Buddy's brilliant future.

Dear Buddy,

Good Lord, you couldn't have been more right. Mrs. Bewley is living in a pig sty. Well, a chicken sty actually. Chicken fecal matter is all over the floor, and I'll bet she has poultry mites in her hair. The house is falling down around her ears. Her physical health seems to be good, except for her hearing problem, but of course her mental condition is deteriorating. I understand from my cousin on the police force that she is also a repeated minor offender.

I think she should be in a nursing home, one like Ferndale

Manor in Waltham. I suppose she would have to be kept in Total Care, because of the kleptomania. Think of those sticky fingers of hers among all those old ladies with their prize doilies and needle-point pillows and bric-a-brac and so on, all crowded into their little rooms! Total Care means a lock on the door, but there would be daily excursions to the sun-porch, the dining room, the TV den and so on, with an aide in constant attendance. She would be a trial to the staff, but I see no other solution.

I cannot allow a human being to continue to exist in such appalling conditions.

Yours,

Dolores Leech, RN

Plumbing still gurgling merrily! Garage still functioning! Thanks to you, Buddy, dear!

Eighteen

BARBARA WAS EARLY FOR HER APPOINTMENT WITH WILLIAM Warren at the town hall. At the last minute she had persuaded John to come with her. John and Barbara found Amelia Farhang in the lobby of the town hall, working on one of her more ambitious flower arrangements, setting it up on a table between the information booth and the water fountain.

Amelia was eager to explain to Barbara the philosophical foundation of her composition. Jamming a flower into a hole in her piece of driftwood, she talked breezily over her shoulder. "You see, Barbara, this tall overarching delphinium stands for heaven. And this little blade of pampas grass symbolizes man. This horizontal cattail — drat, it won't stay flat — represents the earth. Do you see? Universal elemental principles in the language of the flowers." Mrs. Farhang stuck a wad of clay like a piece of chewed bubblegum to the driftwood, attempting to rigidify, sustain, and undergird the earth.

"Where's Mr. Warren's office?" said John.

"Down the hall," said Barbara. "I told Buddy I'd meet him here. We'd better wait."

"He's here already," said John. "Hear him behind that door? That's Buddy."

"So it is," said Barbara. From the next room they could hear Buddy's hearty laugh breaking out over the confused rumble of talk. A loud voice proclaimed, *"Going once, going twice."*

"Sounds like an auction," said John. "What do they auction off in the Lincoln town hall?"

"Only one thing, I guess," said Barbara curtly. "Real estate. For default of taxes or something, I suppose."

The door was opening. Mrs. Barker, the town clerk, came out with one of the selectmen, then Buddy Whipple with the town treasurer, George Shipley. George was clapping Buddy on the back, congratulating him on his successful bid. "Although I must say, Buddy, I don't know what the hell you want that piece of land for. Even the Conservation Commission couldn't see any point in adding it to their collection. Wouldn't join up with anything they've got anyplace else. And too skinny for much of anything except maybe a right of way. And who'd want a right of way to a swamp? Well, I'm glad it's off our hands, anyhow. Say, Buddy, listen here, we're going to have another piece coming up shortly. Taxes haven't been paid in twenty years. We've lost touch with the owner entirely. Another damned useless little piece only a few hundred feet from side to side. Are you interested?"

"Well, I don't know," said Buddy. "I might be. Where is it?"

"Out Tower Road, near Route 117. Little swampy piece."

"Well, no, I guess not. No, not really."

"But the one you just bid on is mostly swamp too, right? What did you take that one for, if you don't want the next one?"

Buddy laughed. He caught sight of Barbara and John and gave them a big wave. "Oh, I don't know. How many swamps do I want to get bogged down in anyway? What do you say, John? You want a swamp cheap?"

"No, thanks." John smiled feebly and shook his head.

"Well, hello there." Someone else had emerged from the auction room and was greeting Barbara. A sharp-faced woman with a complicated hairdo waved her pocketbook. "Remember me? Dorothy Gardenside? I got it back. My bag. I called up the police department, and next day they returned it safe and sound without a word of explanation. Well, then, how are you, dear?

Have you girls made any decision about staying on in the old family homestead? I've got some really scrumptious apartments, some fabulous condominiums. Just call me any time. I'd really adore to show you around."

Barbara shook her head, not trusting herself to speak, and Dotty Gardenside drifted away to gush over Mrs. Farhang's flowers.

"What's she doing here?" muttered Barbara to John. "Oh, well, I suppose as a realtor she's interested in land as well as housing. Never let an opportunity go by. That's her motto."

"In the language of the flowers," agreed John, grinning at Barbara. "Hey, here comes Mr. Warren."

William Warren was holding open the front door for Mrs. Farhang and Mrs. Gardenside. He smiled broadly at Barbara, nodded at John, shook hands with Buddy. His thin hair was awry, his necktie wrenched to the side. He was beaming. "I've just been looking down on you people from ten thousand feet."

"You were up in a plane?" said John. "Oh, wow."

William wiped his red face. "Looking down on everything. It was like—" He waved his hands. "Wait till you see the pictures. The plane flies on a grid pattern, you see, taking pictures automatically every few seconds. They overlap, the pictures, so you can look at them with a pair of stereoscopic lenses, and the trees stick right up at you in three dimensions. It's—well, it's just—" William was still floating in the sunlight ten thousand feet above the earth. "You just wait. I'll show you the pictures when they come in."

John walked behind them to the selectmen's office, seeing them silhouetted against the fanlight at the end of the hall. William's head was surrounded by a thin aureole of windblown hair, Buddy's was shaggy and hirsute, Barbara's small and round like a cobblestone. If John had understood the universal elemental principles of the language of the flowers he might have seen William, fresh from the sky, as the airy heavens; Buddy as man, heavy with sin; and Barbara, her shoes green with grass-stain and her jeans brown with dirt, as the flat and uncompromising ground.

Nineteen

"Fine weather for the next few days," promised the meteorologist at Channel 4. "Cool and dry." In his satellite picture not a single wreathing lacework of cloud obscured the landmass of the northeastern United States. Around the big house at the top of Pine Hill the trees stood glittering, every separate leaf distinct. In the spaces between the trees light was held in suspension, defining voids and volumes of air with the precision of a crystal.

But the brilliant morning was shut out of the great dark hall of Howard Croney's campaign headquarters. The only window open to the world was the vulgar screen of the TV, permanently switched on to catch random scraps of political news and revelations about the current state of the ex-governor's public image.

Croney himself was in residence at the moment, in heavy consultation with Buddy Whipple. A sticky little problem had arisen, and Buddy was dealing with it in masterful fashion. The troublemaker was a young female volunteer with whom Croney had been exercising *droit du seigneur* in the majestic bedroom on the second floor. The stupid girl had been exultant at losing her virginity. She had been throwing her weight around, showing off, claiming rights at the conference table in the great hall as well as in the bedchamber. "She's got to go," moaned Howard Croney. "Goddamn bitchy little interfering goddamn bitch."

"It's all right," said Buddy. "Why don't you just kick her upstairs? Tell her you want her to be your special head fund raiser for the western end of the state. I'll talk to her. She'll keep her mouth shut. Let me handle it."

In the old house at the bottom of the driveway, Barbara and Virginia and John were eager to get to work outdoors. John had three acres of lawn to cut. But it was too early in the morning. The cool fragrant grass was still soaking wet with dew. The grass would fill up the mower and spew out the side in ugly green clots. And Barbara's transplanting and Virginia's violent digging up and clearing out would be easier when every leaf and blossom no longer dipped and spilled its contents down the back of one's neck.

They sat at the kitchen table with second cups of coffee, happy in the absence of Buddy Whipple, intent on different things, hardly hearing the slosh of the dishwasher or the murmur of commuting cars on Route 126.

John was writing a letter to his mother and father.

... I watched my barn spider finish one of her molts yesterday. She was hanging upside down under a lilac leaf beside the porch. It took quite a while. I sat there and just waited, until I saw the skin of her cephalothorax begin to tear, like when you rip the plastic covering off something. Then the skin split right off the abdomen, and she pumped her legs up and down. It was really amazing — how does she do that? those long skinny delicate legs! — and then she pulled out the new legs, and —

Dramatic Announcement!!
Ta-dah!!

There were eight legs! The new one is very small, but perfect. All the parts are there: femur, patella, tibia, metatarsus and tarsus. With my magnifying glass I can even see three tiny claws. She's a really good-looking spider.

Barbara was trying to catch up with her garden diary.

Now that we can do what we want, we've got a really good plan. Virginia calls it THE GREAT COMPROMISE. We're taking out the fancy stuff father liked, all those tricky perennials, and putting in native things that want to grow here anyway — trying to make a sort of halfway station between the wilderness that would be here if we let everything go to hell and the formality of father's grandiosities. All the flowers are coming out of the round border, to be replaced by red cedar and mountain laurel and pasture juniper and meadow lilies, things like that, native stuff — only we're keeping it within the brick edging in the old formal circular shape. We are excited about this.

It feels so good to be doing what we want, instead of those foolish elegancies of father's, like the sunken garden and the impossible roses. He had such absurd notions —

Barbara's pen faltered, and she stopped writing.

John felt her eyes on him, and he looked up. But Barbara was gazing right through him. Politely he looked down again at his letter.

It was really all my fault, wrote Barbara, and threw down her pen.

Virginia was writing too, on a loose sheet of notebook paper.

I think there is a gigantic creature in the sky, looking down at us with eyes like a fly's. Enormous billion-compartmented eyes flickering like a computer panel in a science-fiction movie. Whenever anything gets born — a human being, or a zebra, or a clam — a little compartment flickers on, and when we die it flickers off. There is this colossal impersonal fly's eye, stupendous, gazing down.

Virginia glanced across the table. John was drawing a picture. "Another spider, I see," she said.

"No, it's the same one," said John. "That barn spider I showed you the other day. It's grown a new leg. See? Just a miniature one, so far."

Virginia bent over the drawing, her hair brushing the page. "That's really nice. What's it's name? Oh, I see. *Araneus cavaticus*."

"What are you working on?" said John politely. (Well, not just politely. He was really curious.)

Virginia laughed. She looked back at her page and said nothing. Barbara explained. "Virginia writes these letters."

"Letters?" said John, blushing. "Oh, excuse me."

"Oh, it's all right," said Virginia. "They're not to anybody in particular. Letters to an Unknown Correspondent. Letters to the air." Snatching up her piece of paper she tossed it at the ceiling.

"It's been going on a long time," said Barbara, smiling at John. "It's a long and serious correspondence. Virginia's written an awful lot of letters to the air."

"Well, it's all been rather one-sided," said Virginia, catching her paper as it floated down.

"The air never writes back, I guess?" said John.

"No, never. Oh, of course, I open the mailbox every day, looking for an airmail letter in a pale blue envelope with a patch of rainbow for a stamp. But there's never anything like that. Isn't it sad!"

The telephone rang. Virginia leaped to her feet.

On the other side of town, Amelia Farhang flashed a conspiratorial smile at the other members of the program committee in her living room, then raised her eyebrows and mouthed, Virginia. "Oh, Virginia, dear, this is Amelia Farhang. You remember, I brought over that memorial flower arrangement the other day, after the service. Of course, I've known you since you were a little girl, but it's been a long time since I — how are you, dear? Now, Virginia, I'll have to confess to being very naughty. I had never set foot in that dear old house of yours before, although of course I used to visit the big house when your mother was alive, and — well! I had no idea! I must confess, I peeked around the house and I kept seeing the most marvelous backgrounds for our floral compositions, all those blank white walls. I mean, just perfect, those stark — not to say, bleakly powerful!

— old historical rooms. I mean, I was just so impressed. Well, the point is, what I'm leading up to is, to ask you if the Middlesex County Society of Flower Arrangers could hold our annual meeting in September in your home? You see, once a year we all get together to demonstrate our flower-arranging prowess and creativity in someone's home, in preparation for the state competition in October. In your house, for example, we would concentrate on eighteenth-century bouffant effects, large mixtures in Chinese bowls and jars, and you wouldn't have to do a thing, because we have this committee that brings in the sherry and the goodies and we set the table and then of course we fill the house with lovely arrangements, and the point is, the local chapter does so much enjoy it, and — oh, now, Virginia, you mustn't make up your mind too soon. Just give the idea a little time to —" Mrs. Farhang rolled her eyes melodramatically at her committee. "Well, of course, if you feel so strongly. I expect I rushed in too soon after — well, I'm sorry too. Well, then. Well, all right then, dear. Good-bye."

Amelia Farhang put the phone down and burst into merry laughter. The other women smiled sympathetically and leaned forward to hear her report, careful not to disturb the Japanese arrangement on Amelia's coffee table — an austere masterpiece assembled from a single calla lily, a cabbage leaf, and a long frond of swamp grass shaped into a tight spiral at the end with a curling iron. An onion and an artichoke lay beneath the container on a bed of crushed lava.

"No soap," said Amelia Farhang, shaking her head.

"Too snobbish," said Dora Turnstone.

"Typical," said Debbie Saunders. "I'd call it rather typical, wouldn't you?"

"Do you know, there didn't used to be any Herons even buried in the cemetery," said Effie Fawcett. "I mean, they wouldn't even lie stone dead next to other people. They were all cremated, and then their dust was scattered in the woods. I mean, it was almost like incest. All those family ashes mingling in the fallen leaves! Incestuous necrophilia!" Effie made gay little tossing motions in the air, the dust of the Herons flying left and right, and the committee burst into delighted whoops of laughter. Effie was so clever.

After the last giggles had subsided, it was left to Shirley Camberwell to forward the business of the meeting. "Well, you know, actually, I'm not disappointed. I've seen that place of theirs too, and I must say, I think there's something a little amateurish about it. Unfinished. And the house, after all, is falling down. There's really nothing to compare with the perfection of your home, for instance, Amelia."

"Well, of course," said Amelia Farhang complacently, "you girls are always welcome to come here again."

"Oh, yes, dear Amelia. You're always so generous."

"Some of my camellias blossom in September, and some of the orchids, and of course my big pompom mums. And I'm sure Putnam wouldn't mind at all, as long as our meeting didn't conflict with one of his political affairs. I expect the new gubernatorial race for the Republican nomination will suck him in. You can imagine how everybody cozies up to the president of the Paul Revere Insurance Company."

"Oh, Amelia, that's really grand of you. And your house is, well, it's just so perfect."

It was true. Amelia Farhang's house was only two years old, but it had been brought out of nothing in a single giant effort by a team of architects, landscape gardeners and interior decorators. Bulldozers had cleared the woods and dug a great hole. The house had been erected, roofed over, completed. Rug samples and swatches of fabric had been whisked in and out. Full-grown shrubs and evergreen trees had been dropped into the ground around the foundation. Low walls and sweeping shallow steps and bluestone terraces had been created, all in a momentary slice through time, all in a single summer. The Farhangs' house was harmonious, perfect, finished and done.

"We'll need something really fabulous for my dining room table," said Amelia. "Dibs on that. You girls can do the rest."

"Oh, Amelia, it will be such good practice for the big show

in October," said Effie Fawcett. "But we already know who's going to win the creativity award, don't we, girls?"

"Amelia!" cried Shirley Camberwell and Dora Turnstone and Debbie Saunders. "Amelia Farhang! Let's hear it for Amelia!"

Twenty

THE RASPBERRIES WERE RIPE. JOHN MOVED AMONG THEM WITH his bowl, stopping to admire the black and sulphur-yellow belly of a huge garden spider suspended on her great round web among the thorny brambles. Birds had snatched up a goodly share of the raspberries, in spite of the limp arms of John's scarecrow and the tossing veil of the beekeeper's hat and the trailing shawl. But there were plenty of berries left. Enough so that John could eat as he picked and still fill his bowl with the dull-red, soft, sweet fruit. They crushed deliciously against the roof of his mouth. His hands were soon stained with the over-ripe ones that squished between his fingers.

He took the bowl to the kitchen, then set out on another expedition. This time he was looking for bugs to feed his spiders. Scouting outside the kitchen window, he saw a hornet rise over his head and drop into one of the yew bushes that arched over the stone steps.

Maybe there was a nest in the yew bush. John bent down and peered inside. Yes, there it was, a medium-sized nest deep in the twiggy interior. By the end of the summer it would be huge, with a population of ten thousand white-faced hornets, most of them equipped with mean little stingers in their hind-quarters. Ten thousand hornets, right here where people went back and forth all the time.

John stood up and waited to see where they went in and out. He was pleased when one of them rose from the hedge on the other side, away from the stone steps — then another, and another. That was all right, then. They wouldn't interfere with human traffic on the stairs. He could leave them alone. And it would be fun to keep an eye on them, and record their doings in his notebook. Next fall when he came home from college for Thanksgiving, he could drop over and see if they had been frozen out, and then he could take the nest apart and count the number of cells and see how many stories tall their apartment house had grown to be. (And of course it would be a good excuse to see Virginia.)

The phone was ringing. John ran indoors and snatched it up. Then he winced, and held the squawking phone away from his ear. "I'm sorry," said John. "What did you say?"

The crazed voice on the line screeched again. Barbara was coming into the kitchen. Grinning helplessly, John held up the receiver so that she could hear.

"Oh, I know who that is." Barbara hurried across the room and took the phone. "HELLO, MRS. BEWLEY, WHAT CAN I DO FOR YOU THIS MORNING?"

There were noisy sobs and gulping screams.

"LISTEN, MRS. BEWLEY," said Barbara, "I'LL BE RIGHT OVER. I'LL HANG UP NOW." Barbara turned to John. "She's had a letter. Some kind of letter. She's all upset. I don't know what the hell it is. And her hens won't lay. And something's the matter with her TV. Why don't you come along and take a look at the TV, while I see what her letter is about? Wait a minute." Barbara looked around the kitchen, poked in a drawer, pulled out a bottle brush with a pink handle and put it in her pocket.

"What's that for?" said John.

"Oh, I think it might come in handy."

Mrs. Bewley's house was around the corner, just beyond the sharp curve on Route 126. It had once been inhabited by the chauffeur for the big horsey establishment at the top of the hill. Mrs. Bewley's brother had driven hard-riding Higginsons back and forth to the Lincoln depot in massive touring cars, and later on, in Edward Heron's time, he had become a general handyman. And then he had retired, and now he was dead, and his elderly sister lived on in the house alone. It had once been a pleasant clapboard cottage, but now it was falling into decay. The roof sagged. The floor of the porch had rotted through.

John followed Barbara up Mrs. Bewley's weedy driveway to the back of the house. They found her peering at them through her lorgnette from the kitchen door. As they climbed the back steps Mrs. Bewley reached for Barbara and tugged her inside. She didn't seem to see John. He had to wedge his foot in the door to keep it from slamming in his face. Inside the house Mrs. Bewley was galloping Barbara through the small kitchen. In the living room John was astonished to see a number of tiny hens roosting in a gigantic rubber plant. There were fluffy black ones with white pompoms falling over their eyes, and gold ones with bushy ankle feathers. Under the rubber plant there were encrusted deposits of chicken droppings.

"Wow," said John impulsively, "Polish bantams. I've only seen them in pictures."

"JOHN'S HERE TO LOOK AT YOUR TV," explained Barbara.

John nodded and smiled at Mrs. Bewley. But she had no eyes for John. She was thrusting a letter at Barbara, with cries of "MINE, MINE."

"Well, just a minute," said Barbara, turning the letter rightside up.

John knelt on the floor beside the TV set and switched it on. Immediately it began shouting at top volume and flopping its picture. He turned the volume down and twisted the vertical-hold button. The picture slowed down and stopped, becoming a man with a jar in his hand, talking fast, tapping the jar with his finger. John stood up, his task accomplished.

Barbara looked up from Mrs. Bewley's letter. "Damn," she said. Then she read it through again.

Dear Mrs. Bewley,

After inspecting your home and upon consultation with the Board of Health, I have obtained an order from Dr. Rosenberg, committing you to Ferndale Manor in Waltham on August first. I am happy to inform you that a place is being held for you there. Ferndale is an up-to-date and comfortable nursing home, with the best of facilities and medical care. You will have your own room with upholstered lounge chair, bed, dresser, coffee table and TV. Proper disposal of your home and its furnishings can be made at some future date. We are all anxious to see you comfortably settled in the hygienic surroundings of Ferndale Manor as soon as possible, in the interest of your health and general well-being.

> Sincerely yours,
>
> Dolores Leech, Lincoln Town Nurse

"Oh, hell," said Barbara. She shook her head with disgust and handed the letter back to Mrs. Bewley.

"MINE, MINE." Mrs. Bewley waved her skinny arms at her rubber plant, her chickens, her TV, her living room, her house, her weedy yard, the earth below and the sky above, all of the world that was hers to possess.

Barbara put her hands on Mrs. Bewley's shaking shoulders. "IT'S ALL RIGHT," she said. "I'LL TAKE CARE OF IT. YOU DON'T HAVE TO GO TO A NURSING HOME IF YOU DON'T WANT TO. DON'T WORRY ABOUT THAT OLD LETTER."

Reassured, Mrs. Bewley beamed at Barbara, discovered John for the first time, shrieked with pleasure at the sight of two women weeping on her television screen, and allowed her visitors to depart.

"What was all that about a nursing home?" said John, picking his way carefully in the scrubby undergrowth along Route 126 as cars sped past them around the blind curve.

"Oh, the town nurse is trying to get Mrs. Bewley out of her house and into a nursing home."

"Oh, say, that's too bad."

Barbara shook her head gloomily. "I'll do what I can. I

mean, I'm a nurse too. But I don't know if I can stop them. The letter mentioned hygiene. They're thinking about the chickens. You know —"

John nodded his head wisely. "Chicken shit."

"She should keep those birds in a proper chicken house outside."

"Say," said John, "there's a little shed behind the house. Did you see it? It would be just right."

"We could fix it up for her," said Barbara, looking at John. "Build a fence around it."

"I used to keep chickens," said John. "You know, those bantam hens of hers are really nice."

Barbara was pleased. "That's good, John. You could fix up the shed for the chickens, and Virginia and I — oh, God — we could clean up her house. Then we could call in the nasty-neat hygiene-and-health people and the Universal Cleanliness Is next to Godliness Society and let them take another look. How about it?"

"Fine," said John. "That would be great. Say, Barbara, I see you've still got that brush thing in your pocket. What was it for, anyway?"

Barbara took out the bottle brush. "That proves how upset she was. It was just a polite gesture on my part, bringing her something to snatch. She didn't take it. She was so miserable she even forgot her natural instincts. The poor old soul!"

Twenty-One

BARBARA LOST NO TIME IN WRITING A LETTER TO THE TOWN
nurse.

Dear Dolores,

I've just seen the letter you wrote to Mrs. Alice Bewley,
committing her to a nursing home. I hope you'll reconsider your
decision. She is deeply distressed. As her neighbor and friend, I've
decided to take some responsibility from now on for helping her
maintain her house in a healthful condition.

I hope you'll make another inspection before you remove her
from her home.

Yours truly,

Barbara Heron, RN

Opening the galvanized iron jaw of the mailbox, she put
her letter inside and reached for Virginia's bucket. "Here, I'll
take it," she said.

"No, no, I'm all right. You've got enough to carry, with
the mop and broom. Where's Buddy? I thought he was going to
fix Mrs. Bewley's front porch."

"Oh, I don't give a damn where Buddy is. The front porch
doesn't matter. It will be enough to clean out the inside." Bar-

bara swung her mop over her shoulder and marched down the crumbling driveway. "Oh, God, I don't know how we're going to live through this. But we can't let Mrs. Bewley's life be wrecked like that, can we?"

"Of course not. Besides, you know what they'd do next. They'd come in with a bulldozer and knock her house down to raise the tone of the neighborhood." Virginia picked up a couple of beer cans and dropped them in her bucket. "And I like the tone the way it is, a little seedy, don't you? Look out!" Virginia jumped back as a large shining car whipped between the brick gateposts and shot up the hill.

"Who was that?" said Howard Croney, craning his neck to look back. "Rather attractive, the blonde one. Real class, you can see that. What are those women doing with those buckets and mops?"

The car swayed up the bumpy driveway. Buddy made an instantaneous decision to keep Virginia to himself. "Neighbors," he said briefly. "That reminds me, I said I'd do a little job for Barbara. Oh, well, it can wait." Buddy grinned to himself, comparing the humble task of replacing Mrs. Bewley's rotten porch floorboards with the exalted wheeling and dealing that now took so much of his time. He would explain to Barbara that something had come up. After all, he was on the phone all the time, and all over the map, trying to run Croney's suburban campaign, not to mention all the work of keeping track of his own personal affairs. There were just so many things he had to keep on top of. Some things would just have to wait their turn. First things first.

The car pulled up in the great courtyard of Buddy's house, and he climbed out, feeling serenely competent to handle everything. At times like this it amused him to remember how his senior advisor at Harvard had kept telling him he was irresponsible and sloppy about detail. "Whipple, the overarching master plan of this paper is superb. Congratulations on the grand design.

Look at this sweeping statement, magnificent! But the whole thing is resting on air. Detail is what's needed here, man. You're sloppy about the nitty-gritty. When you get out there in the real world, you'll discover that what separates the men from the boys is attention to small detail. You hear that, Whipple?"

Well, so much for his nitwit senior advisor. Buddy had already been on the way up, right then in senior year, with a girlfriend who just happened to be the daughter of a top-management guy at Cabot and Childs, and before long Buddy had been a member of the firm himself. Of course, things had kind of gone to pot after a while and he had quit before he got fired. But then one thing had led to another, and look at him now! Right in the middle of all this really big stuff.

Howard Croney walked ahead of Buddy, swaggering into the great front hall of his campaign headquarters. Buddy smiled to himself. You could almost see the mantle of ducal splendor descend on Croney's shoulders from the high dark spaces of the surrounding balcony, from the sweeping antlers of the moose, from the glossy eyes of the ten-point buck, even from the cheery greetings of the volunteers at the addressing machine. It pleased Buddy to see how much this borrowed grandeur meant to Croney. His debt of gratitude to Buddy was growing bigger all the time.

Settling down at the telephone to call a list of big-name contributors, Buddy remembered the way his father had always told him to start at the bottom and work his way up. Poor old Pop. If there was one thing Buddy had found out for himself, over and over again, it was to start at the top and go higher still.

Barbara and Virginia found Mrs. Bewley talking at the top of her lungs to John, as he worked on her outdoor chicken yard. John was nodding politely, unrolling chicken wire, stapling it to his new stakes. He had made a hinged flap for his new chicken-sized door in the side of the shed.

Virginia and Barbara admired the work in progress, then went indoors and marched bravely into the living room. "Oh, Lord," said Barbara, putting down her mop and broom. "I don't know if I can stand it."

Twenty-Two

BARBARA'S LETTER TO THE TOWN NURSE BROUGHT A PROMPT reply.

Dear Barbara,

Thank you for your thoughtful letter about Mrs. Bewley. Of course I will make another inspection of her house. I'm glad to hear she has good neighbors to look after her. You are certainly correct in thinking that it would be a serious step to remove a woman of Mrs. Bewley's years from her own home.

We would never do such a thing without good cause, you can be sure of that.

Yours truly,
Dolores Leech, RN

Mrs. Bewley was restless.

She walked around her clean house.

She stared through her lorgnette at her polished rubber plant.

She turned on the TV. It was on the fritz again. All it would do was make wiggly lines.

Mrs. Bewley went to the window to watch her bantam hens step daintily around their little yard.

They were so cute. Just look at Maxie! A bright picture bobbed up in Mrs. Bewley's mind, a memory of a happy childhood on a poultry farm deep in the back country of rural New Hampshire. She had been the youngest of five children. Now she was the only one left.

Mrs. Bewley made up her mind. She opened the back door, marched down the porch steps, undid the hook of the chicken wire gate, snatched up Maxie and hurried back into the house. She would just take Maxie inside for a while, to keep her company.

But then, thinking it over, stroking Maxie's golden feathers, she decided to go outside again for Margie. She would just take the cutest ones back indoors. Just Margie and Muriel. And Minnie, of course! Minnie was so darling!

Twenty-Three

GLITTERING GREEN JAPANESE BEETLES WERE HEAPED UPON EACH other, copulating on the Boston ivy vine that clambered over the foundation of Amelia Farhang's greenhouse. Under the brick coping, *Polistes fuscatus*, the house wasp, was building new layers of cells.

Mrs. Farhang was unaware of the wasps and the Japanese beetles. She was lifting a hammer high over her head and bringing it down with all her might to crush the stems of a bundle of calla lilies from the florist.

Her hair was tumbled. There was a pencil in her teeth. She was glancing again and again at the open pages of a book. In a fit of total absorption, she was trying to copy a seventeenth-century Flemish painting of masses of flowers in a glass vase: gigantic cabbage roses, parrot tulips, lilies. There were butterflies poised among the blossoms in the picture, a caterpillar inching his way along a leaf, a bee on a petal, an ant on a shining stem. Abundance, proclaimed the painting, the fertility and variety of all created things.

Picking up a rhinestone butterfly, Mrs. Farhang pinned it to the stem of one of her calla lilies. Then she fastened an enameled tietack in the shape of a ladybug to the bud of a Peace rose and stepped back to muse over the result.

Something more was needed.

A horsefly was buzzing against the glass roof of the greenhouse. Mrs. Farhang brightened. Just the thing! Snatching up a handful of sphagnum moss, she trapped the horsefly cleverly against the glass and skewered it with a corsage pin. Then with nimble fingers she glued it delicately to the magenta petal of a spray of gladiolus.

Perfect. She was finished. One knew when one was finished. There was that look of calm serenity; that harmony that comes with the balance of opposing forces, lines, textures, colors; that satisfying sweep of curve answering to curve. Amelia picked up her flower arrangement, carried it to the living room and set it down dramatically in front of her husband.

"It's too bad to waste it on the church," she said. "It's got *Best in Show* written all over it. Well, of course, it's good practice for the big competition in October. You know, Putnam, everybody says I'll get the top creativity award. You know what Effie Fawcett said about my flowers for the church last Sunday? She said she stopped listening to the sermon and just listened to the flowers. There's something *cosmic* about my arrangements, Effie says. 'You know what, Amelia?' Effie said, 'Your posies, they really make you think.'"

"You've got a dead fly there," said Putnam, reaching over to brush it off.

"Fooled you!" giggled Amelia, delighted.

Putnam stared at the dead fly. "Well, if you ask me, I think it looks terrible. Just terrible. My God, Amelia, why don't you girls just leave the flowers alone?"

It was an old family argument. Amelia closed her eyes in silent self-pity. For the thousandth time she told herself, *I am married to a philistine.*

The doorbell rang. Putnam jumped to his feet. "I forgot to tell you, Buddy Whipple is coming over."

"Buddy Whipple?" Amelia was surprised. "What does he want with you?"

"You'll never believe it. He wants me to support ex-Governor Croney's nomination."

"You must be kidding."

"Nope. It's a fact." Putnam swung open the door and gave Buddy a hearty greeting. Amelia dodged out of sight, just peeking around the corner to see if Buddy would notice her flowers. He didn't. Snorting in silent contempt, Amelia gathered up her collecting basket and went outdoors to see what she could find. You just never knew what interesting accessories might turn up along the road.

"Now, Buddy," said Putnam Farhang good-humoredly, "what's all this about Croney's nomination? You must know how I feel about Croney."

Buddy grinned at him. "Well, I can imagine what you *think* you think. But wait till you hear what I've got to say. You may change your mind."

Putnam brought two cans of beer from the kitchen. By the time they were half drained he was leaning back in his chair, dizzy with the sense of a once-in-a-lifetime triumph, trying to adjust his mind to the scale of this tremendous coup, feeling like whatsisname when he gazed at the Pacific with a something-or-other surmise. "You say a new Croney administration might be genuinely dissatisfied with the Commonwealth's long association with our competitor, the Benjamin Franklin Insurance Company? They might want to switch to another outfit? All the insurance contracts in the state of Massachusetts? Now, see here, Buddy, I must be absolutely certain this is entirely aboveboard and without hint of any suggestion that I might be acting in my own self-interest, or anything like that. All you want me to do is to encourage an Independents for Croney movement in the western suburbs? I certainly see no harm in that. Good heavens, Amelia, what in Christ's name have you got there?"

His wife was standing in the doorway, dusty, disheveled, jubilant, dragging a rusty chain. "I found it by the road," she said. "It's just what I've been looking for. A really powerful accessory. You know, something really strong and virile. Only it's too long. How do I cut it in half?"

"My God, Amelia, that would take a blowtorch. Who ever heard of arranging a bunch of God's own flowers with a blowtorch?"

Twenty-Four

BARBARA WHIZZED PAST THE WALDEN POND PARKING LOT, HER car full of groceries. There were seven brown bags on the back seat. If Barbara and Virginia had been living by themselves they would have subsisted on air and the vegetables from the garden. And of course the addition of Buddy Whipple to the household made no difference either — Buddy could cook his own food. Barbara frowned, remembering that Buddy had promised to take his turn at the cooking once in a while — he had this fabulous spaghetti sauce, he said. Well, so far he hadn't gotten around to it. And he was often absent from meals without warning in a careless way that infuriated Barbara, even though she was always relieved by his absence, by the buoyancy of lifted spirits when he was not present at the table, not crowding them with the broad-shouldered ferocity of his good humor, not looming over the table with his great sunburned face, not throwing his muscular arm over Virginia's shoulders. The worst times were the days when Virginia responded to his heavy-handed kidding. Yesterday — Barbara winced, remembering — Virginia and Buddy had been standing close together at the kitchen counter, and he had been chaffing her as she made a pile of sandwiches. He had put out his hand to her hair. Virginia had turned to

Barbara. "Whole wheat or rye?" she had said, but with a flushed, distracted look, as if she hadn't really focused on Barbara at all, as if she felt only the physical presence at her side.

No, the seven bags of groceries were not for Buddy. They were for young John. John was a growing boy. He ate with the careless greed of youth. He needed solid square meals: meat and potatoes, fresh zucchini, early corn and tomatoes, Virginia's clever desserts. He needed to come back for seconds and thirds.

The groceries swayed in the back of the car as Barbara made a quick left turn in the middle of the sharp curve on Route 126. As she jounced into the potholes at the bottom of the driveway, she caught a glimpse in the rearview mirror of a car pulling up beside Mrs. Bewley's house. A woman was getting out of the car, a plumpish woman in a white uniform and white shoes.

Dolores Leech! The town nurse was making her promised inspection. Barbara smiled, imagining her surprise at the immaculate living room, so recently cleaned and vacuumed and aired out to the summer breeze by two grim women breathing with difficulty through their mouths. With John's help they had dragged all Mrs. Bewley's furniture outdoors, washed it with brushes and warm soapy water, dried it with rags and left it to bake in the sun. Then they hosed down the rubber plant and spent the rest of a repulsive afternoon scraping up the guano and scrubbing the floor.

Dolores would certainly be surprised and pleased.

Later in the day Barbara finished planting her rooted euonymus cuttings around the base of the barn foundation. She put away her garden fork and dropped all the little plastic pots in the sink. Then she washed her hands and picked up the phone.

"MRS. BEWLEY?"

"WHO'S THAT?"

"THIS IS BARBARA HERON. THE TOWN NURSE CAME TO SEE YOU TODAY. WHAT HAPPENED? WHAT DID SHE SAY?"

"OH, SHE WAS REAL NICE." Mrs. Bewley giggled noisily. "SAY, YOU WANT TO KNOW WHAT TIME IT IS? JUST A MINUTE. IT'S QUARTER PAST FOUR."

"Yes, but, Mrs. Bewley. DID SHE SAY ANYTHING? YOU KNOW, ABOUT MOVING YOU OUT OF THERE INTO A NURSING HOME?"

"OH, NO. AND MAXIE LAID AN EGG! IMAGINE THAT! I THOUGHT SHE WAS A BOY!"

"Well, that's a relief. THAT'S GOOD. I'M REALLY GLAD. I'LL BET THAT'S THE LAST YOU'LL SEE OF HER."

"OH, NO, I'D NEVER GET RID OF MAXIE. YOU WANT TO KNOW WHAT TIME IT IS NOW? JUST A MINUTE. IT'S SEVENTEEN MINUTES PAST FOUR."

"Well, all right. VERY GOOD, MRS. BEWLEY. I'LL HANG UP NOW. THAT'S JUST FINE."

Barbara turned to Virginia, who was coming into the house, the front of her skirt full of green beans. "What did she mean, telling me what time it is?" Then it dawned on Barbara, and she whooped with laughter. "You know what Mrs. Bewley did? She stole Dolores Leech's watch. She did. She just up and swiped it."

"Well, is she all right? Did Dolores say she can stay?"

"I guess it's all right now. Mrs. Bewley didn't seem to be worried. Well, how could she be? After all that gruesome work we did? The day is saved."

Twenty-Five

ANOTHER WINDY NIGHT UNSEATED JOHN'S BARN SPIDER ONCE again, and blew her around the corner of the porch to the front lawn. Swiftly she crawled back to the house and made her way up a drain spout beside the front door. Halfway to the lintel of the door she began building a new web between the spout and the shutter of the living room window. In the thickness of the house wall, only a few inches away from the spider as she dropped and climbed and payed out thread, a mouse was suckling nine naked sacs of milk. And at the top of the house wall where the tossing branches of the maple tree brushed against the eaves, a colony of carpenter ants was hard at work, chewing the rotting wood, carving out spacious galleries in which to lay their eggs.

Next morning Mr. Farley W. Pike, roofing specialist, was pleased to observe the blackened rot in the eavestrough as he drove slowly past the house. It was exactly the kind of trouble he was always on the lookout for.

Mr. Pike stood with Virginia in the front yard. "See there?" he said, pointing upward. "Them's carpenter ants. They'll be into your whole house. Chew it to bits. You got to do something. You get a place like that in your eavestrough, you're in real trouble. Your whole roof will cave in."

"Oh, my God, Mr. Pike, how much would it cost to fix it?"

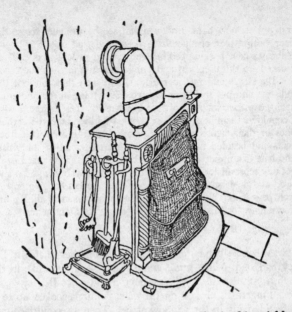

"I'll do it for you special. I mean, see, I'm in this neighborhood anyhow. Do it for four-fifty."

"Four-fifty? But surely that's too cheap for — oh, you don't mean — you mean four *hundred* and fifty —? Oh, I'm sorry, Mr. Pike. We just can't. Not now. Those ants will just have to go right on chewing."

"Well, don't say I didn't warn you. Listen, I could come next Tuesday. You think it over once or twice."

Virginia watched Mr. Pike's small ladder-covered van drive away, and then she went into the kitchen and wrote a letter to the air.

How long has it stood here really? In the face of carpenter ants and post beetles and poverty and carelessness? It sank in the middle a long time ago, I know that, and then Mr. Pike's ancestors came along with wrecking bars and dismantled the rotten timbers and put in new ones. And you can see by the cuts across the floor boards that changes have been made, all over the house. Staircases have been ripped out and erected someplace else. They blocked up the fireplaces and put in stoves, and then they took out the stoves and put in radiators, and then they tore out the radiators and put in hot-air registers. Everything in the house has changed places, leaving no trace of what was there before. I wish I could feel them here, all those people who lived here, the earliest ones in their eighteenth-century clothes, or the ones with frock coats and bearded faces, or those women later on in shirtwaists and hats like upside down bushel baskets. It's strange that I can't get any sense of them at all, all those people who were born and lived and died here. I can't imagine their clothes hanging on the iron pegs in the closets. I never think about them at all. It's my house now, for this flicker of time. Not theirs. Only mine.

Virginia's pen faltered. Barbara had told her what Mrs. Bewley had said. *Mine, mine, mine.* They were just alike in their selfish possessiveness, Virginia Heron and Alice Bewley.

Fingernails clicked on the glass. Virginia looked up to see a face looking in the window at her. Then a second face materialized behind the first, and stared past Virginia at the refrigerator, the television set, the cast-iron fireplace.

Oh, no. Virginia turned her head away, unable to bear it. One of the faces belonged to the real-estate woman, Mrs. Gardenside. Warily Virginia stood up and went to the door.

"Oh, Virginia, Dotty Gardenside, remember? I was here at your father's —" Mrs. Gardenside was holding up a shiny object, a copper teakettle. "Might we disturb the peace of your lovely home to get water for my radiator? It boiled over. Oh, excuse me, this is Mrs. Hawkins. Virginia Heron, Mrs. Hawkins. Mrs. Hawkins is going to move here with her family from Tallahassee. They're looking for a new home, you know, a really lovely old — isn't this a lovely place, Mrs. Hawkins? What did I tell you?"

Virginia towered in the doorway. "It doesn't happen to be for sale."

"Oh, of course not, of course not." Dotty Gardenside glanced at Mrs. Hawkins. "But our radiator boiled over. Just down the road. I wonder if I could fill my container at your kitchen sink?" The teakettle jiggled in the air again, a dazzling guarantee to the factual nature of the testimony.

Virginia backed grudgingly out of the doorway and stood aside, as Mrs. Gardenside and Mrs. Hawkins dodged past her into the living room.

"Not that way," said Virginia dryly. "The kitchen is this way."

"Oh, of course it is. I remember now," said Mrs. Gardenside, while the eyes of Mrs. Hawkins raked left and right. "How could I have forgotten? Isn't that a lovely mantelpiece, Mrs. Hawkins?"

In the kitchen Virginia took a firm hold on the kettle and filled it at the faucet. Behind her she could sense the silent gestures of Mrs. Gardenside pointing here and there, the delighted murmurs of Mrs. Hawkins.

"Oh, thank you, Virginia dear," said Mrs. Gardenside, reaching for the kettle.

Virginia hung onto it. "No, no, I'll carry it."

"But, really, we wouldn't dream of troubling you."

"It's no trouble." Virginia pushed open the screen door and led the way down the driveway.

"But we're fine, just fine." Mrs. Gardenside and Mrs. Hawkins fluttered and clucked at Virginia's heels all the way to Mrs. Gardenside's Mercedes, which was parked beside one of the brick gateposts.

No steam escaped from under the gleaming hood.

"Well, thank goodness, it's cooled down," said Mrs. Gardenside, fussing with the hood, trying to find the latch.

Virginia found it for her and stood back while Mrs. Gardenside explored the interior, searching among the mysteries of the eight-cylinder supercharged Mercedes-Benz gasoline engine for the cap to her radiator. "Oh, dear," said Mrs. Gardenside, gazing vaguely at the spark plugs, "I know so little about cars."

"It's this thing in front," said Virginia. With gingerly fingers she touched the radiator cap. It was stone cold. Unscrewing it, she tipped the kettle and began pouring water ruthlessly. Instantly the radiator flowed over. Without a word Virginia handed the shiny kettle back to Mrs. Gardenside and screwed the cap back on.

"Oh, I'm just a silly woman," giggled Mrs. Gardenside. "It must be something else. I thought it was the radiator."

"The boiler," suggested Mrs. Hawkins desperately, remembering something from an explanation by her husband about steam locomotives. "I'll bet it was the boiler."

"Our house is not for sale," said Virginia, turning away. "It isn't now and never ever will be."

Mine, mine, mine, she said to herself, over and over, stalking back up the driveway.

Twenty-Six

HOMER KELLY CRANED HIS NECK FROM THE LAWN CHAIR TO glance at the open window of the kitchen, listening hungrily to the soft clash of dishes in the dining room, where Mary was setting the table for Sunday dinner. "And how are your spiders, dear boy?" he said, turning back reluctantly to his nephew John. "I must say, I don't miss those eight-legged little creatures at all, not at all."

"Oh, they're fine," said John. "My crab spider died. And my big *Nucteneas* all keeled over within a few days of each other. I guess their purpose in life was finished. They made egg sacs and died. I'll have a lot of new ones, of course, pretty soon."

"Horrible, I must say, the animal kingdom and its single-minded concentration on murder and reproduction," mused Homer. "It reminds me of your mother. Not the murder part, of course, the reproduction. All you passel of little kids. I wish the dear woman had run out of steam before Benny came along. I don't know if Mary and I are going to survive. We'll be the helpless victims of the tyranny of the next generation. We'll curl up our insect legs and die, just like your mama spiders. Listen, John, keep your voice down, and maybe he'll nap right through dinner. Your Aunt Mary had me taking pictures of the little brute all morning to send to his mother. Benny frolicking on the jungle gym. Benny swinging on the swing. Benny playing in the sand-box. If you ask me, his mother doesn't want to be reminded."

"You know, Uncle Homer," said John, "maybe Benny will be okay when he grows up. I know it's hard to believe. But maybe Jean Henri Fabre was something like Benny when he was small. You know, a really smart little kid."

"Fabre, your hero? That old guy in southern France?"

"Listen to this, Uncle Homer. When he was just a tiny little kid, he did this funny experiment. He wanted to know whether he saw the sun with his eyes or his mouth. So he looked at the sun and closed his eyes and opened his mouth, and the sun disappeared. So he knew he saw it with his eyes. Isn't that nice?"

Homer was enchanted. "He opened his mouth and closed his eyes? What a clever little kid. He opened his mouth and closed his eyes!"

"Uncle Homer?"

"Yes?" said Homer dreamily, inhaling the pleasant smell of roast beef wafting from the kitchen window.

"Listen, Uncle Homer, I sort of wanted to talk to you."

Homer's gaze drifted back to his nephew's earnest face. "Talk to me? What about?"

"Well, it's so queer. I don't exactly know how to describe it."

"Well, try, boy, try."

"Well, it's just that —" John groped for words. "Well, it's like the three little pigs. You know."

"The three little pigs?"

"That's right."

"I'll huff and I'll puff and I'll blow your house down? Those three little pigs?"

"Exactly. That's it exactly."

Homer threw up his hands in exasperation. "You're as bad as your little brother. More idiocy from the nursery. That's *what*, exactly? I'm sorry, my boy, for being so dense, but what have the three little pigs got to do with your sense of malaise, of discomfiture, of vaguely unrealized distress and mortification? What sort of huffing and puffing are you talking about?"

"It's us, you see. We're the three little pigs. Virginia and Barbara and me. Only it's not my house, of course, so it's really just Virginia and Barbara. It's their house I mean. The one that's going to get blown down."

"Well, we had a little tornado here in June. Freak wind. Did I tell you about that? It was the same day that —"

"No, no, Uncle Homer. I don't mean a real wind."

"You were speaking metaphorically? I see. Profound poetic symbolism of huffing, puffing, porcine alarm, wolfish gluttony, grandmaw gobbled up. No, no, that's another story. John, for God's sake, get on with it."

"Well, it's Buddy. That's the whole trouble."

"You mean, the wolf is Buddy Whipple? It's Buddy who wants to blow down that fine house of straw occupied by you three plump little porkers with the curly tails? I see. It's funny, you know, John. Barbara said the same thing."

"She did?" John was amazed.

"She said he was like a monster, taking over. I said, 'Why don't you just kick him out?' You mean he's still there?"

"Oh, he's there, all right. Barbara doesn't even try to make him leave anymore."

"Well, why not?"

John's narrow face worked. How could he explain it? That Virginia and Barbara were like helpless specks in a spiderweb, and Buddy was turning them over and over in his claws. Barbara was still beating her wings and struggling, but Virginia didn't move. It was as if the spider had already delivered his fatal bite. Somehow or other they must find a way to prey on the spider himself, to grab him and hold him down and destroy him. The trouble was, Buddy would find a way to wriggle loose, or he would let one of his legs go, just like *Araneus cavaticus*, and carry on. He had seven more legs, after all. No, a hundred legs, a thousand. John's eyes grew large, imagining Buddy hovering over the Herons' house with his thousand jointed legs, clutching it, his hairy femurs dangling over the windows, darkening them, crowding out the light. No, no, that was ridiculous. He was just an ordinary guy, just very shrewd and powerful. Next year he would still be living in the Herons' house, and the year after that, and the year after that. When Virginia was an old, old woman Buddy would still be a mighty presence in the house, crushing everything with his overbearing good will, his clever schemes, his interfering good nature. And Virginia would always be too proud to fret herself. She would escape the way she did now, in indifference, in profound privacy. She would float away in silence above the threatening coarseness of Buddy Whipple. Except that sometimes John feared Virginia wasn't indifferent any more, that she was giving in, that her fragile resolve was weakening.

He looked at Homer and said something in a strangled voice. His astonished uncle thought he was going to cry. Then John got hold of himself and said solemnly, "It's Virginia. I don't know what it is about Barbara and Virginia, but Barbara wants him to go and Virginia lets him stay."

"Virginia wants him to stay?"

"I didn't say that. I said she lets him stay. He's got her, you know, wrapped up in sticky threads, like a —"

"Oh, come now, John, you've got spiders on the brain."

"And it isn't right," cried John, hitting the arm of Homer's chair.

"Ssshhh, ssshhhh," whispered Homer. "You'll wake up Benny."

"It's some kind of threat. I don't know what the hell it is."

"Well, John, until you do, I don't see what I can do about it. Even to help my kith and kin. Not by the hair on my chinny-chin-chin."

"But, Uncle Homer," said John, and then they both jumped, as a happy squeal pierced the sultry afternoon. A small face bobbed up at one of the upstairs windows. Benny was dancing in his cot.

"Hey, John," shouted Benny, "listen to this. I know a song about you!" And in a childish soprano Benny sang a song at the top of his lungs about a fox and a goose and somebody named John.

Homer sank his head in his hands. "It's Mary's fault. She's been teaching him all these nursery rhymes. I don't know which is worse, the imports and exports of the nations of the western hemisphere, or Jack and Jill went up the hill. I tell you, John, it's something awful. He's halfway through the *Oxford Book of Nursery Rhymes*."

"Oh, wow, you don't have to tell me," said John. "I know what it's like. Listen, why don't you get him to help you somehow? Fabre's little granddaughter was only six years old when she kept an eye on his long processions of ants for him. I mean, a smart little kid like that ought to be good for something."

"Help me? Good God, John, how could that little rascal help me?"

"Dinner's ready," called Mary, her face round and flushed behind the screen of the kitchen window. "Oh, Homer, would you take Benny to the bathroom and bring him downstairs?"

Homer groaned.

"I'll do it," said John generously, and for the next hour he manhandled his little brother playfully and ate a heavy meal in the company of his aunt and uncle. But then, picking up his bicycle and riding home along Barretts Mill Road and Lowell Road and across the river, past the Star Market and through Monument Square, down Heywood Street to Walden, down Walden across Route 2, down 126 past Walden Pond, then swooping at last in a clean curve into the Herons' driveway and bumping along the ruts and gullies to the house, he couldn't get Benny's silly rhyme out of his head.

> Oh! John, John, John,
> The grey goose is gone,
> And the fox is off to his den O!
> Den O! den O!
> Oh! John, John, John,
> The grey goose is gone,
> And the fox is off to his den O!

Twenty-Seven

BUDDY CAME GALLOPING UP THE STONE STEPS, HEARING THE IN-
sistent ring of the phone, then stopped cold. He had almost run
into a hornet. Backing away, he ran down and around the other
way to the south side of the courtyard. Then, throwing open
the screen door, he plunged into the kitchen and picked up the
phone.

"Hello?" said Buddy.

"Oh, sorry. I must have the wrong number."

"That sounds like William Warren," said Buddy. "Buddy
Whipple here, William."

"Buddy?" The voice at the other end of the line hesitated.
"Are you still living there with Barbara and Virginia?"

"Yes, as a matter of fact. Just keeping an eye on things. You
know, taking care of the girls."

There was another pause. "Well, Buddy, would you be so
good as to ask Barbara to call me back?"

"May I ask what about?" said Buddy outrageously, in his
most courteous executive secretary's voice.

"Well — well, all right, I'll tell you what it's about." William sounded more confident. "It's my new nine-by-nines. Those
pictures we took from the plane. They just came in. I thought
Barbara and Virginia might like to take a look at their place. You

can see it in three-D. The plane takes overlapping pictures, you see, so you can look at them through a pair of lenses, and you get this three-dimensional —"

"Well, I'm sure they would. I'll pass the word along," said Buddy easily.

"Oh, and say, Buddy," said William, "now that I've got you on the phone — you know, there are some odd patterns of land holdings turning up."

"Is that so?" said Buddy.

There was another pause. "Well, just tell Barbara that I called," said William.

Buddy stared at the phone in his hand and put it down slowly. *Odd patterns of land holdings.* What the hell did the man mean by that? Well, nothing. Nothing that anybody could do anything about. And even if Buddy had made a mistake somewhere, left something hanging loose, what the hell did it matter? Nothing had been put down on paper that wasn't perfectly straightforward. And of course if anything didn't exactly match past history, then past history was wrong. Those old surveyors, everybody knew they made mistakes. Everybody knew you couldn't trust those primitive methods they had in the old days.

The phone rang again. This time it was for Buddy. "Young man, I just want to thank you," said Randall Jones. "I've just heard you're going to take that back land off my hands. You know, when I put that ad in the paper I didn't think I had a chance in the world of selling it. Not after the Conservation Commission turned it down. I mean, you're aware it hasn't even got any frontage? Of course it's a real nice piece of woods. I suppose you just want a chunk of nice woods not far from your own place, right?"

"That's right," said Buddy. "I've always been fond of that stretch of woods. I shot a hawk in there once when I was a kid."

"Well, Betty and I are truly grateful. I won't disguise the fact that we've been pretty short lately. We were casting around for everything we could think of. Those kids of ours, all in college at the same time. It's brutal, even with the two of us working."

This time Buddy put the phone down with a feeling of magnanimity and kindliness, and started upstairs to get his shotgun. Talking about that hawk he'd shot ten years ago made his fingers itch to try it again. Just the other day he'd seen a red-tailed hawk sailing over the cornfield, going around and around in high lazy circles. It might be out there again this afternoon. Then halfway up the stairs Buddy heard the phone ring again.

This time it was Henry Knickerbocker. Henry was grateful to Buddy too. "Now, listen here, Buddy, you can't loan me all that money without getting some interest in return. It's just ridiculous."

"Oh, I wouldn't ask an old friend to pay interest. Forget it."

"I was really surprised by your offer, Buddy, and grateful. I mean, especially after I turned you down about that land of ours. I'm sorry I can't sell it. You understand. Well, you're a chip off the old block. More like your good father every day."

Buddy hung up again, and drew a deep trembling breath. His breast felt charged, excited. His head was full of his own goodness; it was jiggeting with the multiplicity of things in his control. This afternoon he really ought to be taking care of six or seven things for Croney, and there was something he had been meaning to do for Barbara, only he'd forgotten what. And the drug store — he kept forgetting to get that old prescription filled at the drug store. Well, for Christ's sake, a person had to take time off every now and then. What was life for anyhow? Cheerfully Buddy loaded half a dozen shells packed with #4 shot into his old Winchester and headed for the cornfield, still aglow with his own saintliness, untroubled by the gulf between the charity of today and the rapacity of tomorrow, somehow keeping the two things separate in his head with innocent barbarism.

In the selectmen's office in the Lincoln town hall, William Warren adjusted the lens stand over two of his nine-by-nines, shifting the square photographs until the houses on Baker Bridge Road leaped up in exaggerated perspective and the rows of maple trees along the roadside separated themselves from their shadows and stood erect. *There, look at that.* William felt a twinge of shock and pleasure every time the optical effect worked. Then he jumped, as someone touched his sleeve. "Oh, Mrs. Bell, forgive me. Thank you, the morning mail."

William opened the first envelope, and frowned. It was a letter from a local attorney, reporting an exchange of property off Sandy Pond Road from Jones et Ux to Clarence Whipple.

Buddy Whipple again. Swiftly William turned to the great black-bound book of property maps on the cabinet against the wall. Yes, Jones's back land was right in line with the rest.

William's gaze drifted up from the book to the view of the old cemetery out the window. The pattern was there, becoming clearer all the time. Should he discuss it with Barbara Heron? No need to worry her. Not yet. It might not mean anything at all.

Then again, worried William, it might. It just might.

Twenty-Eight

IN THE ARCHING YEW OVER THE STONE STEPS TO THE DRIVEWAY, the white-faced hornets were prospering. Every time John went in and out of the house he ducked his head to look at them. It was too bad he couldn't get an X-ray view of the inside of the nest as it grew larger and larger, and see the inner walls being torn away to add dimension to the outer surface. How many generations of grubs had hatched by now, as the stacks of layered apartments increased in number? All through the month of July and the first week of August John watched the steady stream of worker females emerge from the hedge beyond the tall yew and float purposefully away.

He kept track, too, of his seven-legged spider. He had lost her for a while, but then she had turned up again on the south side of the house in the shade of the great sugar maple that towered over the roof. One breathless night, unable to sleep, John had come down in his pajamas to see if he could catch a glimpse of her at work. Yes, there she was, moving briskly under his flashlight, destroying her old web, consuming the threads — John could see a bit of silken fluff in her jaws, and then it was gone. Now she was starting again, working outward, laying down a spiral building platform. Patiently John held the flashlight and watched her work her way in again, pausing at each radial thread to fasten her line, then running quickly on to the next, measuring the distance between her spiraling circles with one hind leg, pulling out silk from her spinnerets, fastening it with her forelegs, dodging, turning, moving rapidly to her resting ground in the middle, then returning to her niche behind the rain spout to await events. She was bigger now. She must have molted again. Her regenerating leg was fully half the size of the others. Her prey was larger too, moths rushing blindly for the lighted window in the early evening, blundering into her interfering trap. The web itself had increased in diameter. Now it was at least a foot across, with structural threads stretching up and up — John's flashlight followed one of them — to the shutter of the second-floor window, and down, down to the granite foundation of the house.

John went back to bed and lay spread-eagled on his back. He still couldn't sleep.

He began planning the next day's work. First there was the beauty bush in the front yard. An hour for that. Then maybe he could find some four-by-fours and set them up around the compost heap and nail those fallen slats onto them. And then —

It occurred to John that he was thinking up his day's work for himself. He didn't have to ask what to do any more. At first all his assigned jobs had seemed random and disconnected. But now he had begun to see the relation between one task and the next, to get a feeling for the plan. It wasn't a plan on paper, any more than the barn spider's web was built according to a blueprint. It was a picture growing slowly in Virginia's head, following the curve of her arm, the flourish of her pointing hand, sweeping from a cluster of red cedars and spreading juniper to an empty place beside the driveway where another cluster might balance the first. Virginia's Great Compromise was in full swing. There were to be indigenous shrubs and trees placed left and right on the sloping lawn and scattered along the path to the vegetable garden.

John would look up from the bottom of the hill where he had been transplanting a fat infant from the nursery of white pines, to see Virginia gazing down at him, not seeing him, seeing instead the whole landscape with the new tree growing in it. The little white pine was a new stroke of her brush, painting a slow green picture — bush and tree, wilderness and lawn, fence and field and faraway road. The house, too, was part of the picture, part of the slowly emerging hand-fashioned whole. Yesterday John had found Virginia and Barbara staring at the clapboards beside the kitchen door. "You see," said Virginia, "we could put a lattice right there, up and across, and grow something on it, that Sweet Autumn clematis or something." "Mmmm," said Barbara, "I see what you mean." And they had dropped everything and figured out the lattice with pencil and paper, and John had been rushed off to Wilson's Lumber for two hundred feet of lath and some three-quarter-inch finishing nails. And then they had worked on it together, sometimes in companionable silence, sometimes with brisk talk — John keeping up his end of the conversation, sometimes bounding ahead. Once his paintbrush, running along a strip of lath, met Virginia's. Her brush dabbed playfully at his. "There," she said, reaching to the very end of the lath, "that's done," and John had admired the eager stretch of her arm. She was leaning forward into some perfect future, when the paint would be dry, the lattice erected against the door, a vine growing up it, all the trees full-grown and majestic, the shrubs spread wide over the edges of the hillside, the landscape completed. Even the house seemed to be straining forward at its perfected self, as they swarmed over it with spackling tool and paintbrush. Even the newly planted young trees were pulling themselves upward as fast as they could grow.

But under the surface of the work, under the easygoing talk, there was a foundation of silence and helpless inaction. No one mentioned Buddy's name, but he was there just the same. Buddy too was an urgent force moving inexorably forward, arranging things to his liking. John lay on his bed in the dark and envisioned Buddy's broad red face, his brown beard streaked with sun-bleached gold. Buddy's bold laughter echoed and re-echoed among all the tender surfaces of John's brain, and in his bones

he could feel Buddy's heavy tread shaking the house. Buddy was like a clever animal, an enormous dog tugging at a leash, ears erect, nose on the scent for excitement. Even at the supper table there was always the sense that the chain would be torn from their grasp, that the huge dog would lunge free, bounding high over every obstacle in his way. Only Barbara took the trouble to talk back to him, to break into the restless monologue. John would sit silently eating his supper, and Virginia too would say nothing. But Virginia's silence was different from John's and more menacing. In some terrible way she was being picked up in those strong jaws and dragged along blindly, moving neither hand nor foot to save herself.

Oh, God, God, God. John sat up, then threw himself down on his side.

The next morning he was exhausted from lack of sleep. His face was drawn and hollow in the dime-store mirror that hung on a nail over the set tubs. But John was determined to carry out the whole list of jobs he had thought up for himself during the night, so he set to work on the beauty bush right after breakfast.

First he clipped off the straggly arching branches and piled them to one side. Then he circled the bush with his garden fork. Only then did he remember that he needed a tarpaulin to throw his diggings on. And a pair of hand-clippers. And a bucket of good dirt mixed with compost. And a wheelbarrow. Horticulture was mostly going back and forth to get things you had forgotten.

Philosophically John put down the fork and set off at a run up the slope to the shed. His feet were bare. He made no sound in the grass. In his head there was only the image of the place in the back room where the tarp lay folded on the floor. But the instant his hand reached for the latch, a murmur within the shed sent him a warning. Too late. His hand was already flinging open the door.

"Oh, excuse me," said John, blood rushing to his head, as Virginia pulled away from Buddy and ran out the door on the other side of the shed.

Buddy turned to John with a thick slow smile.

Virginia didn't stop running until she came to the top of the hill. Then, breathing heavily, she climbed through the gate, walked across the field and began circling the pond. At one end there was a marshy place from which the water sprang, and grey rocks at the base of a beech tree, and a pool of dead backwater. The gnarled grey roots of the tree were indistinguishable from the mottled rock. Virginia lay on her stomach beside the pool and looked at the cloudy shape of her head in the water, remembering Sunday afternoons long ago, when guests had trailed in twos and threes after her mother and father, exclaiming in surprise at the secret lake and the blossoming azaleas and the white birches leaning over the water.

Heaving herself to a sitting position Virginia looked out over the pond, watching dragonflies dart over the surface. There were black ones with wings like pirate flags and iridescent blue ones. Iridescent was spelled with one r. The dragonflies were mating in midair. Virginia shook her head and got to her feet, impatient again at the greed and hunger in the middle of everything. A bird tumbled the underbrush and moved away swiftly with a small cry. There was a sound in the air; thin, high and constant, like an insect's shrill faraway note. Virginia listened, gazing at the ground. Then she stopped and picked up an apple and a piece of birch bark. The apple was pinched, worm-eaten, malformed. She bit into it gratefully, savoring its sweet wild flavor as if it contained special strengths. The strip of birch bark had curled back on itself and peeled away from one of the trees along the shore of the pond. Holding it in her fingers, Virginia studied the tender fawn color of the underside, the papery whiteness of the surface.

Impulsively she spread it flat on a rock, pulled a pencil stub

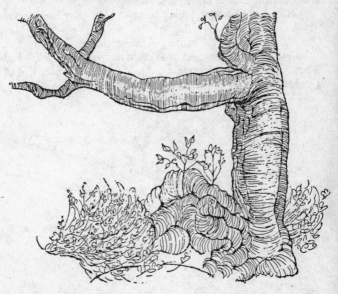

from her pocket and scribbled a letter to the air: *Who am I.* Lifting her arm, she tossed the letter skyward.

John finished the job of uprooting the beauty bush in a burst of angry energy. With gritty fury he spaded the rocks and sand back into the hole, trampled them down, covered them with topsoil, bounced the wheelbarrow over the lawn, filled it with compost, bounced it back, dumped the compost into the hole, stirred it into the topsoil with the fork, trampled the dirt with his feet again, and topped the edges with the clumps of forked-out turf. Then with elaborate care he finished the job and fetched the hose. Only when the sprinkler was turning lazily over his new grass seed was the job done. John gathered up his tools, trundled them up the hill in the wheelbarrow and put everything away. Then in the privacy of the shed he wept three dry sobs, choked them off, and stalked up the hill, looking for Virginia.

Not that he had anything to say to her. Anything to say at all.

Where was she? Crawling between the bars of the gate, John walked across the field and circled the pond. He didn't find Virginia, but he came upon a scrap of birch bark on a bed of Quaker ladies, and he picked it up and carried it home.

Twenty-Nine

IT WAS VIRGINIA'S JOB TO RUN THE LITTLE ELECTRIC LAWNMOWER around the edges of the front lawn before John worked over the rest with the big power mower. The cable was heavy. Lugging it from the shed, Virginia attached one end to the lawnmower, picked up the other end, and opened the lid of the outdoor socket. Then she stopped, and stared at the socket. There were two earwigs in it. Exposed to the light, they dove into the plug holes. Their tail pincers stuck out, waving at Virginia. Should she plug in the cable and fry the earwigs?

John came thundering up with the power mower. He turned down the machine to an idling throb and looked at her mournfully.

Virginia wanted to say something kind, but instead she said, "Look at this. What shall I do?"

John put his head down solemnly and gazed at the earwigs in the socket. Then he turned it over and dumped them into his hand. "For my spiders," he murmured, and went away.

Virginia plugged in the cable. Then she gave a little shriek of surprise. Someone was standing at her elbow. "Oh," said Virginia. "I'm sorry. I didn't hear you."

It was the girl from the church. Her car was in the driveway, a cunning little sports car, fire-engine red. "Here I am. I told you

I was coming. In person! Cherry Peaches Schermerhorn always keeps her promises."

It wasn't fair, thought Virginia, opening the kitchen door. This combination of chubby childishness and sexual bullying wasn't fair. The girl looked like a baby, with her plump cheeks, her long lashes, her orange hair boiling in fuzzy ringlets out of her scalp. But beneath her sleeveless orange jersey succulent bosoms swelled like Barbara's pumpkins expanding in the July heat. Radiance sprayed in all directions, filling the kitchen, rebounding off the wall.

They sat at the table. Virginia kept her eyes on the comforting sight of John as he moved erratically around the edges of the lawn with the electric lawnmower. "You're the Sunday school superintendent, aren't you?" said Virginia.

The girl laughed merrily. "Oh, we don't call it Sunday school any more. Wholeness Seminars for Youth, that's what we call it now. I'm the juvenile coordinator for young adults. You're Virginia, aren't you?" Rapturously Cherry Peaches swung in her chair, raising her arms over her head to shove her hands deep into the thick tumble of her hair. Her unfettered breasts obeyed Newton's laws of motion. Waves of radiance shimmered and wobbled on the ceiling. "Oh, I'm so excited about my idea. I've hardly been able to hold my horses. It's this retreat. Remember? I told you when I was here with Arthur."

"Arthur?"

"You know. My boss, the minister of the Second Parish. I mean, it's just so great to work with somebody who has the same parameters, the same visions for, you know, man and womankind, the whole world! And he's Scorpio too! Isn't that the most fabulous . . . ? Say, you know what, I'll bet you are too. I can always tell. Go ahead, admit it," giggled Cherry Peaches. "I know a fellow Scorpio when I see one."

"Capricorn," said Virginia faintly, veering with Ms. Schermerhorn's erratic breeze, trying to imagine a universe in which astrological and theological forces governed earthly events in harmony.

154

"Of course, the truth is, I may not actually even be a Scorpio, because, the trouble is, I was born at *midnight* — isn't that just *fantastic?* — between two astrological signs! Scorpio and Sagittarius! Which accounts for my split personality. I mean, you know, the tremendous tugging deep inside, like the two lobes of the brain? I mean, like, basically I'm a right-lobe person, artistic, creative, only sometimes — it's really wild! — I feel all rational and businesslike." Cherry Peaches chuckled a warbling little chuckle, and another wave of brilliance washed over the shrinking walls of the kitchen.

Virginia made an effort to get back on course. "You want to bring the kids closer to God, is that it?"

"God?"

"You said you came from the church, right? The retreat is to get closer to God?"

"Oh, God. Well, *naturally*." Cherry Peaches laughed out loud. The joke was on her. "Well, that's what a retreat is, basically speaking. One long prayer. Like a week-long meditation on our relationship to the universe. To God! To angels and principalities! To seraphim and cherubim!" The radiance in the kitchen doubled, tripled, became celestial.

Virginia put a demurring hand into the dazzling air. "You want to bring them here and camp out, is that it?"

"Oh, yes, we do, that's it exactly. It's the high-school group. You know. They get really turned off by organized religion, so we have this special group that meets on Sunday nights, and we have, like, speakers, and we do all sorts of fun experiments, and of course we have snacks and cider, and you know, cookies."

Virginia was mesmerized by the cozyness of the word *cookies* as it popped coyly from the lips of Cherry Peaches. Putting her hand over her eyes, she tried to clear her head. "Experiments?" she said.

"Oh, sure. We try anything and everything. You know. Speaking in tongues, dance, yoga, biorhythms, adolescent-anxiety-oriented behavior-modification. You name it. It's all really just so fabulous."

Virginia shook her head vigorously. "No," she said. "I'm sorry, but no."

"The last week in August. So they can get their heads together before school." In solipsistic rapture, Cherry Peaces gazed inward at her pilgrimage of youth. "Role playing. We're going to do a lot of that. You know. Acting out."

Virginia had to stand up and take her by the shoulders. "Listen, I said no. You can't come here for a Sunday school retreat. No, I said. No, no."

"Oh," said Cherry Peaches. Her expression was transformed. Her great square eyes sparkled with a new kind of greed. The radiance in the kitchen coalesced into a beam of light and focused itself on Virginia. "I didn't understand. There is some . . ." John was rattling past the window again with the electric lawnmower. ". . . and bitterness. Oh, how well I understand. Oh, I'd just love to talk with you. I mean, like, we could work it all out. I mean, after all, what am I here for? Oh, I'm so glad I came today. I could come over any time and we could just, you know, sit down. We could take a long walk and just let it all hang — I mean, us Scorpios got to stick together, right?"

Virginia led the way into the narrow hall and opened the screen door. "I think I'm Taurus, as a matter of fact."

"Listen," said Cherry Peaches, pausing on the doorstep, "you know what my horoscope said this morning? About today? My forecast for today? It said us Scorpios should go out and conquer the world! So hop on your white horse, Virginia, and gallop off into the wild blue yonder! This is the day! Hurray!" Waving her arms overhead, Cherry Peaches Schermerhorn plunged away and capered in the direction of her little red car. Climbing in, she thrust her beaming face out the window and waved her arm. "Any time you say. I'll be back anyway, with Arthur. He's just dying to talk to you." Pumpkins brimmed and tumbled on the edge of the car window. "We'll come for tea! I'll bring the cookies! Hurray for us Scorpios!" Cherry Peaches turned her car around in exuberant dashes, tooted three jolly blats on her horn and went bucking down the driveway.

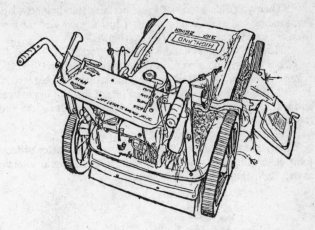

"Actually, I guess I'm Pisces," moaned Virginia, turning away, going back indoors, yearning for a dry gulch in some empty desert where she could hide, where there was nothing for hundreds of miles but prickly dry cactus and mean little horned toads — no luxuriant jungle growth, no copulating elephants, no thrashing in the tall pampas grass. The radiance had vanished from the kitchen. The room was dark and filled with gloom. Virginia stood at the window and looked out at John zigzagging across the lawn behind the electric mower in the light of the blazing sun as it rolled onward through the heavens against the zodiac of stars, producing changes of fortune in the lives of the inhabitants of the planet Earth, propitious days for journeys and business ventures and fortunate encounters with prospective mates.

"Did you see John cutting the grass today?" said Barbara.
"Yes. He did a good job," said Virginia. "He did the whole thing, edges and all."

"Then you didn't see — ? I was upstairs, standing on a ladder, sanding the guest room ceiling. I had a good view of him from above. He cut it twice. The front lawn."

"He did? Twice? What did he do that for?"

"He was writing a word in the grass with the little electric mower, running it up and down the hill, making these big letters. I could read it plain as day. But then he got out the big mower and roared right across it from left to right and right to left, and the word disappeared."

"A word? What word was it?"

Barbara looked at her. "It was a name, as a matter of fact. John was writing your name on the grass. Virginia, it said, as plain as day, right there on the front lawn."

Thirty

SOMETIMES BARBARA THOUGHT SHE COULDN'T DRAW ANOTHER breath. It wasn't just Buddy, although he was bad enough. Everything else was crowding up against her too, plucking at her, like the long fingers of thorny bramble at the bottom of the lawn, reaching out from the wilderness into the grass. Blackberry canes were popping up among the new little white pines. Artemisia Silver King was galloping through the round border like a Mongol horde. There were squash beetles all over the zucchini. Now there was this man. What did he want, sitting there in his seersucker coat? Barbara's chair was tipped awkwardly to one side on the front lawn. Irritably she swatted at the fly that kept settling on her face.

From the stone steps under the arching yew, John couldn't hear what they were saying, but he was aware of them in the front yard — Virginia slouching in her chair, gazing at her feet, Barbara bolt upright (she was angry, you could tell), the man talking and talking.

It was John's day off. His natural history notebook lay in his lap. He was checking up on the hornet's nest in the hedge. He had guessed at its diameter and noted it down. He had drawn a picture.

There was a shiny new hornet only three inches from his

159

nose, crawling on a dead yew twig, opening and closing its wings, drying them, preparing for its first flight. It was queer, thought John, that the hornet was so near to him, there in the bush, and yet at the same time it was really so far away. Its insect intelligence was so remote, the hornet might as well be on some planet in a distant galaxy.

The hornet came closer. John sat very still, gazing at its infinitesimal face. It wiggled its antennae, cocked and uncocked its narrow wings. What was it thinking? Did it see him? Was it amazed at being born? Was it saying to itself, *So this is the world!*

No, no, it didn't really think at all. John knew he was putting his own thoughts into the hornet's brain, and that was wrong.

The hornet crawled closer still, and settled down again in a wobbling splotch of sunshine, moving its abdomen up and down, stroking one of its wings with its hind leg. John sat motionless beside it, trying to sink into insect nothingness, to know only urges, instincts, hungers and desires. *Sex,* he thought. *Hunger and sex. Hunger and sex. Sex. Sex. Sex.*

Impatiently John jumped up. His notebook flopped down, jarring the hornet, which promptly flew at him and stung him cruelly on the forearm.

It hurt like hell. John swore under his breath, "Oh shit," and ran angrily indoors. He put a paste of baking soda on the red welt, then made himself a thick corned-beef sandwich and bit into it savagely.

Hunger and sex. Well, at least he could do something about hunger.

The man sitting on the fragile dining room chair on the lawn was the chairman of the Lincoln planning board. He sat in the dancing shade of the blowing laundry, his light hair lifting in the warm wind, talking mildly about the possible change in the course of Route 126 to eliminate the dangerous reversing curve.

Virginia was paying only listless attention, but she heard soft phrases: "... slippery conditions ... schoolbuses, oncoming cars

160

... no visibility ... killed or maimed for life ... schoolbus accident in Wisconsin last winter ..."

"The other side of the road," said Barbara, waving a dirty hand. "Why don't they straighten it out on the other side of Route 126? There aren't any houses there. Just woods. Why do they have to come up our driveway?"

"Conservation land over there," said the man smoothly. "I doubt very much it can be touched." Taking a map from his pocket, he unfolded it. His hands were very clean, his fingernails immaculate. He ran his silver pencil along a dotted line.

"But that's here," said Barbara angrily. "That's right here."

"Oh, no, it wouldn't touch the house. Of course not."

"But it would be jammed right up next to it. Wouldn't it? Wouldn't it?"

"Forty feet away. The zoning laws require a forty-foot setback."

Barbara whirled in her chair and stared at the round garden, where upended baskets were shading tender transplants from the sun. She saw the garden transformed into a macadam wasteland, blurred with speeding cars, whining with accelerating engines, the whole house shaking with the vibration from the wheels of giant trucks. "How big would the new road be? How wide? As wide as the old one? As wide as that?"

"Oh, yes. More or less. Well, to be precise about it, I expect they'd want to make it safer." The man put his pencil back in the inside pocket of his seersucker jacket. "They'd add a passing lane. On both sides, of course. You'd have to have a passing lane on both sides."

"Four lanes? You're talking about a four-lane highway going right up our driveway?"

"I expect so. I guess that's what they'd be likely to come up with."

Virginia looked up as the man from the planning board folded his map and tucked it away. She could feel his caution, his reasonableness, his courage in tackling the thorniest of the abutters. Calmly now he was mentioning eminent domain, almost dreamily, in a dangling clause that had no subject, as if it were something that existed only in the passive voice.

At the bottom of the lawn a flock of birds was flying up into the oak tree in the same way, as if they had not chosen to do it, but were merely drawn upward by some sort of gentle suction.

Looking down again, Virginia closed her fingers over the hickory nuts in her hand. She had found them piled in a small cairn under the tree from which they had fallen. They had been cracked open. Inscribed on the hard ivory surface inside each of them, as if by the gnawing of an insect, was the letter V.

Thirty-One

"STALLED BERMUDA HIGH," SAID THE WEATHERMAN AT CHANNEL
4, standing in front of his satellite picture, pointing to the clear
outline of the east coast. "Scattered showers tonight. Looks like
a long spell of hot weather. No relief in sight."

The dog days of summer had arrived. The city of Boston was
bathed in humid heat. Mosquitoes crept through cracks in
screens, droned against ceilings, dove with piercing whines to fill
themselves with blood and drift upward again, escaping the blind
slap in the dark. In the fetid dampness other insects grew colossal.
Weird creatures batted against the windows. Cockroaches in-
fested town houses on Beacon Hill and three-deckers in Somer-
ville. At Walden Pond the beach was crowded with bathers, city-
dwellers escaping the furnace heat of their apartments, the sweat-
ing upholstery, the mildewed carpets, the tumbled sheets. In
Waltham an enraged husband, driven insane by a surly wife and
a household of sniveling children, snatched up a shotgun, murdered his family, and roared out into the street, firing random
shots at a world that had driven him — only a little while ago a
strapping, happy-go-lucky kid — into this corner of hell.

UNEMPLOYED TV REPAIRMAN
KILLS FIVE
STILL AT LARGE

163

Even with her eyes shut, Virginia knew there were no stars. Her shoulder above the sheet could feel the thick mist, and now and then there was a patter of water from a movement of air in the drenched leaves. Lifting her head, she stared at the curtain over the east window. It moved slightly, then hung slack again. Even in the dark she could see the watered-silk pattern change as the curtain responded tremulously to the slight breath of the wind. Captivated, she got out of bed and went to the window to touch the miraculous gauze. But of course it was only cheap stuff puckered at the hem. She had run it up herself on the sewing machine. Virginia glanced through the curtain at the window that was John's, and was surprised to see a pale face looking back at her. The face withdrew.

Virginia went back to bed. There had been a great grey moth at the window last night before she came upstairs, one wing marked with a livid V in powdery blue chalk. Virginia smiled and went back to sleep, feeling a momentary sense of safety, a benign complicity in her surroundings, a moth's protection against the enemy.

Thirty-Two

BUDDY POOH-POOHED THE MENACE OF THE FOUR-LANE HIGHWAY.
"I'll talk to the people on the planning board," he said. "Nobody's going to come past your house with any four-lane highway.
I'll go over their heads. Way over their heads. Wait till Howie
gets elected. I happen to know he's got somebody really great in
mind for Public Works. Don't worry about a thing." Buddy said
nothing about the likelihood that the new administrator for Public Works would be a guy named Clarence Whipple, but it was
in the cards. "Not till after your little deal goes through, of
course," Croney had said. "We'll just get that taken care of first."

"There's Muffy Weatherbee, too," said Barbara. "She was
on the phone this morning. She's discovered our house was nearest to Thoreau when he lived at Walden Pond. She's all excited
about Jacob Baker, who lived here then. She wants to spruce us
up and put a marker on the road and open us up to tourists. She's
coming over. I couldn't stop her."

"Oh, that's no problem either," said Buddy. "The Historic
Sites people won't want it. I mean, look at it. There's nothing
architecturally interesting about it. Just another old farmhouse.
No fancy moldings or anything like that. I'll write a letter.
They've got plenty of other places to spend their money on. Leave
it to me. I'll talk to Muffy. Don't worry about it."

165

But when Muffy Weatherbee came to the house, Buddy had forgotten the appointment. Virginia was nowhere to be seen. John was digging up cedars in somebody's sheep pasture. Barbara was fortified only by Homer Kelly.

Homer had dropped in unannounced. He had decided to see for himself what young John was talking about, to sniff the currents in the air, the huffing and puffing that was supposed to be blowing the house down. Walking up the stone steps he looked at the house. Was it really so fragile and ready to collapse? Well, it was certainly shabby and in need of paint. But with forty acres of valuable real estate in their possession it was hard to see what these women had to worry about. Surely they could turn some of it into a really classy development. Half-million-dollar houses. Homer imagined a big sign at the bottom of the driveway, with hand-carved letters in gold leaf: WALDEN ESTATES. Virginia and Barbara would be rich. But then as he paused at the kitchen door, Homer saw Barbara staggering out of the wilderness at the bottom of the lawn. She was carrying a tree stump, leaning backward, hurrying with tottering steps because if she didn't keep up with her center of gravity she would pitch forward. Barbara dropped the stump on a heap of brush and ran up the hill to meet him, her hair wild, her face scratched and dirty. Instantly Homer tore the splendid sign advertising Walden Estates out of the ground and became a partisan to whatever it was that was going on around here — the stubborn refusals, the hanging on by the fingernails.

Barbara was glad to see him. She made him a sandwich and opened a bottle of beer. Homer leaned back in his chair, beaming at her, his sympathy expanding in the steamy heat, ready to encompass her heartfelt confessions and dire warnings of disaster. They were both dumbfounded when Muffy Weatherbee appeared outside the window and hallooed at them.

"Jesus *Christ*, I forgot," said Barbara, clapping her forehead.

Muffy was thrilled to find a genuine Thoreau expert on the premises. Enthusiastically she quoted her morsels from Thoreau's journals about Jacob Baker's cows. Homer shrank into the background as far as it was possible to shrink in his immensity, and gazed at the miraculous diamond patterns and speckles of light in the shadow of his glass of beer. Then he amused himself by studying Barbara's visitor, pigeonholing her with ruthless accuracy. She was so nice, that was the trouble. She had never been anything but nice. She had gone from the comfortable protection of a prosperous father to that of a prosperous husband. She was busy as a bee, volunteering in the hospital, running dances for the benefit of the Boston Symphony, the Museum of Fine Arts. Then Homer was transported by a mystical vision, and in a flight of ecstasy he beheld Muffy Weatherbee at home, trotting out the door after leaving a note for the cleaning woman: *Don't forget wash dining room window where Mops puts dirty paws! Change sheets guest room! Would you mind polishing silver? Thank you! Your check under begonia! See you next week!*

How could you change the woman? How could you smash and destroy the dreadful predictability of her life, the ghastly stereotype? Homer stopped listening to her bright chatter and consoled himself by picturing Muffy Weatherbee in her cunning little wrap skirt and new Topsiders being buried in an anthill in Africa until she was half chewed up, then imprisoned for ten years in the Black Hole of Calcutta, then cast away on a desert island with nothing but a box of matches and a Swiss Army knife. After an education like that, the woman might just possibly turn into a decent human being. As she was now, she was hopeless.

In the long run, Buddy Whipple took care of Muffy Weatherbee and the Save Our Sites Committee as he had promised, by writing to the Society for the Preservation of New England Antiquities.

His letter received a prompt reply.

Dear Mr. Whipple,

We are grateful for your letter of July 15, arguing against the request of Mrs. Townsend Weatherbee to include the Heron house of Lincoln, Massachusetts, among the sites we are recommending for preservation. In the light of the information you have provided, we have decided to remove the house from the list of properties under consideration for registration as an historic site.

Yours truly,
Albert Roper, Director

So that was that. But as Muffy retired from the battle, a more formidable opponent appeared on the horizon.

Jane Plankton of the investment firm of Eliot and Janeway was another kind of woman altogether, testing Buddy's quick wits to the limit, his power of doing battle at the highest level, and his gift for shaping events to suit himself.

Thirty-Three

THE HUMID HEAT CONTINUED. THERE WAS NO RAIN. THE SUN flared day after day in a sky bleached of color. Virginia spent half her time tending the sprinklers, dragging the hoses from place to place, watering the lawn, the transplanted trees, the pots of flowers, the vegetable garden. Crabgrass was springing up in the yard, sending out snaky stalks that lay flat under the mower with rude cunning, then lifted in ugly profusion. Songbirds had given way to vulgar flocks of starlings, waddling and shrieking at the bottom of the lawn.

Virginia was taking her second bath of the day. There was a spider on the steep slope of the tub. She looked at it warily, trying to feel a sporting sense of good will as she stepped into the water. But crouching beside it she was uncomfortable. It sat motionless, august, inscrutable, then cocked a delicate leg as if it were about to rush up her side. Shuddering, Virginia rose dripping from the tub and finished her bath at the sink.

But by the time Miss Plankton drove up to the house, Virginia was grubby again from handling a dusty window sash and chipping out old putty. Jane Plankton sat in her car and giggled at her. "Oh, Virginia, I feel so *effete* in my town clothes. Positively *rococo*, out here where things are so *primitive*, so *bucolic*, where your very *toes*, Virginia, are deep in the soil! Look at me!

Pearls! Gloves!" With a gallant gesture Miss Plankton tore off her necklace and threw it out the car window. Pearls bounced on the driveway. Then, whisk, whisk, she tossed her gloves after them.

"Oh, Jane, not your pearls!" Virginia raced after one that was skittering into the bushes.

"Now, Virginia, never mind. They're just plastic pop'em beads." Jane Plankton got out of the car and picked up a broken strand. "You just pop them in and out, like this, do you see? I bought them at Woolworth's. So amusing, don't you think? Pop, pop!"

"Well, I don't know," said Virginia, smiling. "I must say, I liked that lorgnette of yours better."

"Oh, yes, my lorgnette. Oh, tell me! How is the dear woman next door?"

"Mrs. Bewley? Oh, I guess she's all right. I haven't been over there lately. But we took care of one crisis, I'm happy to say."

At the house they met Buddy, rushing up from his new turnip field, his face hot and red. Barbara opened the screen door and looked at him in heavy disapproval. "Well, Buddy, I don't know if you'll be interested in this discussion."

"Well, of course I will. Anything that concerns you people means a lot to me too." Then Buddy was disgruntled in his turn. "What's John doing here? Listen here, John, what business is this of yours?"

John flushed and stood up from the table, but Barbara grasped his arm and pushed him down again. "Now, Jane, dear, tell us all about it," she said. "What you were explaining on the phone."

Miss Plankton, Barbara, Buddy and John sat at one end of the long kitchen table, while Virginia stood at the other, puttying her window sash on a spread of newspaper. John folded his hands on the table and sat silent, listening, and soon it no longer seemed implausible to him that this funny old woman was actually the pillar of a family firm of bankers, or brokers, or something like that. She was talking briskly about the need for low-income housing in the suburbs, the despair of the urban poor, the spiritual and

ethical impoverishment of suburban children who knew only polite communities like their own, the isolation of city children to
whom cows were as mythological as unicorns, and open fields as
exotic as the landscape of the moon.

Virginia ran her putty knife along one side of a pane of glass.
"How much land would you want?" she said.

"Whatever we could get," said Miss Plankton. "The more,
the merrier."

"Now, Virginia, wait a minute," said Buddy.

"There's the lower field," said Barbara, looking at Virginia.

"Now, listen here." Buddy's voice was trembling. He was
grinning in a pretense of self-control. "I'm sure this is all very
well meant on the part of Miss Plankton. I mean, she is obviously
sincere. But I can't help but raise certain questions. Number one,
do people really want to move out here, the hell-and-gone into
the country, where everybody else is, you know, different from
them? And number two, I question whether they would want to
live in a place so far from stores and transportation. I mean, how
could they get anywhere?"

"Buses," said Miss Plankton promptly. "We would provide
local bus service between our housing community and the train,
and to neighboring towns for shopping."

"You know, Miss Plankton," said Buddy, "there's no law
against their coming out here by themselves. I mean, we don't
have a closed community anymore. If they wanted to live here,
they would have come out already. I'm just not sure the desire is
there. Why manufacture one, if it doesn't exist, just to make
everybody miserable?"

Jane Plankton tossed Buddy's objection aside with a toss of
her head. "They can't afford it. They need help. That's where I
come in, and landowners like Virginia and Barbara."

But Buddy had no intention of giving up. His polite objec-
tions demolished, he tried another tack. "Okay, I'll accept that.
But I don't see why Barbara and Virginia should destroy their
own lives in an attempt to help somebody else. Because that's
what it would come to. You know damn well you're not just

going to get nice families with cute little kids and harmless old folks. You'll get crime and vandalism and destruction of property, that's what you'll get. You'll have big hulking juvenile delinquents making the place a wasteland. Drug addicts. Criminals. No matter how nice your housing is in the beginning, it will be dilapidated in no time. Those people don't have any — you know — middle-class values. They don't know how to take care of things. And this house, right here, it would be in danger all the time. It would get broken into. And it wouldn't be just burglary. It might be a lot worse than that. It might be — " Buddy spluttered to a stop and shook his head. The words *rape* and *murder* hung in the air.

But Barbara was still looking at Virginia. "There's that big piece over there near the road, where the blackberries are."

"The blackberries?" said Buddy quickly. "Where do you mean? You mean over there by Baker Bridge Road? Oh, no. Oh, God, no. You can't let them have that? For God's sake, Virginia. Listen, Barbara, you can't make up your mind without a lot of good sound advice from some really — I mean, be sensible." He turned furiously to Miss Plankton. "Listen here — "

Jane Plankton stood up. "It's all right. I have to run along anyway to my music lesson. Brother Wayland is giving me instruction in the harpsichord. Oh, I've so enjoyed talking to you girls again. If you'd like another meeting, I'd be delighted." Beaming, she turned to Buddy and extended her hand. "And of course I hope you will bring along other advisors, anybody! Everybody! Oh, no, thank you, I can find my way out. Good-bye!"

But Barbara accompanied Miss Plankton to her car. So did Buddy, frantic to overhear whatever fool thing Barbara was going to say.

In the kitchen Virginia was having trouble with her puttied window. Wordlessly John took the putty knife from her and made a neatly chamfered corner.

"You're good at that," said Virginia. "Better than me."

John picked up another dab of putty, rolled it into a narrow snake, and pressed it along the edge of the next pane of glass. In spite of himself he had been troubled by Buddy's violent warnings. He saw Virginia lying on her back, struggling, her clothing torn, a burly shape throwing itself down on top of her. John's hand trembled, and the putty knife jerked, tearing a hole in his silken seam. "Shit," he said.

"It's all right," said Virginia softly.

"No, it isn't," said John.

Thirty-Four

UNDER THE COLOSSAL SPREAD OF MOOSE ANTLERS IN THE GREAT hall of Buddy Whipple's house at the top of the hill, the receptionist-secretary's desk was unoccupied. Buddy stared at the empty chair. Where was the damn girl anyway? And he had expected to find the ex-governor in residence here this morning, but Croney was missing too.

There were noises upstairs, muffled screeches and guffaws. Buddy cocked his head and listened, then shrugged his shoulders. It was common knowledge that Howard Croney had a strong tendency in the direction of miscellaneous lechery. Somebody was always having to call up his wife Madeline and explain that the hectic pace of the campaign had made it necessary for her husband to spend another night at headquarters.

Well, what the hell, thought Buddy, I can type my own letter.

The rented typewriter was superb. Buddy flexed his fingers over the keys and tapped out the name of Hollis R. Smythe, Cabinet Secretary for Public Works, Commonwealth of Massachusetts.

Dear Mr. Smythe,

This is to recommend all possible speed in pursuing Project S-124, submitted for your consideration last month. I repeat that eminent domain will not be necessary in a single property-taking. However, altered circumstances relating to some of the parcels might in the future make the matter far more costly and difficult. You will remember the old saying "Strike while the iron is hot."

May I remind you that the next governor of the Commonwealth will in all likelihood be ex-Governor Howard Croney? I feel sure that in making new appointments or in continuing those of current office holders, he will select only those candidates whose policies regarding public works projects are as forward-looking and public-spirited as his own.

Yours truly,

Clarence Whipple

Buddy jerked the letter out of the typewriter and decided to take it to the post office in Concord immediately. There was no time to lose. And then he could saunter across the Milldam and buttonhole old Peep in the bank, where Mrs. Bewley's long-delinquent mortgage account was crying out for attention.

But Mr. Peep almost upset Buddy's apple cart by going sentimental on him. "Do you think the old lady is competent to understand what the letter says?" worried Mr. Peep. "That we're putting up her place for auction? You know, it was at my personal advice that she remortgaged the property twenty years ago. In a sense it's my fault for assuming she was able to take on an obligation of that nature."

"I'll tell you what I'll do," said Buddy. "I'll go over there myself and explain it to her gently. It won't make any difference to her really. I understand she's going into a nursing home anyway. And of course she'll get most of the auction money, after you people take out what's due to you."

"Poor old soul," said Mr. Peep, with genuine sympathy. "I remember when she used to help Caroline with the children in days gone by. I expect most of the people who employed her as a domestic servant never took anything out of her wages for social security. And we probably paid her too little besides. In a sense, the people for whom she worked have some responsibility. I wonder if —"

"But they are helping her right now, all the time," explained Buddy quickly. "They're paying the taxes that will support her in Ferndale Manor. She'll be well cared for there. It would really be a mistake for her to stay in her own place. Have you seen it? Well, it's pretty bad. Ought to be condemned. It will give the fire department something to burn down. You know how the boys enjoy those bonfires of theirs. I mean, when it's called for by law, of course, and all safety precautions have been taken."

"Well, I suppose so," said Mr. Peep. "Sad, this business of old age." The tragedy of time and tide bore down on Mr. Peep, and he shook his head regretfully. "It's an awful shame."

Thirty-Five

PLUCKING THE THREADS OF THE WEB INGRATIATINGLY TO ANnounce his presence, the male spider approached the female with caution. He was a large spider, almost as big as his prospective mate, but instinctively he knew that she might soon forget who he was. In absence of mind and dimness of sight she might confuse him with her ordinary midnight snack. Swiftly, then, he attended to the business at hand, reaching through the threads in which she was suspended to insert his pedipalp into her epigynum and deposit sperm. Then with all haste he withdrew, while the female spider settled once more into a trance of bloodthirsty expectation.

Virginia and John were working together in the round garden. In the heavy languor of the August afternoon they were weeding opposite sides of the circular border. John was squatting on his haunches, Virginia lying on her side.

Virginia reached into the myrtle ground cover for a stalk of the hairlike witchgrass, feeling for the white casing at the root, jerking it out. She was thinking about Miss Plankton. There she was, Jane Plankton, out there in the world doing good. Miss Plankton wasn't lost in a self-indulgent dream of her own. She wasn't playing around selfishly with a private piece of landscape.

Of course she had been too nice to accuse them of anything like that. Virginia smiled, remembering the way Miss Plankton had clasped her hands at the view and basked among the flowers.

In the motionless air the noise of the traffic on the road was suddenly louder than usual. Virginia and John lifted their heads as a motorcycle roared up the driveway and thundered in a daring turn around the granite post at the end of the stone wall. In a wild slanting swoop it finished the circle, the two passengers leaning into the curve at a crazy angle, then righting themselves as the huge bike careened back down the driveway. On the grassy turf of the round garden it left a deep wheel track.

"Wow," said John, getting up, staring after the cloud of dust.

"Crazies from Walden Pond," said Virginia, staring after them too, shaken by the glimpse of the sleeveless leather jacket over the hairy chest, the girl's pink freckled thighs clutching her boyfriend's denim pants, the gold-flake helmets, the black insect visors.

Calmly John picked up a rake and went to work on the rutted furrow in the grass, while Virginia turned back to her weeding. She was surprised to find herself trembling. She hadn't minded the ugly blat of the exhaust nor the hot breath of careless lust and rude power. Yet they had changed the quality of the afternoon. Somehow the violence of the trespass and the raw desire that hung in the air seemed to call into question the stillness and privacy of the weedy garden, the lank droop of her hair, the smallness of her breasts, the skinny angularity of the wrist that was tugging now at the witchgrass. What difference did it make whether one planted this bush or another bush, or didn't plant anything at all?

When the little red car drew up beside her, it was only more of the same thing, although clenched buttock and excited vagina were less brutally in evidence.

Cherry Peaches Schermerhorn was wearing a T-shirt emblazoned with the word *JOY*. In a single motion she stepped out of the car and kissed John full on the mouth. As a gesture of greeting the kiss was obviously only the brimming over of her cup of health, an impulsive uprush of friendly feeling. John fumbled at his glasses and stepped backward on the rake.

"Oh, forgive me," chuckled Cherry Peaches. "It was just the kiss of peace. Wasn't it, Arthur? The kiss of peace, right?"

Arthur Potter, her overlord in Christ, stepped from the car on the other side and gazed at Cherry Peaches, grinning, his eyes vaguely glittering under a moist film.

"Listen," said Cherry Peaches, winking at Virginia, "it's a song." Swiftly she pulled a guitar out of the car, knocking it clumsily against the window frame, and strummed a twanging chord.

The kiss,

warbled Cherry Peaches,

> The kiss of peace,
> The kiss of pea-ea-eace,
> The ki-i-iss of peace!
> When will you feel it?
> You cities?
> You nationnnnnns?
> You peoples of the woooooooorld?
> When will you feeeeeeel
> The kiss of peeeeaaaaace?

"Well, I'm not much of a singer," she concluded, slapping her guitar and stuffing it in the backseat again. "Say, Virginia, is it okay if I show Arthur the sunken garden?"

Virginia felt grey and pinched, pierced by laser beams of light. "The sunken garden? What for? Remember, I said you couldn't — ?"

"Oh, wait till you hear Arthur." Cherry Peaches tucked her T-shirt into her gathered skirt, which had been put on inside out. "I'm just going to persuade *Arthur*, so he can persuade *you*, to let *us* bring the kids here for our retreat. And then *everybody* will be happy!" She threw up her arms to show universal satisfaction. "Won't they, Arthur?"

Arthur took Virginia's hand limply and mumbled something, then hurried after his Juvenile Coordinator in the direction of the sunken garden. Cherry Peaches darted ahead of him, her wallowing pumpkins saluting the teeming fertility of the earth, the fruitage of midsummer, the plentiful harvest of approaching fall. "Here it is," she cried over her shoulder at her spiritual counselor, beckoning him on, twinkling down the steps, sinking to the sun-warmed flagstones of the floor.

In the round garden John finished the job of loosening the dirt in the track of the invading motorcycle, and began trampling the soil with his new sneakers. It was the second pair of new shoes he had been forced to buy this summer. His feet were getting huge.

"Oh," exclaimed Virginia, "look what I found." She stood up and showed him a robin's egg. The egg had fallen apart in her hand, revealing an infinitesimal piece of folded paper. "A robin seems to have written me a letter."

John glanced at the word *Virginia* on the scrap of paper. "A million robins with a million typewriters, they'd write all the works of Shakespeare sooner or later."

"Oh, is that it?" said Virginia, leaning forward, kissing him gently.

"The kiss of peace?" murmured John.

"The kiss of war. Against weeds and poison ivy. Against cherries and peaches. Against all kinds of scary things."

"Where do I enlist?" said John huskily.

"You already have."

John grinned and went back to work, his head spinning. Virginia knelt down and stared at the next patch of weedy garden. It was a planting of shrub roses and globe thistle, humming with bees. A long claw of bramble had leaped up from below the grafted union of the rosebush, a turbulent wild species that would boil up over the stone wall and reach for the sky, given half a chance.

Virginia looked at it with reluctant admiration. It was like the girl from the church, nature red in tooth and claw.

Thirty-Six

"I'M SORRY, JOHN, DEAR," SAID HIS AUNT MARY ON THE PHONE. "They're your second cousins, and they haven't seen you since you were a baby, and they'll be starting back to California tomorrow afternoon in their camping van. I'm really sorry, dear, but I'm afraid it's a command appearance."

So John biked home to Barretts Mill Road and met his cousins, Bob and Dorothy, and their little kids, Ruthie and Hamilton, and they all had supper, and then Aunt Mary made Uncle Homer take a picture of everybody around the table and Uncle Homer's flash didn't work and he got mad, and then somehow or other Benny managed to push Hamilton off his high chair, and Hamilton bumped his head and cried, and at last John biked back to Lincoln at midnight.

He was tired, exhausted with his long day, but he couldn't sleep. He lay on his mattress in the cool wind of his electric fan, his mind racing. He felt poised on some kind of pinnacle, in a state of nervous exaltation. He could think of a hundred ways to answer Virginia's careless letter to the air. Small ways, miniature ways. John sat up in bed, staring in the dark at the dim jars where his spiders hung suspended in their silken lairs. He felt clever, excited. His fingers were nimble, ready to manufacture a dozen ephemeral pieces of correspondence. "A crush," his mother would have said. John suspected that his Aunt Mary knew what was the matter with him, although she didn't say anything. And Barbara — well, you couldn't hide much from Barbara. Sometimes he would catch her glancing at him keenly, and then she would smile and look away. As for Virginia herself — oh, Virginia. John groaned and fell back in bed. That hadn't meant anything, had it? That time when he had seen her in Buddy's arms? She couldn't really be serious about Buddy, could she? John could feel Virginia's presence, two walls away, lying there in her own bed. Was she awake? What was she thinking? Did she hear the owl hoot? What kind of owl was it? Did owls eat spiders? Would his barn spider be safe?

Another part of John's brain was taking over. From owls and spiders he went on to owls and chickens. Owls liked chickens. Oh, God, Mrs. Bewley's chickens. The roof of Mrs. Bewley's chicken yard had sprung loose, he had noticed it the last time he had passed her house. He would have to mend it, to keep her chickens safe from owls by night and hawks by day. Tomorrow, bright and early, he'd get over there and take care of it.

But next morning he was too late. Only three of Mrs. Bewley's little bantam hens were stepping around the chicken yard. John opened the door of the henhouse and looked inside. It was empty. He stared in dismay at the surrounding woods. Then he walked up Mrs. Bewley's back steps and knocked on her door to ask what had happened, to say he was sorry.

But in answer to his knock, Mrs. Bewley merely opened the door a crack, and cried, "SHOO, SHOO," and then slammed it in his face. John stood there a moment in surprise, then went back to the henhouse. Scooping some chicken feed from the big bag in the corner, he poured it into the feeder. It was nice there in the henhouse. John lingered to watch the three hens duck through their little door and run to the feeder, their foolish ankle feathers dragging on the floor. He reminded himself to get some antilice powder. But on the whole the chickens looked healthy. Their plumage was sleek and fluffy. They were burbling contentedly like pigeons. John went outside and got to work on the roof of the chicken yard.

The job didn't take long. When he was finished, he picked up his clippers and his spool of wire and started for home, walking quietly, trying to be inconspicuous, since Mrs. Bewley seemed to have taken a dislike to him.

But at the end of her driveway he was startled by a commotion at her front door. Buddy Whipple was catapulting down the broken steps. Mrs. Bewley was shaking her fist at him and waving her glasses on their long chain and swearing at the top of her lungs. Mrs. Bewley slammed her front door. A shingle dropped off the roof. The chickens in the chicken yard fluttered up against their chicken wire ceiling, squawking loudly.

Buddy picked himself up and grinned sheepishly at John. There were red scratches on his cheek. "What a nutty old girl," he said. "She really put me through the wringer."

"Wow," said John. "What did she do? Scratch your face?"

"I don't know what got into her," said Buddy. "I was just making a neighborly call. You know, checking up on her."

"She seems to have a grudge against me too," said John. "It's really strange. Say, listen, how are things in there? A lot better than they were before, right?"

Buddy reached down for a handful of grass and patted his bleeding cheek. "Mrs. Bewley's house is in a very satisfactory condition," he said. "It's just fine."

Thirty-Seven

THERE WERE SUMMER TOURISTS ON THE STREETS OF CONCORD. They were not a pushing crowd but sober visitors, politely interested in local history. Parked beside the information booth on Heywood Street their cars bore license plates from North Dakota, from Tennessee, from New York State. Fathers of families asked questions in regional accents, mothers consulted maps. They had spent a rainy morning in the neighboring town of Lexington, touring the Hancock-Clarke house and the Buckman Tavern, and they had crossed the wet grass of Lexington Green to gaze up from under their umbrellas at the glistening bronze statue of Captain Parker with his nicely buttoned gaiters and his musket. Then the sky had cleared, and now they were on their way to the North Bridge in Concord to admire the equal determination of the Concord Minuteman to abandon his plow and take up arms. Then they would walk patiently up the hill beyond the Concord River and sit in the dark to watch cartoon minutemen reenact the stirring events of April 19, 1775. Later they would visit the Old Manse and Orchard House while guides repeated again and yet again, "Nathaniel Hawthorne came here with his bride on his wedding day in 1842," and "At this desk between the windows Louisa May Alcott wrote *Little Women*." At last the exhausted tourists would come back to the Milldam to buy ice-cream cones at Brigham's and saunter among the old gravestones beside the parking lot.

On Main Street Amelia Farhang hurried importantly past a travel-worn family — mother, father, daughter, and small male child whining and sucking his thumb — and paused on the corner of Walden Street to examine critically the wooden barrel of petunias on the sidewalk.

Not bad, thought Amelia. A workmanlike job. Someone from the Concord Garden Club had assembled it, no doubt. Of course if anybody had asked *Amelia Farhang* to manufacture an arrangement for such a prominent place, something for the tourists to admire, something to symbolize Concord, Massachusetts, with all its distinguished history and its place in the American heritage, she would have come up with something truly inspired. Amelia drifted along the sidewalk with half-closed eyes, imagining a patriotic creation in red, white, and blue, using the American flag as an accessory. When Buddy Whipple gave her a cheery

wave from the driver's seat of his car, she failed to see him. The sun was in her eyes. She was transported, inspired by a sudden fit of cosmic understanding. The sun itself was a blossom, a great dahlia in the sky, God's own glorious flower arrangement, with the planets cunningly placed here and there as fascinating accessories. And the stars! What were they but celestial posies!

Buddy's greeting had been perfunctory. Mrs. Farhang was merely a female fruitcake who happened to be the wife of Putnam Farhang, the president of the Paul Revere Insurance Company, a man with whom Buddy had important matters pending. Buddy's business at the moment was with the post office. There was a parking place right in front of the building, behind a big camping van from California. Buddy nipped into the parking place, ran up the steps of the post office, bought his stamps and mailed his letters. Then he took a quick peek at his private box.

Was there anything in it yet? No, not yet. No interesting little package was blocking up the window. But wait — there was something in there after all. Opening the box with his key, Buddy took out a pink slip.

Package too large for box. Present slip at desk.

Shit! What was the point of having a private box if it didn't stay private? He couldn't ask for the box at the desk. Not in person! Not when he'd taken all that trouble to arrange for the box by mail under an assumed name.

Furious, Buddy strode out of the post office and ran down the steps. Then he stopped and looked curiously at the camping van parked at the curb in front of his car. The license plates of the van said California. Its windows were plastered with stickers from Yellowstone Park and the Grand Canyon and the Carlsbad Caverns. A small boy was sitting in the front seat, all by himself. The van obviously belonged to some California people who were making the grand tour of the whole goddamn country. Today they were here in Concord looking at the Old North Bridge and Walden Pond, but soon they'd be someplace else, a thousand miles away.

Buddy strolled across the sidewalk to the window of the van. "Hi there," he said to the little boy. "Hey, how'd you like to make a quarter? Want to get a package for me in the post office? You just take this card up those steps to the counter, and they'll give you the package, okay?"

The boy looked up from his book and stared at the pink card. Buddy was faintly surprised to see that his reading matter was a heavy college text entitled *Introduction to Astronomy*. Gazing brightly at Buddy, the boy said, "It won't blow up or anything, will it?"

"Blow up? The package?" Buddy laughed hugely. "Oh, no. But it's a secret, you see. It's a birthday present for my brother, and he's in there in the post office, and I don't want him to know."

The boy looked wisely at Buddy for a minute, and then he reached out for the card, slid down from the high front seat and trotted up the steps of the post office.

Five minutes later he was back, carrying a small square package, holding it to his ear. "Gee," he said, "what's in here? It says, *Live Material, Rush!*"

Buddy was ready for the question. "Worms," he said. "My brother loves to fish. It's a big supply of fishing worms."

"Oh, I see," said the boy. He shook the package beside his ear, as if he hoped to hear the worms tumbling over themselves with soft thudding sounds.

"Hey, don't do that," said Buddy. "You'll get them all black and blue."

Reluctantly the boy released the package and put out his hand for his quarter. Reaching in his pocket, Buddy pulled out a handful of change. A grubby scrap of paper fluttered out of his pocket at the same time. The boy plucked it deftly out of the air, handed it back to Buddy and took the quarter. Then he marched back to the van on his fragile legs and struggled back up onto the front seat.

Buddy looked at his package. Pleased with himself, he spun on his heel, intending to run around the corner to Vanderhoof's hardware store and get some heavy working gloves, good thick ones with leather palms. He almost ran into Mary Kelly, as she came out of the ten-cent store with her husband Homer. Buddy gave them a loud, "Whoops, sorry!" and a grin and a wave, then bolted across the street, leaving behind him a floating piece of paper. As Mary and Homer ambled along the sidewalk, the slip of paper drifted unnoticed into a slender stream of water that was trickling slowly along the edge of the pavement below the curb. Carried along by the little rivulet of fresh rainwater and bits of sticks and fragments of last year's crumbled leaves, the scrap of paper journeyed to the drain at the corner of Walden Street and Hubbard, stuck for a moment in one of the clotted openings of the grillwork, then slipped through in the next miniature surge of dirty water.

Mary and Homer found Benny holding the fort in Uncle Bob's big camping van all by himself.

"Sorry to keep you waiting, Benny old boy," said Homer, crowding his large bulk into the back seat.

"We just had to pick up some things for your Aunt Dorothy, you see, Benny," said Mary, "so they can start home again this afternoon for California. Oh, there you are, Bob. Come on, Ruthie, you sit with us in back. Move over, Benny, so Hamilton can sit on his mother's lap."

"Oh, Benny, dear," said Aunt Dorothy, "thank you for minding our stuff for us. You're a real good scout."

Benny was excited. "Hey, listen, Aunt Mary," he said, as his Uncle Bob pulled the van out of the parking space and started around the block, "guess what?"

"What?" said Mary. "Here, Ruthie, just squeeze over a little bit. Uncle Homer's squashed the picnic basket. Oh, Homer, for heaven's sake."

"Mr. Whipple gave me a quarter. He got some worms in the mail, and he gave me a quarter and I went in and picked up the worms. Right there in the post office!"

"Worms? That's nice, dear," said Mary vaguely, trying to rescue the picnic basket.

"*Ouch*," said Homer. "There's something sticking into me.

What's that, a paring knife? Listen, Bennie, that's a crazy way to earn a quarter. Why didn't Mr. Whipple pick up his worms himself? Was he squeamish or something?"

"Well, he said his brother was in there," said Benny in his shrill piping voice, "and the worms were for his brother's birthday, because his brother likes to fish, and he didn't want his brother to know he was getting these worms for a present. So he asked me, see?"

"His brother?" said Mary. "What brother? Buddy Whipple doesn't have a brother. Are you sure it was Mr. Whipple?"

"Oh, yes. He used to visit Pop and borrow stuff. And the package said *Fragile, Live Material, Rush!* on the outside, and it had eighty-one cents in stamps on it, and it was mailed on August fifteenth from the South Georgia Biological Supply Company in Brunswick, Georgia, with laboratories in Portland, Oregon. And he dropped his prescription."

"His prescription?" said Aunt Dorothy. "Oh, Benny, I hope you gave it back?"

"Oh, sure. It was for epi-neph something. He must be sick, right, Uncle Homer?"

"God knows." Homer shrank sullenly down in his corner of the back seat, disgusted by yet another exhibition of his little nephew's photographic memory. Damned show-off little kid.

But Benny's Uncle Bob was a pharmacist. "Epinephrin, probably," he murmured, turning the van left onto Heywood Street. "Maybe he suffers from asthma."

Homer sat up. "Hey, maybe he stole the prescription from Edward Heron, and that's why Edward didn't have his medicine that day. No, that won't work." Homer slumped down in the seat again. "Barbara swore she saw the stuff in her father's pocket."

"Buddy doesn't have asthma, does he?" said Mary. "Barbara would know. I'll ask Barbara. He couldn't hide anything like that from Barbara."

And then Benny began tormenting his two-year-old cousin Hamilton, who was sitting pudgily beside him on his mother's lap. "Maybe that box had a *tarantula* inside it," he said, leaning close to Hamilton, breathing in his face. "And it got loose, and it's going to crawl all over you with its eight big *HAIRY LEGS*." Benny crooked his fingers wickedly and ran them up Hamilton's stomach.

Hamilton howled and threw his fat arms around his mother.

"Oh, Hamilton, don't be such a baby," cried his mother.

"Now, Benny, stop being mean to Hamilton," shouted Mary.

Thirty-Eight

IT WAS JOHN'S DAY OFF AGAIN. HE SPENT AN HOUR SWEEPING UP
flies in his butterfly net and feeding them to his spiders. It was
tricky getting a fly past the plastic film on the front of a web
frame and safely into the reach of one of his *Nuctenea sclopetarias*. As often as not the fly got away, and John had to try again.
It took a lot of stubborn perseverance.

The weather was still insufferably sticky and hot. The only
thing to do about it was to forget it and keep busy. John picked
up his tweezers and his little brush and his plastic pillboxes and
went on a collecting expedition. He found a bowl-and-doily spider
in a white pine tree, but they were a dime a dozen, and he left it
there. In the raspberry patch he looked for the garden spider, and
found her still poised in the middle of her giant web. He let her
be. Then, crawling on his hands and knees under the sugar maple
tree in front of the house, John found a wolf spider with an egg
sac attached to her abdomen, and he scooped her up in one of
his pillboxes. And then he ran down into the jungle at the bottom of the lawn and waded through catbrier and honeysuckle
and blackberry into the old orchard, to see what he could turn
up along the stone wall.

Slowly he made his way along the wall from one end to the
other, peering into crevices, bending down to look under project-

191

ing stones. At the far end of the wall he found the torn nest of yellow jackets once again. But there were no spiders. That was odd. John walked back along the wall to the beginning. This time he found a single linyphiid hiding deep within a cranny behind her horizontal veil. There were a lot of other sheet-web veils here and there, but most of them were only broken strands, as if earlier habitations had been destroyed.

Just as the wasp nest had been destroyed.

Standing up with his linyphiid safely in a pillbox, John stared at the long length of stone wall running off into the green jungle. It was almost as if there had been some catastrophe, as if all the organic life in the stone wall had packed up and left home. Idly he picked up a stone and turned it over, looking for something alive on the under side. But there was nothing. Only a set of yellow chalk marks. TOP, said the chalk marks, 17. John picked up the next stone. That one too said TOP, but the number was 32.

For an instant John was reminded of his own playful love letters to Virginia. But these hieroglyphs were of another kind entirely. Staring at the two upended stones, John remembered a story about some man who had bought a Scottish castle and taken it apart, and numbered every stone, so that the castle could be reassembled in Arizona or some place, like a giant puzzle.

The stone wall too had been moved. The numbers had been chalked on the stones so that the wall could be taken apart and then put back together again in the same order, with the weathered sides of the stones facing out, the lichen-covered upper boulders still on top, every stone edge-to-edge with its brothers, in the same pattern in which they had been carelessly dropped into place by the farmer who had cleared the fields a century or two ago.

Even the vegetation proved it. Tall weeds had been crushed flat by the new wall. Their dead stalks were sticking out under the lowest stones. Lopped honeysuckle bushes on either side were sending up green shoots.

The whole wall had been moved. What a colossal job! How

long would it have taken? John imagined himself moving the wall, piling the round boulders into a wheelbarrow, then pushing the wheelbarrow here from someplace else and dumping it out and going back for more. How many days would it take? A week? Maybe one man could move two hundred yards of stone wall in a week, if he really worked at it.

John looked left and right at the great bristling heads of the old apple trees. What had Edward Heron been doing down here, the day he died? It had been that real-estate scheme of his — he had been working on that. Maybe he had wanted a bigger territory to sell to the developer. Maybe he had moved the boundary of his property to give himself more land. Well then, where had he moved the wall from? Slowly John pushed off into the orchard, beating his way through the undergrowth, looking for traces of an ancient stone wall. Surely there would be a long bare line in the vegetation, a rectilinear emptiness where stones had lain for a century or more, and then vanished — where some of them still lay, perhaps, buried too deep for a hasty transferal.

It would be a hard thing to hide, the line of an old stone wall. But on the other hand, John reminded himself, nature abhorred a vacuum. New growth would close in fast. How long ago had the stones been moved? The chalk marks on them were a little smeared by dampness, but they were still legible. It must have been this year.

In the orchard there was no sign of a vacuum, no yard-wide absence of undergrowth in a long straight line.

John gave up. He took his wolf spider and his linyphiid and the stone marked TOP 17 back to his room. It was funny. Funny-peculiar, as his mother was always saying. Really weird.

Thirty-Nine

VIRGINIA WAS PEERING INTO ONE OF JOHN'S SPIDER CAGES, HER
head close to his. She showed no fear. "Are any of them poisonous?" she said.

"Oh, no. There aren't any poisonous spiders around here.
Oh, there's the black widow spider. But it's pretty rare. I haven't
got any. I mean, it isn't something you worry about in Massachusetts, getting bitten by a poisonous spider. Would you like to
hold this little lady in your hand?"

"Why not?" said Virginia bravely.

John lifted the screen from his aquarium, reached under a
veil of silk and dumped a spider in Virginia's cupped hands.
Virginia closed her fingers over it, then shuddered, without meaning to.

"It's all right," said John encouragingly, turning away to get
another spider for himself. "It will just sit there. It isn't going to
run all over and get in your hair or anything. Isn't it a nice one?"

"What did you say it is?" said Virginia, opening her fingers.

"Amaurobius ferox. I don't even know how to pronounce it."

"It's handsome," said Virginia. "So black and shiny."

"Shiny?" John looked up. "I wouldn't call it —" With a
sudden exclamation and a sweep of his hand he knocked the
spider to the floor. "My God," he said, "my God, how did that

get in here?" John picked up Virginia's hands and gazed at them. Then he snatched up a collecting cup and fell to his knees. The spider was moving slowly across the floor. John clapped the cup over it and stood up.

Virginia's blood was rushing into her head. She looked at her hands and wiped them on her jeans. "It's all right," she said. "It didn't bite me."

"But how did it *happen*?" John was almost crying. "It couldn't have got in there without my — I mean, I know an *Amaurobius ferox* when I see one." He shook his head despairingly. "But it was. It was. And I put it in your hand without really looking at it. Oh, my God, how could I do a thing like that?"

"But what was it?" said Virginia, trying to laugh, to seem unconcerned.

"Oh, for God's sake, it was a black widow. Now don't worry. They're so sluggish they hardly ever bite. You didn't feel it bite you, did you?"

"No." Virginia looked at the palms of her hands again. John looked at them too.

"That was terrible," he said. "Just terrible."

"Do they ever really bite people?" said Virginia. "Or is it just a sort of old wives' tale, that people get killed by black widow spiders?"

"Oh, yes, they sometimes bite people. Usually just in parts of the country where there are outdoor privies. The spider makes a web under the seat. It must be pretty ghastly. People get bitten in, you know, really vulnerable places. And it's very painful, and I guess some of them die."

"Well, I feel fine," said Virginia. She wiggled her fingers to show their good health and put them in her pockets and watched as John slid a file card under the cup on the floor and gathered up card, cup and spider, and dumped the spider into an empty jar. Then he capped the jar with a screened lid and turned the jar over and over in his hands to show Virginia the red marking on the spider's belly. And then they examined the other spiders in John's collection, his huge batches of infant house spiders and *Nuctenea sclopetarias*, his pair of cellar spiders, his trapdoor spider, his tarantula named Fred. The jars shook in John's hands as he picked them up. His fingers were still trembling.

Virginia smiled around at John's room. "I like it here," she said, and went away.

Left alone, John picked up the jar containing the black widow spider and stared at it again. How could he have collected a black widow without knowing about it? Either he had found it in the wild, and identified it carelessly as an *Amaurobius ferox*, or else somebody had put it into his aquarium with the intention of doing him harm.

In his mind's eye John could see the *Amaurobius ferox* perfectly, nestled in a loose web under a stone in the wall beside the mailbox. The spider had been roughly the same size and shape as a black widow, but he could remember seeing the brown pattern on her back perfectly clearly.

There was one way to find out for sure. Lifting the dry twigs

out of the aquarium, John examined every corner. He found only the silk-wrapped carcasses of the mosquitoes and flies and mealworms he had fed it. But one of the carcasses looked too big to be a fly or a mealworm. John poked it with a pencil. Surely it was bigger than anything he had put into the aquarium for spider food? Picking up the bundle, he spent five patient minutes pulling away the silk with a pair of tweezers. Then he looked at the remains with his hand lens, and sat back satisfied. It was his Amaurobius ferox in person, stone dead, sucked dry by the interloper in its house, the imposter, the black widow spider that had been dropped into its cage on the sly.

Well, thought John, at least his own honor as a spider collector and amateur arachnologist had been restored. The black widow was entirely somebody else's doing.

At the supper table that evening he passed the jar around for the others to see. He said nothing about the peculiarity of its presence in his collection. Neither did Virginia. Barbara was interested, and asked questions. Buddy was disgusted, and left the room.

And after that, for the rest of the summer, John made sure that the black widow was still securely contained in her jar before he went to bed. And he shook out his quilt and his sheets and looked under his pillow too. Every night. Just in case.

Forty

IN THE TELEVISION STUDIO AT CHANNEL 4 THE METEOROLOGIST waved his hand at the perpetually stalled Bermuda high on his satellite picture and apologized gamely for yesterday's optimistic forecast. The siege of hot and humid weather was not going to end after all. In a hundred thousand kitchens people swore at the TV screen, as though the heat wave were the weatherman's fault. They glowered at their soggy toast and slammed their salt shakers on the table to loosen the damp crystals. Refrigerators and air conditioners rattled and shuddered, working overtime. Everything seemed grubby to the touch, glittering with splotches of grease. Paint mildewed on north-facing porches. Babies were querulous. Employees quit their jobs in sudden explosions of bottled-up resentment. Thunder rumbled. There were sinister flashes of light. Four-letter words steamed up, savage and thick, from the city of Boston, collecting in a peevish low-hanging cloud of concentrated spite.

On the second-hottest night since the year 1882, the murdering TV repairman from Waltham cut a swath through the suburb of Belmont, killing a schoolteacher and wounding a policeman.

The hot weather didn't bother Buddy Whipple. Nothing bothered Buddy. Buddy was busy on a dozen fronts at once, moving forward, bringing one project after another to fruition.

His hands were tingling with the vibration of the wires and strings gathered together under his control.

Leaning back in his tilting office chair, Buddy smiled up at the distant ceiling of the great dark hall and imagined the place as it must have been in the old days, with the men and women of the Middlesex Foxhounds drinking stirrup cups beside the immense fireplace and dashing their glasses against the stony hearth. Then he put aside his romantic dreams of yesteryear and glanced at the headline in the morning *Globe*, MURDERING REPAIRMAN STRIKES AGAIN. Was there anything on the front page about Croney's TV debate last night? It had been a great moment, a real attention-getter, a triumph. Howie had never been in better form, and poor old Brumble had made a fool of himself. But there was nothing about it on the front page, only a little item with the editorials, a couple of paragraphs showing an obvious sympathy for the governor. Brumble was described as "underdog Brumble." Croney was "dapper, glib and sleek." The damn newspaper would probably come out for Brumble sooner or later. Well, the hell with it. Buddy put down the *Globe* and tried to come to grips with the shape of the day to come.

What was on the official political schedule? Well, there was his private conference at ten o'clock with a certain amiable justice of the state supreme court. And a clambake in Revere at two in the afternoon. And then there was the ad to be placed in the local paper for a new secretary-receptionist, because the last one had been banished in a hurry, assigned to manage the distribution of ten thousand campaign leaflets in the city of Fitchburg. And, goddamnit, what was the other thing? Mrs. Bewley, that was it. Buddy had promised to help Dolores Leech get Mrs. Bewley out of her house and into Ferndale Manor. Dolores was afraid she might need muscular assistance. Mrs. Bewley was being obstinate about the whole thing, and she was a tough, wiry old girl, a fact Buddy had reason to remember very well. And, oh, God, he should call the doctor. What the hell was the name of that stuff he was supposed to be picking up at the drug store? The goddamn prescription had turned up missing.

And then there was something else to be taken care of in the long, ongoing silent war with that snotty little kid, John Hand. John had been sending cute little letters to Virginia on leaves and flowers. The kid was a menace. Well, two could play at that game.

"Jesus *Christ*, what the *hell* do you think you're doing?" said Barbara, running across the lawn.

Buddy looked around at Barbara, and at Virginia and John, who were getting out of Barbara's car. In a moment all three of them were standing around him, staring at him in horror.

"Just making a little romantic statement on this here tree," said Buddy comically, waving his jackknife.

In livid white on the great trunk of the maple tree that towered in front of the house was a crude heart, with the message *B W + V H*.

Virginia turned away, not trusting herself to speak. Barbara spluttered indignantly at Buddy. John touched Virginia's arm and pointed skyward. Geese were flying over the house in a long ragged plowshare, uttering their hoarse cry.

"V," said John softly.

The geese vanished over the treetops.

"Oh, shit," said Buddy, throwing down his knife.

The Concord bank was open till four. Buddy rushed away from the clambake in Revere just in time to get to the Harvard Trust ten minutes before it closed. In the fluorescent light of the little room in the basement, he opened his safe deposit box.

His mother's ruby ring shone as red as ever.

Red is for my valentine, thought Buddy sentimentally, walling off Virginia from all the other chambers of his mind, from the complexities of the business apparatus he was carrying forward, from the multiplicity of his feverish schemes, separating her even from her own stubbornness, her anger, her silence, her furious passionate tears. Putting the ring in his pocket, Buddy poked through the papers in the box until he found the one he wanted, his will. It would have to be changed. Then he tucked that, too, in the inside breast pocket of his light summer jacket.

When the ring appeared on Virginia's finger the next day, Buddy had his revenge.

John took it hard. He couldn't believe it. He turned, appalled, to Barbara.

But Barbara had been forewarned. She glared at Virginia. "When is it going to be?"

Virginia gazed out the window. She was airy and calm. "Oh, some time in December. Maybe next year."

"November," said Buddy. "Just as soon as we get Howie elected. Plenty of time for a big church wedding then. Right, Virginia?"

To John in his despair there was something both wheedling and threatening in Buddy's loud voice, in the wrenching turn of his big shoulders as he swung around to look at Virginia. John looked at her too, his face white. His stomach was reacting violently. He felt sick and feeble. His knees were ready to give way.

Virginia merely studied the ring on her finger and said nothing.

Buddy was in his element. He waved a bottle over his head. "Now listen here, you people, this calls for a celebration. Look what I've got here, champagne. And wait till you see this." He picked up a rumpled paper bag from the floor and dumped it on the table. "Grouse. I bagged me some grouse with my little shotgun."

"Grouse?" Barbara was suspicious. "Where'd you get grouse? Is this the right season for hunting grouse? I've never heard of anybody eating grouse."

"Out Littleton way," said Buddy. "They haven't got any foolish regulations against firearms in Littleton. And, yes, of course it's the hunting season for grouse. You can hunt any old thing you want to at this time of the year."

Barbara looked at the skinny little plucked carcasses dangling from Buddy's hand. "Well, it just seems a shame," she said. "I'll bet they were nice little birds. Who's going to cook them? Not me."

"I am, Barbara. You just stand back. Proper engagement celebration." Buddy slapped the grouse down on the counter, picked up his bottle of champagne and jammed it into the refrigerator. Then, as John watched in sickened revulsion, Buddy reached for Virginia, threw his arms around her, and sank his face into her throat.

Forty-One

"She shuddered, Uncle Homer, and jumped away," said John. "I saw it. She really did." John's voice was strangled. "She doesn't want to have anything to do with him, not really. I swear. He's got her in his clutches somehow. She's trapped."

Homer stroked his chin and looked at his nephew. The boy was obviously entangled himself. Jealous. You couldn't trust a jealous man. You couldn't even trust a jealous kid like poor old John, with a crush on an older woman. "Hmmmm. Well, who knows the ways of women in love? Virginia's at least twenty-one, isn't she? She can do what she wants. Now, listen, what are the other things? You said there were three things. What are you doing with that rock?"

"It's from a stone wall, down in the old orchard. Buddy moved it, the whole stone wall, because it's a property bound." John displayed the chalked numbers on his granite boulder, and explained his discovery to Homer. "At first I thought Mr. Heron had done it. I thought he moved the stone wall because he wanted to enlarge the development he was going to put in down there with that other guy — remember that developer who turned up at the funeral? I thought I could find the place where the stone wall used to be, back in the orchard that was really Mr. Heron's property. You know, you'd think there would be a line

where nothing was growing, because the wall had been on top of it for a couple of hundred years. But I couldn't find any place like that, and I was really puzzled.

"But then I thought about the person who owned the land on the other side of the boundary. You know, Buddy Whipple. What if it was Buddy moving the boundary the other way, so he'd be the one to get more land? Listen, Uncle Homer, he got in there very soon — it was the very day after the funeral — with the big rotary mower from the town barn. And he chopped up all the brush on his side of the line, and then he plowed it up, all on the same day. The same day. And then he planted it with alfalfa, and he's already got one crop off it and planted winter wheat. So if there was a long bare strip there any place, there where the stone wall used to be, he had it all covered up right away, do you see?" John's face was flushed with excited color. "And I'll bet I know how Mr. Heron really died. He came along just as Buddy was nearly finished with the stone wall, and he said, 'What do you think you're doing?' And Buddy picked up a stone from the wall and threw it at him. And that brought on an asthma attack.

And it explains how he got that bump on his forehead. So it was Buddy's fault. That's what really happened."

"What makes you so sure he was there when Mr. Heron died?" said Homer. "As far as we know, Edward Heron was alone when he had that attack. He could have got that bruise on his forehead by falling on the stone wall in a paroxysm of gasping for breath."

"It was the yellow jackets, Uncle Homer. Remember, I told you there were yellow jackets there? I think Buddy was just finishing the job of moving the last stones, when by mistake he picked up this stone with a yellow jacket nest under it. And it was just at that moment that Mr. Heron came along and said, 'What are you doing here?' and Buddy threw the rock at him and knocked him down, and then Mr. Heron was so disturbed and hurt that his asthma was excited, and he began to cough and wheeze and gasp for breath."

"But you don't have any proof that Buddy was there when Edward died. You're just making that stuff up."

"No, I'm not. Buddy was already stung himself when he came along the first time that day and asked to see Mr. Heron. He didn't get these stings later on, when he pretended to be going to find him." John's eyes were focused inward on a memory of Buddy bending over a honeysuckle stump, his red neck exposed, inflamed with scarlet welts. "I didn't think of it until the other day, and then I realized he must have been there in the orchard before Mr. Heron died, right there with him beside that broken nest. They both got stung at the same time."

"What about Mr. Heron's medicine?" said Homer sharply. "What happened to that?"

"Buddy took it away from him." John waved his arms. "You see? That explains what happened to it. Buddy grabbed it away, so Mr. Heron couldn't save himself, and then Buddy just stood back and watched him die."

Homer strummed his lower lip thoughtfully with a forefinger and gazed at his nephew. "And the third thing?" he said solemnly. "What about the third thing?"

"Well, the third thing is that Buddy tried to kill me with a black widow spider. There was this black widow in my collection all of a sudden, only I never put it there. And then I did a really stupid thing. Oh, never mind the stupid thing." John waved his hands in dismissal of the stupid thing. "The point is, Buddy put it there."

·"But where would Buddy get a black widow spider?" said Homer. "What makes you think it was his doing?"

"Well, who else would it have been? And anybody can order one through the mail. It's easy. I've got this catalogue."

There was a pause. Homer and John looked up as Mary came out of the house and lifted Benny into his wading pool. "Oh, Homer, you've got to take his picture," said Mary. "Wouldn't that be a cunning picture to send to Gwen, Benny splashing in the water?"

"Good God, not now," said Homer, staring balefully at his small nephew, who was jumping up and down in the water and shrieking, "THE SKY IS FALLING, SAID HENNY PENNY! THE SKY IS FALLING, SAID TURKEY LURKEY! THE SKY IS FALLING, SAID DUCKY LUCKY!"

"That's right, dear," murmured Mary. "Have a good time." She smiled at John and settled down in a lawn chair beside the pool, as Benny tossed a bucket of water into the air and shouted, "THE SKY IS FALLING ON YOUR HEAD! LOOK OUT BELOW!"

Homer closed his eyes, wiped his hand across his face, and turned back to John. "You said anybody can order a black widow spider through the mail? That's interesting. I didn't know that." Homer leaned back in his chair and gazed into space, remembering an encounter in front of the dime store on Walden Street, and Buddy Whipple rushing away around the corner, and Benny's crazy story about a box of worms. And that piece of paper that had fallen from Buddy's pocket —

Homer sat up and looked at John. "You live in the same house with Buddy Whipple. Tell me, does he have asthma?"

John looked blank. "Asthma? Buddy Whipple? Not so far as I know."

Homer sighed. "That's what Barbara says too. She says she

never saw anybody with healthier lungs. Then what the hell was Buddy doing with a prescription for epinephrin? You know, the same stuff Edward Heron was supposed to have been carrying with him on the day he died, only he wasn't."

John made a puzzled face and shrugged his shoulders.

Homer waved his hand in helpless resignation and fell back in his chair. "You know, John, I'm slow. I know I'm slow. That story you told me about Fabre — what's his name? Jean Henri Fabre. You know, when he was a little boy, that experiment he did, opening his mouth and closing his eyes to find out how he saw the sun in the sky? Well, I've had my stupid mouth open all the time, and my eyes closed. But even imbeciles like me catch on at last and see the light. Buddy Whipple moved the stone wall to get himself another little slice of real estate. He let Edward Heron die without lifting a finger to help him. He tried to do you in with a black widow spider. And he's got some kind of stranglehold on Virginia Heron. But what is it? What the hell is on his mind? Something nasty, you can be sure of that. Something big. Something to do with land. I don't like it at all."

"I know who we should talk to," said John, jumping up impulsively. "William Warren, over there in the Lincoln town hall. He knows everything there is to know about local real estate."

"Good," said Homer, standing up grimly. At the same instant his nephew Benny, transported by the apocalytic melodrama of his nursery saga, leaped out of the wading pool, raced across the lawn and tossed a whole bucketful of water at his uncle, screeching that the sky was falling, the whole sky, along with the sun and moon and planets and asteroids and meteorites and comets and red giants and white dwarfs and black holes and galaxies and all the rest of the expanding and contracting universe, the whole entire SKYYYYYYYYYYYYYYY.

Forty-Two

As HOMER AND JOHN DROVE ACROSS ROUTE 2 THE HEAVENS opened. It began to pour.

"The sky is falling, all right," said Homer peevishly, turning on the windshield wipers. "Damn little kid. It's all his doing."

"Wow," said John, watching the rain sheet across the glass. "I can't believe it. It must be raining in the vegetable garden and the front yard and the back yard all at once. I mean the rain doesn't take turns, the way we have to do with the sprinklers. Isn't that great!"

"Hold it," said Homer, as they pulled up in front of the Lincoln town hall. "I've got a busted umbrella in the trunk." Homer's umbrella was mildewed and one of its ribs had collapsed, but it shielded them from the drenching downpour as they made their way into the town hall. In the lobby they were greeted by an extraordinary flower arrangement beside the water fountain, a staccato composition of dried pulque pods from Mexico, a contorted branch of diseased locust, and three defoliated branches of the fried-egg tree, on a bed of smashed Coca Cola bottles. A kinked rusty wire meandered toward the ceiling.

Homer glanced at the flower arrangement, then averted his eyes hastily. "What are we going to say to him?" he muttered to John, putting down his dripping umbrella on the floor.

"I don't know, Uncle Homer. You're supposed to be the big lieutenant detective. Haven't you got a right to go in and ask questions?"

"Well, for Christ's sake, I'm not anything official anymore. You know that."

The door to the selectmen's office opened as they stared at it doubtfully. "Well, good morning, John," said William Warren, smiling at him warmly. "Come on in. What's on your mind? And this is your Uncle Homer, if I'm not mistaken. How do you do, Professor Kelly? I've got a book you wrote."

Homer was flattered. "You do?" he said, beaming.

"Yes. And I want to talk to you about it some time. You made a mistake, I think. You said Thoreau built his house with boards and nails from an Irishman's shanty. That's right about the boards. But somebody stole the nails. He had to buy a lot of extra nails."

"Oh," said Homer, crestfallen. "Well, thank you. I guess the whole thing is one big mess of boners."

"Oh, no. Some parts of it were quite good, I thought. Now, what is it you two want to see me about?"

"Well," said Homer, "we just wondered if we could take a look at your maps. You know, the maps of property holdings in the town."

"Well, certainly. Which ones, precisely, would you like to see?"

"Which ones?" Homer looked at John. "The Heron place, I guess. And the Whipple property next door."

William Warren looked at Homer soberly, then reached for one of the giant black books that lay on his long table and hefted it in his arms and laid it on top of the others. "Here you are," he said, opening it to the right page. "Actually, there's a slight error on this map. At least so I've been told." William's voice was dry, his face expressionless. "This property line right here is too far to the east by several hundred yards. This stone wall boundary right here. Buddy Whipple claims the old survey was incorrect. And I guess he's right. I checked it myself with a theodolite the other day, from Baker Bridge Road. There's no stone wall at all along the boundary line shown here."

John nudged Homer's elbow. "That's the one. That's the stone wall we were talking about. See? What did I tell you?"

"Well, as a matter of fact, Mr. Warren," said Homer, "my nephew thinks the stone wall has been moved."

"Moved?"

"Stone by stone. Somebody picked it up and moved it farther to the west. There are chalk marks on the stones, numbers, so they could be picked up and put down again someplace else in the right order."

William Warren stared at Homer. His grave face became graver. He looked at John. "I should think, in that case, you could see a bare strip of ground where the stone wall was moved from."

"But he plowed it all up," said John. "Buddy did, I mean. He got in there right away with a tractor and a rotary mower, and chopped down all the wild growth and plowed it under and planted stuff. So you can't see any bare ground there anymore at all."

"I see." William pursed up his mouth and frowned. Then he glanced out the window at the rain. "I usually take a little coffee break about this time of day. Would you like to join me? I generally take my thermos outdoors and sit under the trees in the middle of the afternoon."

"Well, certainly," said Homer. "Of course, it's raining cats and dogs, but who would mind a little thing like that?"

Behind the town hall an old cemetery sloped down the hill. Huge slate tombstones leaned at gloomy angles. Homer's umbrella was only big enough for two ordinary-sized human beings. Heroically he sat outside its perimeter of protection and leaned against one of the gravestones. Rain poured down upon his head, plastering his hair to his forehead, drenching his eyelashes, running in rivulets into his mouth.

William was proud of the cemetery. "This stone was erected in honor of Eleazer Brooks," he said, "good Lincoln farmer, soldier and statesman. Move over, Homer, and you'll be able to read the inscription. Ah, here's my coffee. We can take turns with the cup."

Out-of-doors in the pouring rain, physically removed from the professional chamber where he conducted the business of the town, William Warren was hospitable and talkative. On official premises there were things one preferred not to discuss. One's office was a place of stern ethical principles. But under the trees in the open air William was his own man. "It just so happens," he said, taking a bulky folded map from inside his raincoat, "that I've noticed a couple of funny things myself." With difficulty he unfolded the map. John held one end high under the dry circle of the umbrella. "Look here, this small-scale map shows the northwest end of town. See there, that's the Heron place. There's Buddy's house up the hill, right next door. Here on the other side is Mrs. Bewley's place, and then we have a piece of back land Buddy picked up at auction this summer. Then you get Randall Jones, only he just sold this strip of his property to Buddy. Then Knickerbocker — well, I guess Henry Knickerbocker still owns all of his place. Then a couple more parcels of back land that just happen to belong to Buddy Whipple. He bought them outright from their former owners this summer. What I want to know is, what does he want all that back land for? He can't do anything with it. He can't build on it, or anything. The parcels are all too small, even if they had frontage, which most of them don't."

Homer poked his dripping head under the umbrella and tried to see what William was pointing at. "Where?" he said. "Where, where? Show me."

"Right here, Uncle Homer." John ran his finger along a curving line. "This is what he's talking about. I see what you mean, Mr. Warren. It's a long narrow piece, all more or less connected, except for Mrs. Bewley's house and that scrap of land that belongs to Henry Knickerbocker. Is that it? What could he do with a long strip like that?"

"Goddamnit anyway," said Homer, craning his neck, pawing at the map. "I can't see a damn thing. Oh, Jesus, there goes my coffee all over northwest Lincoln. Sorry, William. Here, we might as well hold the map out under the rain and wash it off. Is this what you're talking about? You mean, this strip right here?" Homer stared at the map. "But it isn't a strip unless Bewley and Knickerbocker give up their parcels, is it? And of course Buddy's own little connecting strip doesn't even belong to him, if what John says about that stone wall is correct. Of course —" Homer flicked a sidelong glance at John, "— he might be able to persuade the Heron girls to give him the piece anyhow."

"Never," murmured John.

"Well, just suppose, for the sake of argument," said William, "that Buddy Whipple succeeded in gaining ownership of the entire strip. Then do you see what it would look like?"

"A long skinny piece of back land," said Homer slowly, gazing at the map, "between Route 2 and Baker Bridge Road."

"That's it, do you see?" said William. "Between Route 2 and Baker Bridge."

"A new road," said John softly.

"Oh, oh, I see," cried Homer. "A road, a cutoff road, going through the back land on this side of Route 126 behind the Walden Pond parking lot. A great big four-lane highway, I'll bet, slicing the Herons off in a tiny corner between two major thoroughfares. Jesus X. Christ. I see it now. He'd sell all those pieces at a vast profit to the state highway department, with the blessing of that bastard Howard Croney."

William screwed the plastic cup back on his empty thermos, shook out his soggy map and struggled to his feet. "Well, there's still Henry Knickerbocker and Mrs. Bewley to be thankful for," he said. "Let's hope they hang on." Together the three of them squelched up the wet grass to the back door of the town hall. In William's office Homer and John spread the map on the rug, careful to utter no word to the tight-lipped selectman who was seated once more at the table, carrying on in righteous silence the daily affairs of the town. Squatting on the floor, Homer dabbed at the wet splotches that fell on the map from his dripping rain-soaked hair, and studied the long strip of patchwork that represented the driving force of Buddy Whipple's will.

Forty-Three

THE DOWNPOUR WAS ENDING AS JOHN GOT OUT OF HOMER'S CAR AT the bottom of the driveway. Walking up to the house, he saw the clouds part and the sun send broad rays over the drenched trees, the dripping front yard. Birds came out from the shelter of the tumbled bushes and took off across the empty air. There was a distant surly rumble of thunder.

His room was still stuffy and hot. An elm-leaf moth was batting against a window. John captured it in his butterfly net. But as he reached into the long bag and grasped it by one wing, he heard the telephone ring dimly through the wall from the other part of the house.

He took the moth with him. Charging down the dark stairway, he rushed through the laundry into the room that had been Edward Heron's study, snatched up the phone in his left hand and shouted hello.

There was a very angry man on the other end of the line. "Listen here, you told me you wouldn't call in that loan for years. That's what you told me. You knew I couldn't pay you back for a while. I told you that at the time. What the hell did you loan it to me for anyway — *Christ!* — if you were going to want it back as soon as this? My god, Buddy, listen here — "

The man was so enraged, it took John a minute or two to persuade him he was talking to the wrong party.

"What do you mean, the wrong party? Who the hell are you?"

"John. John Hand. I live here too. Buddy isn't here right now."

"Oh, Christ." There was a fuming silence. "Listen, tell him Henry Knickerbocker wants to talk to him right away. Henry Knickerbocker, you got that?" The crash of the phone rang in John's ear. He hung up and stood gazing at the feeble struggles of the moth in his right hand. Henry Knickerbocker owned one of the last parcels of land that kept the curving strip belonging to Buddy Whipple from making a complete arc, a single narrow band plunging through the woods in the direction of Route 2. Then John checked himself. Mr. Knickerbocker had been talking about money, not land.

Taking his moth back upstairs, John consulted his chart to see which of his spiders was hungriest. Number Six hadn't been fed in a long time. John pulled down the filmy covering over the web frame of Number Six, one of his *Nuctenea sclopetarias,* and put the moth into the web with a pair of tweezers. Then, watching the spider rush at the moth and throw silk all over it and paralyze it, he decided money and land were the same thing. Buddy would be so obliging! If the money was not to be had, he would be perfectly willing to take a small piece of land instead.

One down, one to go. But the remaining land holder was Mrs. Bewley. With pleasure John remembered the forcefulness with which she had thrown Buddy out of her house. It had been a good sign. Mrs. Bewley would surely stand like a bulwark between Buddy Whipple and the fulfillment of his repulsive plan.

Forty-Four

"OFF WE GO!" MISS PLANKTON WAVED A CHEERY GOOD-BYE TO John.

"Don't work too hard," said Barbara, leaning out of the car.

Virginia smiled at him, but John merely nodded good-bye, looking at her reproachfully, then stood motionless in his paint-spotted clothes, gazing after the car as it aimed itself down the driveway to begin the journey to New Haven, where Virginia and Barbara were going to take a look at some of Miss Plankton's low-income housing units. Heaving a great sigh, John turned around and went back to the house to paint the ceiling of the dining room.

He had been working on the ceiling all summer, off and on. He had gouged out a channel where two drooping surfaces met, and filled it with Spackle. Then he had sanded it, filled it again, and sanded it again. Then he had filled in all the other cracks and sanded them and filled them in and sanded them again. Now the whole ceiling was ready for painting. The painting would be easy. After all the hard work of preparation, painting the ceiling would be nothing. John wandered around the house looking for last week's *Concord Journal*, brought it back to the dining room and spread it on the floor in the corner. Setting his ladder on the newspaper, he picked up his can of Chamber White latex paint and his broad brush and set one foot on the bottom rung of the ladder. Then he stepped down again and stooped over the newspaper. A name in dark print had caught his eye: *ALICE BEWLEY.*

What was Mrs. Bewley doing in the legal notices in the *Concord Journal?* She hadn't *died* or something, had she? John got down on hands and knees and read the notice.

> BANK AUCTION, Thursday, August 27, 2 P.M. Property on Concord Road belonging to ALICE BEWLEY to be sold to the highest bidder. House, 1.2 acres land. Auction on premises. Certified $2000 check required as deposit.

John couldn't believe his eyes. He read the notice again. What had happened to poor old Mrs. Bewley? How could things have gone so wrong? Mrs. Bewley had been right there at home last week, still holding the fort. "Mine, mine," she had shouted at Buddy, pushing him out the door. Well, of course, this disgusting turn of events was Buddy's doing. Buddy was at work again, wiping out the last obstacle on the map in the way of his new road.

John jumped to his feet. What should he do? When was the auction? On Thursday, the notice said. What was today? Wednesday? No, yesterday was Wednesday. Today was Thursday! The auction was today at two in the afternoon. Two o'clock? Jesus, what time was it now? John ran to the kitchen to look at the clock. Oh, God, it was two o'clock right now. For an instant John stared at the clock. Then he made up his mind. Running his hands through his hair, he pushed open the screen door, raced down the driveway, slipped on a loose piece of asphalt, fell on his face, picked himself up and ran again, blood running down his cheek.

There were cars parked in Mrs. Bewley's driveway and along the road, tipped at odd angles. John stopped running. His heart was thumping. In the driveway something crunched under his feet, and he looked down.

He had stepped on somebody's glasses. But they weren't ordinary glasses. They had a long handle. It was Mrs. Bewley's lorgnette, the one she had stolen from Miss Plankton. What was it doing here on the driveway, all smashed into pieces like that?

Grimly John picked up the broken metal frame and put it in his pocket. Mrs. Bewley must have been dragged out of her house, kicking and screaming. She had been shoved into a car and carried off to that nursing home against her will, Ferndale, or whatever the hell it was called.

The back door of Mrs. Bewley's house was wide open. Shivering with nervous excitement, John walked up the steps and looked inside.

Through the kitchen he could see into the crowded living room. People were standing shoulder to shoulder. Someone had taken the porcelain table from the kitchen and placed it beside the rubber plant as a kind of auctioneer's block. Behind the table a balding man in a business suit was sitting in a chair, shuffling papers. John stumbled over his big sneakers as he came in, and caught himself only by lurching into someone and grabbing the edge of the table.

"Excuse me," he said to Mrs. Gardenside, feeling a hot blush rush up from his collar.

Everyone was looking at him. Buddy Whipple was staring at him with open mouth. John was suddenly aware of his paint-splotched shirt and jeans and the blood trickling down his cheek. He shrank back behind Mrs. Gardenside and looked around furtively. Who were all these people? What did they want with Mrs. Bewley's house?

The man behind the table was getting up, introducing himself as Rutherford Peep of the Bay Bank Harvard Trust Company on Main Street in Concord. "I will begin the bidding this afternoon at twenty thousand dollars," said Mr. Peep, "because that is the sum owed by Alice Bewley to the mortgaging institution, namely the Harvard Trust Company. Anything over that sum will go to Mrs. Bewley, after the town of Lincoln has been reimbursed for delinquent taxes and the Boston Edison Company for unpaid electric bills. Would anyone like to begin the bidding?"

Mrs. Gardenside raised her hand and cleared her throat nervously. "I'll bid twenty-one thousand," she said.

"Twenty-two thousand," said Buddy Whipple softly.

"Twenty-three thousand," said a fat man in a checked jacket.

"Twenty-four thousand." Mrs. Gardenside's voice was brittle and high, her eyes were sharp, her face flushed.

"Twenty-five thousand," said Buddy Whipple, smiling as if he were mildly amused.

"Twenty-six thousand," said Mrs. Gardenside.

"Twenty-seven thousand," said the fat man.

John swallowed uneasily, watching from his corner as the bidding rose to thirty thousand, thirty-five, forty. Beyond Mr. Peep, Mrs. Bewley's enormous *Crassula argentea* seemed the embodiment of its owner, a rubbery witness on her behalf. John was surprised to see traces of chicken droppings on the floor beneath it. As the bidding rose to forty-four thousand, as the fat man shook his head and bid no more, John understood why Mrs. Bewley had shooed him away from her back door. She must have been keeping some of her little hens indoors again. She hadn't wanted him to see.

"Forty-five thousand," said Buddy Whipple.

And then Mrs. Gardenside faltered, and made a tactical mistake. "Forty-five thousand five hundred," she said timidly.

"Fifty thousand," said Buddy boldly.

There was a pause. "Mr. Whipple has bid fifty thousand dollars," repeated Mr. Peep. "Are there any more bids?" He looked expectantly at Mrs. Gardenside.

Her face was red. Her hands were trembling. "I guess — I guess I — no, I guess not." Defeated, she stood with drooping shoulders as Mr. Peep repeated Buddy's bid once more. "Does anyone else wish to bid on this property before I award it to Mr. Whipple for fifty thousand dollars? If not, I declare the bidding — "

"I do," said John, raising his hand. He could feel the color drain from his face. His voice was thick. He cleared his throat and tried again. "Please, I'd like to make a bid."

Everyone turned to look at him. John caught a glimpse of Buddy's flabbergasted face. "Ten thousand," said John. "I mean ten thousand more than he just said."

"But he can't make a bid like that," spluttered Buddy Whipple.

"Sixty thousand dollars," said Mr. Peep, looking encouragingly at John.

"But that's crazy," said Buddy. "He doesn't have a dime."

"Of course I shall expect a registered cashier's check for two thousand dollars to seal the bid," said Mr. Peep crisply. "Sixty thousand. I have a bid for sixty thousand dollars. Are there any other bids?"

"But this is ridiculous," shouted Buddy. He leaned over the table and took Mr. Peep by the arm. "He can't bid, I tell you."

Mr. Peep shook his arm free and scowled at Buddy. "Do you wish to make another bid, Mr. Whipple?"

"Not ten thousand more than I already said. Look, I already won, I tell you." Buddy was furious.

"Going once," said Mr. Peep, whose dander was up. "At sixty thousand dollars, going twice. At sixty thousand dollars, going thrice. *Sold* to the young man in the back of the room for sixty thousand dollars." Mr. Peep smiled at John, and beckoned him forward. "Congratulations, young man, the house is yours."

John's bones had turned to water. He thought he was going to faint. Dimly he heard Buddy laughing angrily and stamping out of the house. Walking forward with limp unsteady legs, John put his shaking hands on the porcelain table. "I'm sorry," he mumbled. "I mean, I don't — I can't — " He couldn't speak. His voice drowned in his throat.

But Dorothy Gardenside was taking his arm. She was standing beside him with a check in her hand. "I'll take care of it," she said loudly to Mr. Peep. Sticking an elbow in John's side, she nearly pushed him off his feet. "John can pay me back later on.

I'll vouch for him. Will you accept my check to secure the sale?"

The room was clearing out. The other people were leaving, clattering down the back steps. Out-of-doors John could hear engines starting up, cars driving away. Mr. Peep looked at Mrs. Gardenside's check. "I see no reason why not," he said. With swift authority he began filling out forms. Than he handed a piece of paper to John, stood up, slapped him on the arm and congratulated him again.

John took the paper and shambled out of the house, followed by Mrs. Gardenside. "Listen, dear," she said, "we'll work this thing out together. Now, I know you can't really pay for the house. I know that was just a little bit of boyish mischief on your part. But here's what we'll do. You go ahead with the deal. We'll be in business together. Just you and me. I'll make the payments in your name, and give you a little something to make it worth your while. Okay? We'll be partners, sort of. Won't that be fun?"

"You mean, you'll pay them the whole sixty thousand dollars?" John gaped at her, hardly able to speak.

"Well, sooner or later. I mean, I'm going to get it fixed up real quick, and turn it into a cute little Cape and sell it for twice as much money. Then I can transfer the mortgage to the buyer, and we'll all come out ahead. And maybe you could do some of the work for me on the side, so I wouldn't have to pay union wages? How would you like a hundred right now? Of course we'll have to have a real grown-up agreement on paper, just between the two of us, just you and me."

John felt shaky and feeble. He was breaking out in a cold sweat. Goggling at Mrs. Gardenside, he put his hand to his mouth, rushed away from her, fumbled through the scrub pine at the edge of the road, and threw up his lunch.

Forty-Five

"GOOD MAN," HOWLED HOMER INTO THE PHONE. "BY CHRIST, there's good blood in your veins."

"But, Uncle Homer, what am I going to do now? I owe Mrs. Whatsername two thousand dollars, and I can't pay the bank fifty-eight thousand dollars in a million years. I already mortgaged my entire future last spring, getting a loan for the first two years of college."

"Listen, boy, you stopped him. That's just superb. You hurled yourself in the way of his juggernaut. Oh God, I wish I'd been there. I wish I'd seen the whole thing. Listen here, I'll tell you what I'll do. I'll make you a no-interest two-thousand-dollar loan for fifty years. Don't worry about Mrs. Gardenside. I'll send her a check. I don't trust her. No relative of mine is going into partnership with a tough cookie like that woman. I mean, I knew one of her ilk on Nantucket, and I tell you — well, never mind."

"But what are we going to do with the place, Uncle Homer? We can't afford to buy it and give it to Mrs. Bewley. I mean, of course, I'd like to, and all, but — "

"Wait and see," said Homer soothingly. "Right now, I'm just glad you've kept Buddy's big greedy hands off it. I just have this strong feeling — well, it's more than just a feeling, it's an overpowering conviction — that we've got to stop that eager beaver, no matter where he starts chomping with his big sharp teeth."

On the day after the auction of Mrs. Bewley's house there was a thunderstorm. John covered himself with a poncho and set off on his bicycle in the wild wind and rain to deliver Homer's check to Mrs. Gardenside without delay.

On the way back, pedaling doggedly along Baker Bridge Road, trying to avoid puddles and fallen twigs, he told himself the world was coming to an end. Lightning was splitting the sky around him with dangerous sharp cracklings. Cannonades of thunder and explosive reverberations blundered around the horizon. *K-k-k-BLAM*, there it went again — *bimmety-bammety-boom-boom-boomety-boomety-boom*. Hardly a split second between the lightning and the thunder. Really close that time. Splashing through the running rivers in the driveway, John jumped off his bike. He was relieved to find the house still there, unharmed, and overjoyed to find Barbara sitting at the kitchen table reading her mail. "Welcome home," he said, pulling off his dripping poncho. "Hey, wait till you hear what happened."

Barbara was astounded at his news about Mrs. Bewley's house. She couldn't forgive herself. "Oh, my God, we should have checked up on her every day. Oh, the poor old woman. I'll call that damned Dolores Leech. Calls herself a nurse. More like a mortician, that's what she is. She's in the same league with that crazy TV repairman who goes around shooting people. And to think she was in cahoots with Buddy all the time."

Then John was struck by a memory. "Hey," he said, "what happened to her chickens? It just occurs to me, there weren't any chickens in the chicken yard." John stared vaguely at the rain pelting down on the stones of the little courtyard outside the kitchen window. "Oh, no," he said, "the grouse. Oh, Jesus, remember those little grouse?"

Barbara looked at him, appalled. "You don't mean —?"

John groaned, remembering the tiny morsels of breast and

the dainty drumsticks. "It was Maxie. We were eating Maxie and Minnie and Mickey and all the rest of them. Eight of them, remember? There were four of us, and we had two apiece."

"Oh, that bastard," said Barbara. Then she leaped to her feet. "Good God, what's Virginia doing out there in the rain?" Running to the door, Barbara threw it open and shouted at Virginia. "You silly fool girl, what are you doing?"

Virginia brushed past her. "That emergency number, what is it?"

"What for?" said Barbara sharply. "What's happened?"

"I've got to call the fire department." Virginia snatched up the phone book. "Have you seen Mrs. Bewley? I ran in there to get her out, but she wasn't there. I saved her rubber plant. I dragged it out the back door and pitched it off the porch. Her house is on fire. I saw the smoke from upstairs. It's burning down."

Forty-Six

BUDDY CAME RUNNING THROUGH THE WOODS WITH THE NEARLY empty kerosene can sloshing inside his shirt. For a moment he was taken aback by the sight of the small car parked at his own front door. The car was as bright as the scarlet coats of the Middlesex Foxhounds, as red as the fire trucks of the town of Lincoln. Checking his rapid plunge through the driving wind and rain, Buddy studied the car. But then he smiled and began running again, dodging around to the back of the garage. There was no official insignia on the side of the car. And it was far too small to be an official vehicle of the Lincoln fire department. Opening the door of the garage, Buddy took the can of kerosene from his shirt and put it back carefully on the shelf, setting it down precisely on the dark oblong ring that proclaimed its status as part of the domestic paraphernalia of the household. From the garage he ducked into a side entry of the house, ran upstairs, took a shower, washed his hair, put on some old clothes that had belonged to his father, and appeared at the top of the stairway in the great hall.

"Oh, here he is," said the woman on duty at the desk below. "Buddy, this is Cynthia Schermerhorn. She's inquiring about that job we put in the paper."

"You see, I just got canned," said Cherry Peaches, laughing, lifting her radiant face. "From the church, I mean. And I'm afraid I got my boss in hot water too. Wow, that parish governing board! Talk about uptight! Anyway I guess I don't really want to be in organized religion anymore anyhow. I mean, I think politics is really more where it's at right now, you know what I mean? You know, right out there in real life? Hey, wow, maybe I'll run for something! You know, someday! Anyway, like right now I'm ready to start at the bottom. You know, like a good sport. So how about that job? Say, isn't this place just fabulous!"

In the gloom of the dark day and in the shadow of the enormous overhanging porch the great hall was pitchy black. But the girl at the foot of the stairs seemed a glowing object, self-luminous, effulgent.

Wait till Croney gets a load of this one, thought Buddy. Of course it would make a lot of sense to turn the girl down flat. They should hire a secretary-receptionist with fewer physical credentials, somebody more like today's volunteer, a heavy woman in enormous polyester pants. But the trouble was, nobody else had come along. Work was piling up on the secretary-receptionist's desk — thank-you letters to contributors, important requests for really significant gifts.

"Can you type?" said Buddy, descending the stairs, smiling at Cherry Peaches, waving her into a chair.

Forty-Seven

IN THE MIDDLE OF THE S-CURVE ON ROUTE 126, HOMER PAUSED dangerously to gaze at the blackened ruins of Mrs. Bewley's house. The fire department was cleaning up. The wreckage was just as bad as John had said on the phone. Stepping angrily on the gas, Homer swerved the Volvo wildly between the two brick gateposts and bounced furiously up the hill.

He had never seen Alexander Higginson's splendid false-Tudor hunting lodge before, but today he was in no mood to admire its grandeur. Parking beside a small red car in the courtyard, he leaped out of the front seat and strode into the house.

At first his eyes were blinded by the solemn high gloom of the great hall, and by a bright spot of light in one corner. But then Buddy Whipple appeared in the shadows, marching up and down. He was dictating something to a secretary. For a moment Homer was boggled by the secretary, who looked familiar somehow, and out of place in this setting. Vaguely Homer became aware that the dazzling radiance in the corner of the room was given off by the golden ripeness of the secretary's skin and the incandescence of her orange hair, rather than by some sort of spotlight glaring in his eyes.

"Well, hello there." Buddy stopped walking up and down and looked at Homer, smiling politely. "What can I do for you?"

There followed a scene of some violence. The roughhouse was all on Homer's part, because Buddy remained serene and cheerful. He merely grinned and let his body shake limply from side to side as Homer took him by the shoulders and shook him and accused him loudly of setting fire to Mrs. Bewley's house.

Buddy was all astonished ignorance. "It burned down? Good God. You know, I *thought* lightning might have struck around here somewhere, it sounded so close. I worried about this house, as a matter of fact, because we stick up so much higher than anything else. But we were lucky, I guess. Hey, come on, what's the big idea?" Buddy laughed with long-suffering good humor as Homer hugged him in a grizzly-bear embrace and smelled him with great inquisitive sniffs like a dog. "Hey, let go of me. Come on, let go."

"I swear, if I smell lighter fluid on you, or gasoline—" Homer backed away and shook his head, disappointed. There was no odor of anything intensely flammable in Buddy's hair, or in his beard or in his clothes. The man smelled a little musty, if anything. Goddamn.

"It's too bad about that nephew of yours," said Buddy, grinning at him. "Did the place burn to the ground? I guess the kid is stuck with sixty thousand dollars worth of uninsured smoking ruins, right? I'm just as glad I didn't make the winning bid after all. Say, why don't you ask him if he'd like to get rid of the place now? I'd be glad to take it off his hands for a sensible price. Nothing like that crazy sixty thousand, of course."

"Go to hell," said Homer, heading for the door.

"No, no, I'm serious," said Buddy, trailing him to his car. "I'll give him twenty thousand. He won't get that much from a realtor. Hey, look, it's stopped raining." For a moment Buddy and Homer stared up at the limpid blue of the clearing sky. Then Buddy backed away as Homer scowled at the gearshift and turned the key in the ignition. "Don't forget," said Buddy. "Tell him what I said, okay?"

Forty-Eight

THE SAVAGELY PELTING RAIN WASHED JOHN'S BARN SPIDER TO THE ground, and in the boiling puddle at the foot of the rain spout she nearly drowned. But then the rain stopped and the puddle guttered down. The sodden spider managed to get a foothold on the gravel under the spout and crawl free. Her belly was swollen with eggs. Making her way blindly along the granite foundation of the house, she climbed to the stony terrace and began to ascend the clapboards beside the kitchen door.

In spite of himself, Homer was affected by the change in the weather. The air had been washed clean by the rain. It was dry and cool at last. As he drove down the hill, cautiously negotiating the streaming ruts, he could see a great shelf of cloud retreating between the branches over his head. His anger at Buddy faded. His spirits rose. He felt sociable and inquisitive. He would stop in at the house at the bottom of the driveway and see Virginia. Sooner or later he wanted to discover the reason for her peculiar slackness, her odd refusal to take sides, to fight back. Why not now?

There was a pickup truck in the driveway. One of the firemen was helping Virginia grapple with a gigantic potted plant. Homer got out of his car and lent a hand.

"Just put it in the border here," said Virginia. "It will be

glad to be outdoors for a while." Clumsily Homer and the fireman heaved Mrs. Bewley's colossal singed rubber plant over the
low wooden fence. "Good," said Virginia. "Thank you. That's
just great."

"Funny-looking damn thing," gasped the fireman. Climbing
back into his truck, he gave Virginia a genial wave and drove
away.

Homer turned to Virginia. "You were the one who discovered the fire, right? John told me on the phone. My God,
what do you think happened?"

She looked at him soberly, then glanced away. "I suppose it
was struck by lightning."

"Lightning!" Homer controlled himself. "Listen here,
where's John?"

"John? He went with Barbara to see Mrs. Bewley at Ferndale
Manor. Did you want to see him? They'll be back in an hour or
so. It isn't far."

"No, as a matter of fact, I didn't want to see John." Homer
stroked his chin and gazed at a small furry spider crawling up the
trellis beside the kitchen door. "I was just passing by. Thought
I'd stop in. Look — " Homer made a sweeping gesture that in-
cluded the brilliant sky, the immaculate trees, the low juniper
breaking like a cresting wave at his feet, " — it's such a lovely
evening. Do you suppose I could have a tour of the garden?"

"The garden?" Virginia laughed. "Imagine calling it a garden. Of course you can have a tour. What would you like to see?"

"The best, whatever that is," said Homer grandly. "The
most beautiful part. You know. The aesthetic pinnacle of the horticulturalist's art."

"The pinnacle? Well, that's easy. If you had asked for the
worst, the ugliest, it would have been hard to choose, because so
many places around here vie for honors in that department. But
the best? That's simple. Come on, I'll show you."

They walked down the slope past the vegetable garden with
its transvestite scarecrow, its burgeoning tomatoes, its sprawling
cucumber and squash vines, its shiny green peppers and purple

knobs of eggplant, then up again through a drenched field of wild
asters and goldenrod and along a narrow path between wet bristling wands of blackberry. At last they came back out on the driveway and approached a gate made of rough poles. Swiftly Virginia
ducked through the gate and entered the field. Homer struggled
through in his turn, knocking down one of the bars. They crossed
the field.

Homer kept his eyes on the ground and carried on an easy
flow of small talk, probing gently now and then, looking for a
tender spot. He felt like someone who has miraculously captured
a bird and holds it lightly in his hand, allowing it to fly away if
it will, amazed when it does not. One by one he lifted the feathers
of the wings, looking for the scar that refused to heal.

Virginia's mother — did she remember her mother?

"Oh, no. She died when I was too small to remember. Barbara was always there, taking care of me. All I can remember is Barbara."

"Your father's death must have been a blow."

"Oh, yes. But it's surprising how quickly we got over it. I feel a little guilty about it. Of course, his death was an awful shock. But I'm astonished how little I miss him. In a way he was another child for Barbara to take care of. In some ways it's a relief. Certainly to Barbara." Virginia turned to Homer. "I want her to be let alone, to have her own life. She's spent so much time taking care of the two of us, father and me."

"She's a nurse, isn't she? You want her to practice nursing again?"

"Nursing?" Virginia's eyes flickered away. "Well, of course, if she wants to."

There was a surprise at the end of the field. The ground dipped down into a hollow, where a stream had been dammed up to make a pond. The water was amber with organic matter and dark in the shadow of the tall white pines. Homer followed Virginia around the pond, getting his shoes wet on the stepping stones that made a path across the boggy inlet at one end. "This place here," he said, "it must mean a lot to you, I guess."

"Well, of course it does. We're devoted to it. Barbara even more than I. It's her whole life now." Virginia held a branch aside for him. "And the pressures have been so — you know — unrelenting."

Pressures? That could only mean one thing. In his eagerness to hear Virginia talk about Buddy Whipple, Homer jumped on the word too quickly. "Pressures?" he said. "What pressures?"

"Oh, there are a lot of them." Walking ahead of him along the mossy path, Virginia waved her hand vaguely. "If it isn't one thing it's another. There was that woman with the dried kelp and the rhubarb. And the other one with the overheated radiator, only it turned out to be stone cold. And another one who likes Williamsburg drapes. And that girl who was born under the sign of Scorpio. And then there are the carpenter ants in the eavestrough, and the thorns, the honeysuckle, the catbrier, the poison ivy, the blackberry, the firecherry. It presses in on all sides. All we can do is keep it at bay. We cut and slash at it, but there's such a teeming lunge of it everywhere, do you see?" Virginia's hands thrust into the air to describe the upward rush of growing weeds and the feeble strokes of their helpless tools. "Sometimes I think all that scoundrelly force and energy should be harnessed somehow, the way people want to do things with the tides. Oh, look, Homer, there's a frog. See him there in the mud?"

"A frog? No kidding! Where, where?"

"Right there. See his big eyes above the water? Look, I'll throw a little stick and make him jump."

"Where do you mean? I don't see any frog." And then in his eagerness and enthusiasm, Homer leaned too far, slipped on the mossy bank and fell in the pond up to his knees. The frog disappeared. Homer climbed out again, splashing and cursing. Virginia laughed and helped him onto the path again.

So it was not until Homer was struggling once more through the bars of the gate that he remembered there had been an avowed purpose in setting out. "Hey, listen," he said, "which was the great beauty spot? I've been expecting marble statuary and hedges shaped like birds or tennis rackets or electric guitars or upright pianos or something."

"Oh," said Virginia, "it was back there. We already saw it. That field there, on the other side of the gate." They turned back to the gate and looked over it. "Those big old white pines. Don't you think they're really nice? Nobody even planted them. They just grew by themselves."

"You mean those trees over there? Well, yes, I suppose so. Yes, now that you mention it. Very nice indeed."

"I think they look like soft green explosions, only it takes fifty years instead of a few seconds."

"Right. I see what you mean. Right, right."

"They're what I like best anyway. Those trees on the edge and the way the field slopes a little bit to the south. Nobody even planned it. It just happened that way." Virginia turned away from the gate, and together they began walking down the hill. "Barbara likes the pond best. I like the field."

Barbara likes the pond best. They always came back to Barbara. Homer took a leap in the dark. "Buddy Whipple is threatening Barbara in some way, isn't he? What does Buddy have against Barbara?"

Virginia looked at him, startled, missed her footing, turned her ankle, hopped once or twice, then settled again into a smooth stride. "I don't know what you mean."

"You're protecting her from Buddy. Isn't that it?"

Virginia nudged his elbow and eased him in another direction, down a path through the woods. "There's a shortcut here. It leads to the place where the old piggery was, when the big house was a hunting lodge."

It was no good. The bird in his hand had opened her wings and flown away. Homer sighed, and made up his mind to try again. Only this time he would send in his wife.

Forty-Nine

AT THE SUPPER TABLE BUDDY REPEATED HIS OFFER. "TWENTY thousand dollars for a pile of charred wood. You've got to admit it's a princely offer. I mean, what do you want to do with the place anyhow? It won't do the old lady any good, not with the house gone, right?"

John flashed him a suspicious glance. "What do you want to do with it yourself?"

"Investment for the future," said Buddy patiently. "If it was IBM stock, or something, you wouldn't ask me what I wanted it for, would you? And the trouble with stocks is, they go up and down. Real estate only goes in one direction, straight up."

"I don't want to sell," said John stubbornly.

Buddy's good humor vanished. He shouted at John. John shouted back, and Buddy slammed out of the kitchen.

"Good boy." Barbara patted John briskly on the shoulder and went upstairs to bed.

John picked up his book with trembling fingers and stared at the open page, trying to concentrate, reading it over and over.

Virginia sat calmly beside him, her head down, running her needle in and out of the hem of a new dress. The dress was for New York. Virginia was going to New York with Barbara to unveil a plaque in honor of Edward Heron's contributions to horti-

culture. A lot of silly stupidity, thought Virginia. Horticulture
would have been a lot better off without her father's poisonous
green roses and rusty canna lilies. She didn't want to go, but Barbara had said she had to.

Sitting so close to Virginia without speaking was torture.
"Good night," said John. Picking up his book, he nodded and
smiled wanly at her, made his way through the darkened house
and climbed the dark laundry stairs to his room in the shed.

Virginia put down her sewing and stood up. Nervously she
switched on the television, then switched it off. She looked at the
clock. She waited five minutes. Then she too walked through the
house in the direction of the shed. Opening the laundry door
softly she gazed up into the hollow black rectangle of the stairway
to John's room. The stairs looked vulnerable. They were ap-
proachable from all directions, from the door to the house, the
door to the workroom, the door to the porch. Upstairs she could
hear John bumping around. Was he going to bed? What if he

came down again and surprised her here at the bottom of the stairs? But in a few minutes the bumping stopped. There was silence overhead. Quietly Virginia crossed the laundry, picking her way past the baskets of dirty clothes, and drew the bolt on the door to the porch. Then she groped her way through the workshop and the lumber room and the wood room and fastened the latches of three more doors. But even as she pushed the last bolt home, Virginia knew she had secured nothing. The bolts were old. They were small and fragile. One sharp kick at a door and they would burst from their rusty screws.

Slowly Virginia made her way back to the stairs and sat down on the bottom step. Leaning sideways, she stretched out her legs and rested her head patiently against the wall. Through the small window on the other side of the room she could just see the new moon lying like a white cradle over the trees. The laundry clock ticked loudly on the wall. In the daytime she never noticed the sound of the clock, but now it seemed to make the quiet house quieter, as if its click-clock-click were warning the washing machine and the dryer and the wooden drying rack and the baskets of laundry to keep still.

Fifty

"I CAN'T DO ANYTHING WITH VIRGINIA," SAID HOMER. "YOU'RE going to have to ask her. Go ahead. You ask her."

Mary looked at him doubtfully. "Ask her what?"

"I just told you. Ask her what Buddy's got on Barbara. She'll tell you. She won't tell me."

"If she won't tell you, why should she tell me?"

"Because you're — you know. Women tell each other things."

"Well, I'm not going to ask her a thing like that. I hardly know Virginia. Not really."

"Oh, come on, girl."

"No, I won't."

"But, goddamnit!"

"I'll tell you what I'll do, I'll go over there. I'll bring her something. I'll bring her some of my grape jelly."

"Your grape jelly?"

"And that's all. I'm not going to ask her anything."

"But you could just — I mean, after the grape jelly, you could just say —"

"Not a word."

"You're so damned stubborn!"

"Not a single word."

Mary took down a jar of her wild grape jelly and left Homer playing Monopoly with Benny. It was a painful morning. Benny turned out to be a promising young capitalist. Before long he was building hotels on Boardwalk and Park Place. Homer landed on one or the other without fail, every time he edged timidly around the board. Three hours later the game was still in progress far past its natural point of resolution, because Benny had loaned his bankrupt uncle ten thousand dollars at fifty percent interest, and Homer had holed up craftily in jail. When Homer heard the familiar dying rattle of the Volvo in the driveway he leaped to his feet and ran outside.

"Well?" he demanded, leaning into the car window. "What did she say?"

Mary smiled up at him. "She liked the jelly."

"Oh, the jelly. Never mind the jelly. Did she say anything else?"

Mary turned around and reached for the paper bag on the back seat. "You know, Homer, those foxy wild grapes make a really nice tart jelly. Look, we found some more, see?"

"Well, fine, that's fine, but what the hell? Is that all?"

"You remember the way they taste when you eat them raw, all skin and pits, with a musky flavor?"

"What, the grapes? The hell with the grapes! Mary, for God's sake, will you forget the grapes and tell me what Virginia said?"

"Listen, Homer, the grapes are important. The grapes are everything. Here, take the bag and I'll tell you all about it while I start lunch. It was the grapes that did it, you see. I gave her the jar of jelly, and she was pleased, because she said Barbara loved good homemade grape jelly . . ."

". . . only we're not very good at making it ourselves," said Virginia, admiring the jar.

"Well, I didn't think I was either," said Mary. "But there they were, last fall, all along the shore of the river, those big black grapes. I picked a lot of them and brought them home, but they weren't really fit to eat, so I tried making the jelly. And it wasn't hard after all."

"It wasn't?" said Virginia. "I thought it would be just too —" She gestured helplessly at Mary. Her face was drawn and tired, but she smiled, and Mary was encouraged. The jar of jelly was comfortable to talk about. It was an object you could hold in your hand and look at.

"No, no, it's easy. You just boil them down and mash them through a strainer and put in some sugar, and that's it. It's funny, this year the river grapes don't seem to be bearing, I don't know why."

"We've got some wild grapes of our own," said Virginia, pointing through the kitchen window, "down there in the old orchard. It's all overgrown with briers, but there are grapevines climbing up into the trees. Would you like to pick some?" The strain in Virginia's face vanished. Her eyes brightened. "We could go down there right now."

"Oh, yes, I'd like to. And then, if you want, I could show you how to do them up."

"You're not wearing your best clothes, are you?" said Virginia. "Good. Everything grabs and tears at you down there."

Mary lifted her feet high, trying to free herself at every step from the looping strands of bramble that went romping over the ground, rooting themselves, then arching up again in thorny snarls. "How old is the apple orchard?" she said.

"I don't know. Do you think it could have been planted a hundred years ago? Maybe only fifty or sixty? Maybe the farmer put down his shovel and went off to a speakeasy and danced the Charleston. Anyway, he put in a lot of different kinds. It's fun to taste them, and try to imagine him planting a Baldwin here and a Roxbury Russet there."

"You mean, the trees are still bearing?"

"Oh, no, not very well. But sometimes we get enough wormy

apples to make applesauce." Virginia covered her face with her arm and pushed through the twiggy outer branches of one of the trees. Mary ducked after her, and stood up under the high umbrella of scabby twisted limbs. She was just in time to see Virginia tip sideways and fall to her knees.

"Good heavens, are you all right?" Stumbling forward, Mary helped Virginia to her feet.

"I'm fine. I just fell into a hole. Look at it. Did you ever see such a hole? Rabbits, I guess. A colossal rabbit hole. A palatial country estate for the king of all the rabbits in Middlesex County."

"The county commissioner, you mean," said Mary. "By divine right, of course. Or do you think it's a woodchuck hole?"

Virginia stooped and peered into it. "Hey, in there," she said. "Any of you folks at home?" Then she gasped and dropped once more to her hands and knees. Reaching into the hole, she drew something out and sat back on her heels to look at it. Then she began to laugh.

"What is it?" said Mary.

But Virginia couldn't speak. She was leaning over, hugging something to her breast, laughing a silent laugh that was more like dry sobbing.

"Well, for Christ's sake, what was it?" said Homer, staring at his wife. And then he knew. "The allergy medicine. The syringe, the adrenalin, the antihistamine. The little red box. Was it all there?"

"Yes, but the syringe was empty. The pills were gone. Buddy must have emptied them out in sheer spite. Listen, Homer, Virginia told me Buddy said he saw Barbara take the box from her father that morning."

"Take it? Barbara?"

"That's what Buddy told Virginia. He said he was just approaching the house around ten o'clock that morning, the morning Edward Heron died — he was just coming up the stone steps into the courtyard there, when he heard them arguing. He could hear Barbara shouting at her father, and her father yelling back. And so he stopped on the top step, Buddy said, because he didn't want to embarrass them, coming along in the middle of an argument. He could see them through that big window in the kitchen. Edward was wheezing and coughing, and then Buddy saw Barbara reach out and snatch something out of his hands — a little red box of some kind — and then Edward cursed her and ran out the door. Buddy had to move fast, he said, to get away before Edward saw him. But Edward was so angry and he was coughing so hard and moving so fast, Buddy said he wasn't looking left or right anyway. He was running down the hill in the direction of the apple orchard. And that was the last anybody saw of him, until Buddy came back later on to ask for that job and the room in their house, and discovered Edward's body."

"Buddy told her that?" said Homer. "Virginia told you Buddy said that?"

"And Barbara herself made it worse. She was always muttering to Virginia, 'It's all my fault,' or words to that effect. So Virginia thought Buddy was right."

"Well, then, that explains what Buddy had on Barbara." Homer shook his head. "I still don't see why it would have given him such a handle on Virginia. You could hardly even call it manslaughter. Well, at any rate, now she knows the truth. It must have been Buddy who stuffed it in that hole. What did Virginia say to that?"

"Nothing else. She seemed to catch herself, and stop talking. I could feel a wall going up between us. But there was a glitter in her eye, a kind of angry glee."

"A wall went up between you? You mean, she just stopped talking to you?"

"Oh, no. We went on looking for grapes, and we found some, and then I showed her how to make jelly, and then I came home. But she didn't say anything more about the little red box, and I wasn't about to ask her."

"You wouldn't." Homer watched Mary dump the big black

grapes on the counter and reach into a cupboard for her sister's preserving kettle. "Damn the man. We still can't call it murder. And how could we connect Buddy with a little box in a rabbit hole? The defense would call in some big asthmatic bunny rabbit."

Mary laughed. "Listen, Homer, what about that black widow spider? Did you get in touch with that place in Georgia? You know, that address Benny knew by heart?"

"Oh, sure. They had sent a black widow to Concord, Massachusetts, all right. But they didn't have a check with a signature on it, just cash and a box number to mail it to. And when I asked the postmaster in the Concord post office about the box number, he said it was arranged by mail too, anonymously, and paid for in cash." Homer plucked a grape, popped it in his mouth, winced, and spat it out in the sink. "So there he is, Buddy Whipple, planning his goddamn road, moving a stone wall, burning down Mrs. Bewley's house, and he as good as murdered Edward Heron, and I suspect he's still putting the screws on Virginia. We know all that, or we think we do, but there's no way of really proving anything. Nothing to stop him with. You know what I think? The only thing that will stop that huge driving mass of beefy muscle is an act of nature. An earthquake. Some stupendous natural force. Let the sea roar and disembowel itself."

Then Homer remembered the great trees that had been uprooted in the hurricane a dozen years back, a violent natural upheaval that had almost cost Mary's life, and he flinched, and put his arm around her. "Or maybe we could get all the woodchucks in Massachusetts to attack him." Homer stood dreamily beside his wife at the sink, watching her pick over the grapes, thinking about Henry Thoreau's encounter with a woodchuck. Henry had kept it mesmerized for half an hour. Somehow he had been able to make a kind of primitive communication from man to beast, from tame to wild, to that kingdom unknown and undiscoverable, that immense inaccessible majority of living things. But Homer doubted whether even Henry Thoreau could have aroused the woodchuck population of Massachusetts to do battle.

The phone rang. Mary dumped her colander of grapes into the kettle, and reached for the telephone on the wall. Then she smiled at Homer. "It's William Warren. He says how would you like a helicopter ride?"

As Homer took the phone, his nephew Benny ran into the kitchen and tugged at his sleeve. "Come on back, Uncle Homer. You've got to come out of jail on this throw of the dice, and guess what? I've got hotels all the way around the board!"

"You bet I'd like a ride," said Homer to William. "I owe fifty thousand dollars to a pint-sized loan shark and I've got to get out of town. I'll be right over."

Fifty-One

THE HELICOPTER WAS WAITING FOR THEM ON THE TARMAC AT
Hanscom Air Force Base. The pilot helped Homer step up into
the sun-drenched bubble. "What if the blades stop turning?"
said Homer nervously. "What if the engine stalls? Do the blades
stop going around and around?"

"They better not," said the pilot. Climbing in on the other
side, he put a new disk of paper in the meter.

Homer sank down beside William Warren and looked up
at the smear of whitewash over his head. Anxiously he studied
the black column of instruments, then shrank back as William
reached across him with the seat belt. "Here, this goes over both
of us," said William.

"Clear," shouted the pilot. The rotor blades began to whine,
making a flickering shadow in the quivering light-filled interior,
then speeding up until they were an invisible tremendous throbbing. Homer clenched his teeth and stiffened his back as the
helicopter lifted, tipping uneasily backward and sideways. His
stomach lurched. What if he threw up his lunch and made a fool
of himself? He turned to William and whispered, "I'm scared."

"What?" shouted William.

"I'M SCARED," roared Homer.

William only grinned and patted his knee.

They were leveling off, churning slowly over the green landscape. William pointed forward. "Look, there's Cook's stand. See all that red stuff out in front?"

"Tomatoes," cried Homer. "Baskets of tomatoes." He was delighted. He felt fine. In fact he had never felt better in his life. He stopped cowering and began pointing and exclaiming. "The dump! Hey, William, look at the dump. Wow, what's all that sparkle? Look at it glitter in the sun."

"Recycled bottles, I think," said William .

"Oh, is that it? Hey, William, look at the air base. All those houses. Like anthills. That's what we are, William, ants. Just billions of ants, crawling on the face of the earth."

"What?" shouted William.

The dry bright air was going to Homer's head. "So damn many of us," he cried, gesturing at the rows of houses as they wheeled beneath him and fell away. "And you and I, we're just a couple of crawling insects creeping over the ground — no offense, old man — while overhead," — Homer flourished his hand at the sky — "the heavens stretch their impassive blue to the indifferent sun and the unfeeling stars to the farthest reaches of eternity."

"Is that so?" said William politely. Then he joggled Homer's arm. "Look, there's Buddy's house. See it down there? All those big rooftops?"

"My God, right you are. What a huge place it is. Hey, William, what's going on down there? Somebody's chasing a girl on the front lawn. My God, it looks like Croney to me. You see? What did I tell you? The planet is just one heaving mass of crawling organic life. Behold the mating instinct, raw sex on the hoof. Say, listen, do you think the girl needs help?"

"Not her." William grinned at Homer and shook his head. "She can call on God any old time. Kid from the church."

"Well, actually, I feel like God up here, don't you? All-knowing, all-powerful, omniscient, mighty in wisdom, in the far-reaching sweep of my gigantic arm — whoops! Sorry, sir, didn't mean to knock you off course. Ouch, stop it, William. What are you poking me in the ribs for now?"

247

"It's what I wanted to show you," bawled William. "See there at the bottom of the hill? That's the Herons' house."

"Oh, I see. So it is. Needs a new roof, right?" shouted Homer.

"Look down there below the house at that green field. See there, that crop of winter wheat? Buddy planted it. See anything funny about it?"

"Funny?" Homer leaned forward and craned his neck while the pilot obligingly circled the field. But Homer could see nothing strange about the green rectangle below him except that it was the only orderly piece of geometry in the homely landscape of empty meadow and tangled orchard.

"Don't you see that straight line?" said William. "Not far from the orchard?"

"Oh, now I see what you mean. Sort of a yellow line in the grass?"

"That's it. Look, it runs right through the whole crop. A straight line lighter than the rest."

"What's the matter with it?" shouted Homer, turning to William. "Ground not as fertile there?"

"Right." William glared at Homer. "But why not? That's the question."

Fifty-Two

WHEN THE PHONE RANG, JOHN WAS STANDING IN THE LAUNDRY, looking at the stairway that rose steeply to his bedroom.

He felt uneasy about the stairway. Last night he had been padding down the steps with his flashlight, and he had nearly caught someone there. He had heard a stumbling rush and then the soft click of the latch on the door between the laundry and the house.

He had been looking for his spider. She had been missing ever since the big storm. The best time to find her was in the small hours of the night. It was when she would be most active, building or rebuilding a new web. But John's flashlight roving on the front of the house had turned up nothing.

Now with the afternoon sunlight shining through the small window in the laundry, John thought about the presence on the stairs, and wondered who it had been, and why somebody had come there in the night. There was no lock or bar on the door upstairs. How could he keep anybody out?

The phone was ringing in the house. John made a dash for it.

His Uncle Homer was excited. "We'll pick you up. We're on our way to the town hall to look at William's nine-by-nines."

"His what?"

"His aerial photographs. Wait till we see. We'll be right there."

*

"Wow," said John, crouching over the dark picture on William's light-table. "I see what you mean. That's great. A straight line right across Buddy's field."

"I don't get it," said Homer. "It's darker, that line. Only it was lighter than the rest of the green stuff when we saw it from the air just now."

"This is a negative," explained William. "Dark is light, light is dark."

"Oh, of course," said Homer, groaning to himself. "What a stupid jerk."

"It means the soil is poorer," said John. "So that strip of growing wheat isn't as dark green and healthy as the rest."

"Right," said William. "The soil was crushed under that stone wall for a couple of hundred years, so it was impacted, deep down." William made impacting motions with his hands.

"And bits of stone would have leached down into the soil," said John. "You know, tiny particles would have washed down, changing the chemical makeup of the dirt, so it was more in need of lime or something. So the crop growing there would be a little deprived, and come up stunted and pale."

The three of them stared at the negative, gazing at the dim dark line across the patch of lighter grey.

Homer shook his head with wonder. "He moved those stones one by one. What a colossal job. It must have taken him weeks. I suppose he used a whatchamacallit. You know."

"A stoneboat," said William. Then he pounced with his finger at the negative again. "Look where the stone wall is now, here in the orchard. What's a stone wall doing in the middle of an orchard? See? Most of the trees are on this side of it, but there's one row of trees on the other side. Nobody would have planted an orchard like that, would they?"

"And here's something else," said John. Carefully his finger traced a circle. "You can just see the old cart track that used to run around the orchard, so they could bring in a horse and wagon. There's one just like that around Pop's orchard, where his tractor goes around with the spraying equipment, and the truck, when he's got people in there picking. See that faint line, curving around the corner trees of the orchard? See how the stone wall cuts right through it?" John looked up and beamed. "That really proves it, doesn't it? That stone wall couldn't have been there before."

"Good for you, John," said William, patting him on the shoulder.

On the way home in the Volvo, Homer related Buddy's story about Barbara and her father, and told John about the grape jelly and the rabbit hole.

John was interested at once. "Buddy said he saw Barbara and her father through the kitchen window? He was standing on the top step there where you come in off the driveway?"

"That's what he told Virginia."

"What time did he say it was?"

"Well, what he said was, around ten o'clock in the morning."

"Then Buddy couldn't have seen anything through the window," said John triumphantly. "If he was standing where you said, and if it was during the daytime, then he couldn't have seen in that window at all. The light would have bounced off the glass right into his eyes. *The angle of incidence equals the angle of reflection.* I learned that in physics class last year."

Homer looked reverently at his nephew. "*The angle of incidence* — by God, boy, that's right. At the angle where he was looking in, most of the light would have been reflected off the glass. Hardly any of it would have been refracted through it."

"I know. I've tried," said John earnestly. "I'm always trying to read the kitchen clock through the window, and at that time of day you have to get right up next to the glass and shade your eyes to see in."

"Oh, what a glorious thing is the brain of an intelligent boy," cried Homer. "What's Benny got that you haven't got? Benny's all recitation by rote and worthless dry bones of meaningless memory, whereas you, my boy, have the gift of rational thought, reason, blessed reason, that godlike power that distinguishes man from the beasts! Ratiocination, that heav'nborn —"

"Except, Uncle Homer, there are these really amazing gorillas. They've got these young gorillas in a sort of nursery school, and they're teaching them to do the most extraordinary things, wait till you hear —" But then John caught a glimpse across the field of the long shambling farmhouse that belonged to Virginia and Barbara Heron, and his excitement vanished. He hung his head and gazed darkly at the long bony wrists sunk between his knees. "He's still got her, you know, Uncle Homer."

"Who do you mean? Virginia? You mean, Buddy's still got Virginia?"

John nodded his head slightly in dire agreement.

"Well, it's like I told Mary," said Homer, glowering at the maple trees beside Baker Bridge Road, "it will take some violent natural force to stop him. Some grizzly bear, some elephant. A tidal wave, an erupting volcano. The black plague. That's what I think."

"I'm afraid it's hopeless," said John. "She's going away this evening. I almost wish she'd never come back."

"Going away?"

"There's some ceremony in honor of her father in New York. The New York State Horticultural Society is unveiling a brass plaque. Virginia and Barbara are spending the night in some hotel."

"Oh, I see."

And as they drove up to the house, there was Virginia, lugging her suitcase down the stone steps. John leaped out of Homer's car, snatched the suitcase, stuffed it in the trunk of Virginia's car, murmured a stifled good-bye, ducked past Virginia and ran into the house.

Homer was shocked by his nephew's behavior. He got out of his car and made polite remarks. "What's all this about the Horticultural Society?" he said.

"Oh, they're unveiling this plaque."

"In honor of your father's achievements, I understand."

"Oh, yes, all those ghastly canna lilies. I'd rather stay home, but Barbara says I've got to keep her company. Why should she suffer alone, says Barbara." Virginia touched Homer's arm.

"Homer, I wonder if you would do something for me? John will be here by himself while we're gone, and I just wondered if you would stay here with him, just for this one night?"

"Stay with John? Oh, come on, Virginia, John's a big boy now."

"Of course he is. I know that. Of course he is, of course."

Homer gazed at Virginia, and wondered how he could ever have compared her unfavorably with the dawn. Even drawn and pale as she looked now, and harried and uncertain, with wrinkles in her forehead that would one day come to stay, even beside a Virginia like this, the dawn would come off second best.

There was an unblinking urgency in the way she was looking at him. "You'd like me to spend the night here?" said Homer.

"Oh, yes. Oh, would you, please?" Virginia scrabbled in her pocketbook. "Here's the key to the kitchen entry. It's just for tonight. Just this one night."

Homer looked away and examined the airy sprays of sea lavender in the border where he had so often seen her working. "Where's Buddy going to be?"

"Oh, he'll be around, I suppose. He has a key of his own, I think."

"Right," said Homer slowly. "Well, of course I'll stay. I'll be glad to. No problem. You can count on me. I'll just go home and get a few things."

Child care again, he thought morosely, turning his car down the rutted drive and heading for home. It had got to the point where anybody who wanted their kid taken care of just called on Homer Kelly, that famous ex-lieutenant detective in the office of the district attorney of Middlesex County, that celebrated scholar and international authority on the works of the American transcendentalists, that sometime Harvard professor — Homer Kelly, babysitter.

Fifty-Three

JOHN WAITED IN HIS ROOM FOR THEM TO GO. TAKING THE TOP OFF his tarantula container, he let Fred roam on the plywood table. Fred wasn't interested in roaming. He stayed put. When John heard the smooth humming of Barbara's car, he bundled Fred back into his plastic cage and ran downstairs and out to the front yard, suddenly deciding he wanted to say good-bye.

He was too late. They were gone. The driveway was empty. John stood for a while beside the mailbox, staring at the stony emptiness of rutted gravel, angry with himself for acting like a sulky kid.

Moodily he turned away and wandered across the lawn in the direction of the vegetable garden. Then he remembered the faint dark line on William's negative, and it occurred to him that he hadn't yet examined Buddy's patch of winter wheat to see if the impoverished strip was visible from the ground with the naked eye. His pace quickened. Running past the vegetable garden, he crossed the edge of the jungle, skirted the stone wall and the last row of apple trees, and walked all the way around the small field.

At first he could see nothing but thick healthy growth of a uniform dark green. Where was the undernourished line of yellow that had been apparent from the air? And then John saw a furrow, a slight shadow, a line of seed heads nodding at a lower level than the rest. The difference in color was negligible, but it was there. John reached down to scratch with his fingers at the soil, wondering if a handful would be different in texture from the rest of the dirt in the field.

"What the hell are you doing, trampling down my crop?"

Startled, John stood up to find Buddy staring at him angrily.

What was he doing? John didn't know what to say. He felt queer and defenseless. It crossed his mind that he had not very often been alone with Buddy before. He told the truth.

"I was just wondering if the soil is poor right here. This line of wheat, you see, right here? It's not as tall. Not as healthy, I guess. I wonder why that should be?"

Buddy stared at him. His eyes did not glance down to see the blades of wheat brushing against John's knees. "Get out of there," he said. "Come on, get out." Then he threw something past John's head. Instinctively John ducked, but Buddy had missed him deliberately. The thing sailed far off into the jungle of bramble and honeysuckle. Gazing after it as it clove the air past his head, John knew what it was. That rock had spent the last two weeks on the table in his room, holding down his spider notes. He had studied it and handled it, he had wiped the dust off it, he had killed ants with it, he had shown it to his Uncle Homer. It was the boulder he had taken from the stone wall, the chalk-marked cobblestone. Buddy must have been in John's room. He had taken the rock from the table.

Together they walked silently up to the house, the truth walking between them, naked and embarrassing. But at the kitchen door John forgot the heavy menace of Buddy's presence, and the sense of threat in the red hands hanging at Buddy's side. "My barn spider," he said. "There she is. I thought I'd lost her. See her there on the trellis? Look at that web. It's really huge." Delighted, John leaned close to the house wall and took a good look at his spider. He was pleased to see that her new leg was nearly as long as the rest.

He was unprepared for Buddy's spoiling anger. With a sweep

of his hand Buddy knocked the spider to the stone floor of the small courtyard and started after it, lifting a heavy shoe. John leaped at him, and together they fell in a tangled sprawl. "For Christ's sake, Buddy," he said, sitting up, "it's just a harmless little spider. Why can't you let her alone?"

"Goddamn you," said Buddy, getting to his feet. Whirling on his heel, he ran down the steps and set off up the hill. John could hear his heavy footsteps thudding on the road.

Sighing, he got to his feet and began looking once more for *Araneus cavaticus*. She was nowhere to be seen.

Fifty-Four

"HOMER, BEFORE YOU GO, WOULD YOU RUN UPSTAIRS AND TAKE A picture of Benny? Just one last picture to show his mother and father? They'll be home any day now, and I'd love to show them how cunning he's been this summer, sound asleep."

"If we'd had any sense, we would have put him into a coma in June," growled Homer, slinging his camera around his neck. "We could have borrowed some of John's spiders and paralyzed the little darling and left him cuddled in his bed the whole entire time. We wouldn't have had to suffer with a wide-awake Benny all day long every day of the week for three interminable miserable months."

Mary opened Benny's door softly, and Homer took the picture, admitting to himself grudgingly that the little bastard did look kind of cute in the glare of the flashbulb, all tucked up in his cot.

"Thank you, Homer, dear," said Mary. "Have a nice night over there with John. You'll take good care of that boy, won't you?"

"Well, naturally," said Homer gruffly. Stuffing a pair of pajamas into a paper bag, he was on his way out the door when the phone rang.

"Uncle Homer?" John's voice on the telephone sounded thin and far away.

"Yes, my boy?"

"He knows about the stone wall. I mean, he knows I know."

"Who knows? Buddy? You mean, Buddy knows?"

"I just thought I'd tell you."

"Well, good for you. Right you are."

"Well, so long, Uncle Homer."

For a moment Homer thought of telling his nephew that he was coming to spend the night with him, but then he thought better of it. It wouldn't do to insult the boy's pride. Homer would

sneak in and out of the house and John would never know he had been babysat with.

"So long, old man," said Homer.

He found the house dark. The only lights were dancing at the bottom of the lawn, the pale phosphorescent sparks of fireflies. For a moment Homer stood still and watched them. Then, turning around, he looked up at the second-floor windows of the house. Had Buddy gone to bed? It was still early, only eleven o'clock. Well, of course, Buddy was probably up the hill with that thieving politician Croney, who was about to snatch the governor's job away from Homer's old friend Mike Brumble. Goddamn the lot of them anyway.

John's room was at the other end of the house, in — what did they call it? — the shed. Homer had never been in the shed. Walking past the front door and around the corner of the house, he saw John's lighted window. But even as he stared up at it, looking for a glimpse of his nephew, the light went out. The boy was going to bed.

Homer went back to his car for his flashlight and his paper bag, and then he walked up the stone steps and entered the kitchen door, inhaling the pleasant smell of wood ashes and disintegrating plaster, and the indefinable scent of two-hundred-year-old boards. Flashlight in hand, he went upstairs, looking for Buddy.

The four upstairs bedchambers were empty, the beds unoccupied.

Buddy was elsewhere.

Homer went back to the large bedroom at the rear of the house. He guessed it had been Edward Heron's. Newly emptied of Edward's possessions and left impersonal, it stood ready for the miscellaneous guest.

The bed looked inviting. Homer turned off his flashlight, set down his paper bag, drew out his pajamas and fumbled at the buttons of his shirt. His camera was in the way. He began to lift it over his head, and then he stopped and sat down on the bed to think.

Was Virginia right in worrying about John's safety? Was Buddy a genuine threat? Turning the matter over in his mind, Homer slowly came to the conclusion that her fears were perfectly sensible.

The boy was a thorn in Buddy's side. It didn't take an expert in affairs of the heart to see that John's modest claims on Virginia's affection were a menace to Buddy's heavy-handed courtship, if you could call Buddy's territorial takeover of Virginia by so polite and old-fashioned a name. That was bad enough. But John had also thrown a monkey wrench into the great Buddy Whipple Roadworks by buying Mrs. Bewley's property, snatching it right out from under Buddy's nose. And now he had discovered the moving of the stone wall. John was in a position to expose Buddy's grubby devices for robbing Virginia and Barbara of their patrimony. For a skinny kid, the boy was a serious obstacle to the onward progress of wheeling and dealing and empire-building. There was no doubt about it. And there had already been one nasty little incident involving a black widow spider —

Sighing regretfully, Homer patted the plump pillow of the bed and got to his feet. Tonight his duty as a babysitter meant just what it said. He would be sitting up, not lying down.

Slowly Homer made a tour of the downstairs with his flashlight, latching doors, fastening bolts. In the kitchen entry he stood for a moment, staring at the door. There was no bolt to draw, no latch to fasten. There was only a Yale lock, and Buddy had a key.

Oh, God, what did a babysitter do in a time like this? Well, damnitall, he guarded the door. He sat up the whole bloody night and guarded the door. Homer sank heavily to the bottom step of the stairway to the second floor, remembering sentimentally the stalwart defenders who had stood at every entrance to Memorial Hall on a certain eventful evening in the past. That is, at every door but one. That door had been a fatal omission. Well, there were no secret entrances to this house. Homer had locked them all. All but this door right here, where he would sit stoutly awake the whole night through.

Leaning his head on the newel post, Homer closed his eyes for just a second, thinking bitterly about white-collar crime. Give him an honest burglar any day, a hardened criminal or a habitual strangler. Then you knew where you were at. These college-educated types were so erratic and undependable. You never knew what the hell they were going to do next.

Opening his eyes, Homer gazed up at the window on the landing, where a single star was visible, wheeling around the celestial pole. The star reminded him of Henry Thoreau, lying out-of-doors on a summer night, aware of the earth turning under him as a star moved slowly over his head. Maybe this star was Henry's star, this very star, still proving the rotation of the earth every night of the year as it circled the north pole of the sky. Homer stared at the star until it disappeared behind the stick of wood dividing one pane of glass from the next. Would the star come out on the other side? What if it didn't? What if the earth stopped turning on its axis at this very instant in the late summer of this year of God? Gazing faithfully upward, Homer pillowed his head on his arm and waited for the star to come back.

But he failed to see it emerge on the other side of the stick of wood and drift across the next pane of glass. It was not that the earth had ground to a halt. It was simply that Homer had fallen asleep. He was dreaming that he could fly. It was his favorite kind of dream, and Homer was delighted. Of course it wasn't flying, exactly. It was more like bounding. You just jumped gracefully upward and kept soaring slowly, higher and higher, until you landed in a tree. This time the tree was a colossal blue spruce, really immense. Homer came lightly to rest on a branch and looked all around at the snow-covered landscape. Brrrr, it was cold. What had happened to the rest of the summer and the autumn of the year? Winter had certainly come early. Vaulting gently upward, Homer landed on the windowsill of a tall building next to the tree. Other people were already poised on the edge of the window, drinking tea. "Lemon and sugar?" said a woman, her leg flung casually over the seventy-floor drop. There was a tremendous explosion. Homer dropped his teaspoon and woke up.

He was freezing. Where was he? Echoes of some monstrous noise were ricochetting in his head. Shambling to his feet, Homer fell off the step and hit his head on the opposite wall.

The noise, there had been a noise. It had sounded immense in his dream, like a gun going off in his ear. But now the reverberations had a muffled sound, as though something had exploded very far away at the other end of the house.

And then Homer remembered who he was and where he was and what he was supposed to be doing. He was supposed to be taking care of John. John! His nephew John was sleeping at the other end of the house! Homer's heart leaped into his mouth. In his blind rush he forgot his flashlight. Blundering through one dark room after another, he found himself struggling with the door to the laundry before it occurred to him to worry about his own safety. Someone might come at him with a gun. Well, who the hell cared? Homer didn't give a damn. All he could think of, as he tripped over one laundry basket after another, was his nephew John and the terrible silence in the house. Why in the hell was it so quiet? If John were alive and well, why wasn't he moving around upstairs?

With an anguished sense of foreboding, Homer stumbled clumsily up the pitch-black staircase. In a moment he was standing in John's open doorway, gazing in horror at the shadowy room, at the broken body on John's bed, at the fragments of John that lay all over the floor. A terrible sob burst from Homer. "Oh, the bloody bastard." Turning, he plunged, half falling, down the stairs again. Where in the hell was the bloody bastard? Oh, God, God, God, what would he say to John's father and mother?

Now there were noises in the house, jarring collisions of furniture — beyond the laundry, beyond the room next to the laundry. From the living room at the front of the house came a clatter and thud and a strangled oath.

With passionate presence of mind, Homer abandoned caution and pounded heavily through the book room, the coatroom, the dining room, and the narrow front hall where he had spent the night, and then he burst into the living room from an unexpected direction. In the grey light of dawn he found Buddy in front of him, his hand just reaching out for the knob of the hall door.

Homer took him by the throat, sobbing so hard he could hardly speak. "You filthy — filthy — he was only seventeen, you murdering bastard."

Buddy was bigger, younger, stronger. Taking hold of Homer's arms, he lifted him off his feet, then dropped him heavily. "What the hell do you think you're doing? What the hell?"

"What do you mean, what the hell? You know goddamn well what the hell. You blew my poor boy's guts out." With hot tears running down his face Homer lunged again at Buddy.

But Buddy merely held him at arm's length. "Look, you fool, I just came in. I was up the hill. For Christ's sake, why don't you go lie down? You see that door?" With one hand Buddy reached for the door of the kitchen entry and yanked it open. The vague grey morning light fell over them. "I just came in that door. If anything happened to that kid nephew of yours, it was that crazy TV repairman that did it. Listen, he may still be around here someplace. Why don't you call the police?" With a violent shove, Buddy pushed Homer backward against the stairs.

Falling, Homer threw out his hand to save himself, and encountered the flashlight. He picked it up and went for Buddy again. "You liar. You goddamned liar. You killed him yourself, you bastard."

Buddy seized the flashlight. "Stop making an ass of yourself. Call up Croney, why don't you? He'll tell you where I was. I tell you, I just walked in that door a minute ago."

Homer was nearly fainting with sorrow and rage and frustration. The bastard would get away with it again. He would weasel out of it again. But not if he were dead first. Blindly Homer threw his arms around Buddy and tried to grapple him to the floor. A lumpy object was grinding into Homer's chest — his camera, his goddamn camera. And then Homer grunted with shock, as something smashed against the side of his head. Blood began running down his ear as Buddy lifted the flashlight again.

With all his strength, Homer seized the arm that held the flashlight and hung on. *Jesus!* He was in no condition for hand-to-hand combat.

It was no good. With one jerk Buddy freed himself and pulled away.

Only then did Homer see what was in the open door. Beyond Buddy's upraised arm he caught a glimpse of something astonishing, something miraculous. For a moment he stopped breathing, and then before Buddy could bring the flashlight smashing down again, Homer sagged to his knees. The misdirected blow pitched Buddy forward against the wall. As he gasped and backed away and reared up over Homer again, Homer fumbled at his camera and lifted it to his eyes with trembling fingers. *Thank God for all that practice. Thank heaven for all those pictures of Benny splashing in his wading pool, Benny sleeping in his cot — would the flash work?*

It worked. In the dazzling momentary glare, Homer caught Buddy's shocked face against the spiderweb. Behind Buddy the great orb of silk stretched its concentric threads across the entire opening of the door. Upward to the lintel ran the supporting threads, and downward to the wooden sill. The falling temperature of dawn had strung the fragile strands with dew, and they were sharply visible in crystalline perfection. As a work of art, the spiderweb was not delicate and intricate like the webs of early summer. It was irregular and loosely woven, with careless gaps in the pattern, as if the whole thing had been thrown together heedlessly by a drunken craftsman.

But Homer was enchanted. "What do you mean, you just came in that door? That door isn't open. That door is locked like the tomb of the pharaoh and sealed with the pharaoh's seal." Homer's voice surprised him — it was loud and hoarse and panting. "You were in this house. You were in here all the time. You were waiting, just waiting. You fired that gun." Brushing roughly past Buddy, Homer spread his hand against the spiderweb and turned in triumph.

And then Buddy saw it too. He gaped at the spiderweb and dropped the flashlight. He tossed his arms. "Look, it's nothing.

It's just — for Christ's sake, it's only a spiderweb."

"Only a spiderweb?" Homer's voice broke with his sense of doom fulfilled. "Only a spiderweb! Only a force of nature, like an earthquake or a tidal wave. Only a volcano blowing up in your lying face." Reaching down, Homer snatched up the flashlight. It was slimy with something, and he was mildly surprised to discover that it was wet with his own blood. He lifted it over his head, trying to threaten Buddy with it as Buddy had threatened him, doubting at the same time that he could bring it down hard enough on Buddy's skull to do any good.

But Buddy seemed to be giving up. He was backing away, bending down, clawing at the floor. Homer faltered, the flashlight heavy in his hand. But Buddy was only looking for something. He found it. Raising it to his shoulder, he jammed it against Homer's face. Instinctively Homer brought down the flashlight and swept the muzzle aside as the gun went off. The shot shattered the kitchen window with a tinkling smash of glass. Buddy merely laughed and lifted the shotgun to fire again.

Homer's knees seemed to have lost any connection with his body. Stumbling backward, he turned and ducked under the tattered web in the doorway and dodged across the courtyard.

But he was a clumsy ox. As Buddy lunged after him, Homer tripped on the uneven flagstones and fell headlong. Behind his shuddering back he could sense Buddy taking aim again, and he struggled to his knees.

But instead of a point-blank explosion, there was only a high furious whine. Fiery needles pierced Homer's face and arms. Behind his back he heard a shriek, and then the rattling clatter of Buddy's shotgun as it fell to the ground. Batting feebly at the maddened cloud of flying hornets around his head, getting clumsily to his feet, Homer looked back to see Buddy claw at his face and fall to his knees.

There was a shout from the driveway. "He's down, Uncle Homer. They've got him. It's all right now."

Homer was completely befuddled. Whimpering with pain, he had only enough presence of mind to reach for Buddy's shotgun. Then he peered down the stone steps and was staggered to see a monstrous creature with an enormous head poking something into the bushes. The creature had a rake in its hands. It was jabbing the rake into the bushes, poking and twisting and grinding.

"John," croaked Homer, "oh, ouch, is that you? Oh, thank God, oh, goddamn. My God, boy, what's that on your head? What the hell do you think you're doing?"

It was John, all right. Homer's beloved nephew wasn't dead after all. He was wearing some kind of big hat with a veil hanging down all around. He was poking the rake into a hornet's nest. And now John was dropping the rake, running up the steps, flailing at Homer with gloved hands, brushing off hornets, dragging him down the steps and out of harm's way.

"Stay here, Uncle Homer," said John firmly. "Now just don't move, okay?" And then John ran back up the steps and stood over Buddy. "Hold still," he said, yanking at Buddy, trying to take hold of his shoulders.

Buddy couldn't hold still. He was rolling over and over as if his clothes were on fire, but the flames were a thousand infuriated white-faced hornets, affixed to his throat, his face, his bare arms. With one violent motion John dragged him to his feet. Then, sweeping and slapping at him, he began helping him down the steps. But Buddy was arching his spine, throwing back his head and staring sightless at the sky, and the sound of his agonized struggle for breath was a long-drawn-out grating, like dry pebbles over stone.

The sun was brimming over the treetops to the east as Homer's car pulled out of the driveway and plunged down the hill. On the lintel of the kitchen door, the barn spider was unaware of the morning's carnage. She failed to hear the shrill aimless droning of ten thousand homeless hornets, vengefully circling the wreckage of their gigantic shattered nest. Nor was she interested in the hanging remnants of her own broken web. Her eggs were heavy within her. Wedging her fat belly between the trellis and the clapboards, she settled herself in patient expectation of the moment for which she had been born.

Fifty-Five

MARY HEARD ONLY A GARBLED VERSION FROM HOMER ON THE phone. Snatching Benny out of bed, she popped him into his clothes and drove to Emerson Hospital. At the entrance to the emergency ward a policeman was lounging against the wall. Mary left Benny in his astonished charge and ran inside.

She found Homer and John in one of the curtained partitions. They were sitting side by side on the edge of the high cot. Homer's face and arms were blotched with welts. A bandage was wrapped around his head. Mary looked at him in horror. "A *spider* did that to you?" she said.

"No, no," said Homer. "Buddy clipped me on the side of the head. The rest of it was hornets. More of John's little friends. John smashed the nest, you see, just in time, and the hornets came roaring out, mad as hell."

"But what *happened?*"

"It was simply a case of Androcles and the lion," explained Homer, beaming at his wife, throwing his arm around his nephew. "John, here, he was Androcles. He nursed that spider along, and then she did him a favor in return. We've gone back to the Peacable Kingdom, you see, Mary, when the lion lay down with the lamb. You know, the Golden Age, when human beings lived in blissful harmony with their natural surroundings. It's sort of like, you know, the garden of Eden. That's all there is to it. Go ahead, John, you tell her."

John looked at his Aunt Mary and opened his mouth to speak. But then the white curtains parted and a doctor entered the partition. He was shaking his head, uttering words John had heard before.

"It was Buddy's own fault. I warned him to be careful. I told him another episode might kill him. Why wasn't he carrying his medicine? How could he have been so careless?"

Mary was astounded. "Buddy was supposed to be carrying medicine? You mean Buddy had asthma too?"

"Asthma?" The doctor looked blankly at Mary. "Not asthma. Allergy to insect bites, wasp stings and so on. Buddy Whipple was an old patient of mine. He'd been in serious trouble a couple of times before." The doctor shook his head in disbelief. "I told him over and over again he had to carry that stuff with him wherever he went, even in the heart of Boston. I told him about the man who was fatally stung by a bee on the floor of the stock exchange."

"How horrible," breathed Mary.

"I finally guessed it," said John. "I mean, I put two and two together at last. Homer said Virginia found the red box of medicine in that rabbit hole, but the epinephrin in the hypodermic needle was all gone. So I thought, what if Buddy had used it on himself? What if he snatched it away from Mr. Heron and took the dose himself? And I remembered the yellow jacket bites on Buddy, and I looked up epinephrin, because Benny said Buddy had a prescription for it, and the dictionary said it was adrenalin."

"Adrenalin!" said Mary.

"Of course," said the doctor. "Anybody who has a hypersensitivity to insect bites should carry adrenalin."

"Did you know that?" said Mary, looking at John with wonder.

"Well, I wasn't sure, but I remembered what Buddy was like after Mr. Heron died. He had this really terrific strength. It was the adrenalin, right?"

268

"Ah, you noticed it, did you?" said the doctor.

"You should have seen him. He tossed Mr. Heron up on his shoulder and carried him uphill as if he were, you know, a baby. And Mr. Heron was big. I mean, he must have weighed two hundred pounds."

"You pay for it later, of course," said the doctor. "The super energy lasts for a while, and then you're super exhausted." The doctor departed, after asking a grim question or two about the disposal of Buddy's remains.

Outside the hospital Benny was wearing the policeman's hat and entertaining his guardian with grisly tales from the brothers Grimm. "Worst things I ever heard," said the policeman, looking up with a white face. "Murder, incest, cannibalism. Take him back. He's all yours. Cute little kid though."

Homer was worn out. "A little nap," he said. "All I want is my nice soft bed." But when Homer and Mary and Benny drove up to the house on Barretts Mill Road, they found Benny's mother and father and his sister Miranda and his brother Freddy tumbling out of a taxi in the driveway, fresh from Logan Airport and two days on a jet and three months in the foothills of the Himalayas. There were cries of welcome, embraces, horrified gasps at Homer's bandages, incoherent explanations. John was summoned. There were presents from the mysterious East and a noisy, alcoholic lunch. It wasn't until John went home again and the homecoming travelers had dragged themselves upstairs to bed for long afternoon naps, it wasn't until a yawning Homer had undressed too, and struggled into his pajamas and pulled back the covers and climbed between the cozy inviting sheets, that he remembered the body in John's bed.

He was electrified with horror. If he could forget a *dead body*, he was really over the hill. Rushing downstairs, he snatched up the telephone and shouted at the chief of the Lincoln police department. A moment later he was hurtling down Barretts Mill Road, zooming around the rotary, and barreling along Route 2.

But the chief's car was just pulling out of the driveway as Homer bounced to a stop and catapulted out of the driver's seat.

"Hey, wait a minute," he bellowed, running over to bend down into the window and stare goggle-eyed at the chief. "Whose body was it? Where are you going? What's the big idea?"

"Listen, friend," grinned the police chief, "it was just an old stuffed shirt, that's all. One stuffed shirt more or less in the world, who cares? Not me. Hey, what do you call that?" The chief snickered and poked a finger at Homer's striped pajamas. "Some kind of fancy new leisure suit?"

Homer stared after the chief's car, scandalized by the display of callousness to human life on the part of the man responsible for law enforcement in the town of Lincoln, Massachusetts. His nephew set him straight. "I'm sorry, Uncle Homer," said John, leading the way through the house in the direction of his bedroom in the shed. "I forgot to tell you what I did." At the top of the narrow stairs he stood back to let Homer survey the disemboweled scarecrow that still lay on the bed, and the bits of rag and stuffing scattered all over the floor.

"I just holed up in my sleeping bag in the closet," said John. "You could have smelled the difference, if you'd tried. Smell that hay?" John sniffed the air. "It doesn't smell much like blood and guts, does it, Uncle Homer? Just nice old hay." John cocked his head and went to the window. "Listen, there's a car outside."

It was Virginia and Barbara, back from New York.

John hung back and watched through the kitchen window as they got out of the car. They were smiling with surprise at Homer as he came down the stone steps in his pajamas and took their hands. He was telling them about Buddy. Would Virginia be unhappy? She was listening intently. She wasn't crying. She was taking a breath —

Virginia felt the air enter her lungs and fill them. It was dry and light. It flowed into deep passages, and there was room for more. Taking another breath, she looked up to see the sky lift and lift until it was remote and blue and infinitely far away, no longer a lowering roof, imprisoning her in a thick haze. The gigantic fly's eye that had been gazing down at her all summer with its billion flickering lenses withdrew too, and vanished.

"Well, then," said Barbara, "that's over then." She grinned at Homer and gave a great whooping laugh. "I must say, I like your outfit. I've always been partial to purple stripes myself."

Virginia went indoors to find John, and together they looked for the spider. They found her easily. She was clinging to her egg sac. It was a nest of yellowish-white gossamer at the top of the kitchen door.

"I guess she's made her last web," said John. "Now she'll die, and her eggs will hatch next spring."

Impulsively he turned to Virginia. There was something important he wanted to tell her before he went off to school, a matter of tremendous consequence, the most crucial thing of all, the thing that had been building up in his chest all summer, only he didn't know how to put it into words. So he said something absurd, and then Virginia said something preposterous, but together they made themselves understood.

"I'll get older as fast as I can," said John earnestly.

"I'll stay just the same," promised Virginia.

Fifty-Six

HOWARD CRONEY'S LAWYER WAS ON THE PHONE. "LOOK, MR. Kelly, all my client wants to know is, can he go on using Buddy Whipple's house for a campaign headquarters? There's still a couple of weeks to go before the Democratic caucus, and it would be a real hardship to move out now. Is the place in probate court? Did Whipple leave it to somebody? Has anybody found a last will and testament? Who's in charge?"

"Not me," said Homer testily. But when nobody else came forward, he was left holding the bag. With a court order in hand, he was permitted to see the contents of Buddy's safe deposit box in the Concord bank. Homer sat with Mary in the basement of the bank and turned the key in the big metal container.

"Look at that silver-plated tea service," said Mary. "Black as coal. Imagine trying to clean all those little curlicues."

"Not much paper in here," said Homer. "Just these two things at the bottom. Looks like a couple of letters."

The first piece of paper had been folded many times. It was nearly worn through at the creases.

"Oh, look, Homer," said Mary, "that's Barbara Heron's signature at the bottom." She read it aloud to Homer, pausing once or twice to suck in an astonished breath.

On the evening of December 10, 1980, I administered a fatal dose of morphine to Mr. George Whipple at his home in Lincoln, Massachusetts. Mr. Whipple had been ill for many weeks with terminal cancer. I had been acting as his nurse during that time, and living in his house. Mr. Whipple was in intense and continuous pain, nearly uncontrollable by drugs. During the entire period of my care I was under constant pressure from my patient to bring his torment to an end. At last his suffering was so excruciating that I couldn't bear it anymore. I agreed, in the belief that such an action on my part would be humane, and that I would myself wish it if I were in his position.

Barbara Heron, RN

The other piece of paper in the safe deposit box was an envelope addressed in a faltering hand, to Clarence. The letter within was a message of farewell from George Whipple to his son Buddy.

To Clarence, a loving good-bye and a last request. I am deeply grateful to my kind neighbor and nurse, Barbara Heron, for caring for me in my last illness. I am especially indebted to her for taking the courageous action that will bring my ordeal to an end. She has refused to accept wages. Please make her a gift of ten thousand dollars from what you yourself will receive at my death.

I know you will carry out my wish faithfully. Your loving father . . .

"Look at that scrawled signature," murmured Mary, and for a moment they gazed at it, imagining the old man dropping the pen, sealing the envelope and holding out his trembling arm for the injection that would relieve his suffering forever.

"So that was it," said Homer. "That was what Buddy had on Barbara. I'll bet he never gave her that ten thousand. I'll bet he made her write that statement, and then he called her a murderer and threatened to expose her and get her debarred or decapped or decapitated, or whatever they do to forbid registered nurses from practicing their calling."

"What a rotten piece of interfering malevolence that man was," said Mary. "So that's why she stopped working."

"And then after Edward Heron's death, Buddy began bullying Virginia. He told her Barbara was a — what do you call it? — patricide. First she had killed *his* father, and then she had brought about the death of her own. And he said he would spread the news, and ruin Barbara's life, unless Virginia went along with his schemes. And of course Virginia's mouth was sealed. She wouldn't tell Barbara about Buddy's threats, because she thought Barbara would rush out in the street and admit to any kind of ugly crime rather than see Virginia herself go down Buddy's rancid drain. It was a case of doubly mistaken generosity and puritanical self-immolation. Oh, these old-fashioned New Englanders! Any sign of another document in that box? Last will and testament of Clarence Whipple, Esquire?"

"No, nothing at all," said Mary. "Where can it be? Maybe he didn't have one. Or maybe he stored it in his room at the Herons' house with all his other stuff." They drove to Lincoln to take a look. Barbara was there to meet them. They gave her the envelope and the folded piece of paper.

"What's this?" said Barbara.

"We found them in Buddy's safe deposit box," said Mary. "You might just want to dispose of them somehow."

"I suggest a small bonfire," said Homer wisely. "Now, Barbara, may we go upstairs and take a look at Buddy's things?"

"I cleared them all out," said Barbara. "It was a pleasure. I just dumped everything in cardboard boxes and stowed them in the laundry."

And there in the laundry, Homer and Mary found what they were looking for. Kneeling on the floor behind a wooden drying rack dripping with wet socks, they fished a thick wad of legal papers out of the inside pocket of one of Buddy's sports jackets. Mary smoothed the folded sheets on top of the washing machine, and together they read Buddy Whipple's intentions for the disposition of his earthly effects.

His possessions were many and great — an enormous, heavily

274

furnished house, a number of parcels of land, and a large holding in securities and investments, itemized on an appended sheet.

"But who gets it all now?" said Mary, flipping over the pages. "I don't think he had any close relatives, do you?" Then Mary found the name of the beneficiary, and tapped it with her finger. "Virginia Heron. It all goes to Virginia."

"No kidding? Some tax dodge, I'll bet," growled Homer. "Some wily scheme or other."

"No, Homer, you're wrong about that. I think in his clumsy overbearing way Buddy really loved her. He didn't know what to do about it. He didn't know how to make her love him in return. He thought if he could once get hold of her by force, then he could persuade her to be happy. What would it matter that giant trucks were careening past her old front door, now that she was up the hill among all the moose heads and hunting prints and all that faded grandeur? How could she help but love him back?" Mary shook her head with wonder. "Poor old goofy sinister simpleminded Buddy."

Homer took his wife's hand. "It's funny how physical force just doesn't seem to work with some women. They're stubborn. They get their backs up. You have to edge around them when they're not looking, and then sneak up behind them and just" — tenderly Homer pulled back Mary's collar — "drop a live frog down their neck."

"Homer, you beast!" Mary arched her back, reached awkwardly inside her shirt, pulled out a wet sock, and threw her guffawing husband to the floor.

Fifty-Seven

FIRST RESIDENT MOVES
INTO "THE LODGE"

Bringing with her only a large house-
plant, Mrs. Alice Bewley, 79, today
moved into one of the ground floor
apartments of "The Lodge," Lincoln's
new low-income housing complex, once
the hunting estate of Alexander Higginson. House and grounds were the
gift of neighboring resident Virginia
Heron to Cambridge Housing Associates, Jane Plankton, president.

The same firm will build another unit
of low-income housing on Route 126
on the foundation of a house destroyed
by fire. This property was recently acquired by Ms. Heron, along with an
additional 15 acres of woodland. Six of
the 15 acres will be zoned for conservation, the rest given to the Walden
Pond Reservation.

"Oh, Lord," said Homer, putting down the *Concord Journal*,
"imagine Mrs. Bewley in Alexander Higginson's great hall. She'll

have her little chickens roosting on those moose antlers, you see if she doesn't."

"Oh, no, she won't," said Mary firmly. "Barbara gave her an enormous cat. You should have seen it, Homer. She found this crazy longhaired kind, and it has six or seven toes on each paw. She said Mrs. Bewley took to it right away. You know the way Mrs. Bewley talks — OH, THE DARLING KITTY. It was a big success. She's going to call it Maxie."

Homer laughed, remembering all that he had heard about the original Maxie and his fellow chickens, gone but not forgotten, departed and, alas, digested. "Well, it's a mercy the strip of woods around the corner is going to the Walden Pond Reservation. With good old Mike Brumble in the governor's office for another four years, his conservation lawyers will be able to make the donation stick. If Croney had been elected, God knows what would have happened to it. Thank God, he lost the nomination."

For Howard Croney had been defeated. In the long run it was not his cupidity that did him in, nor his flagrant and manifold conflicts of interest. It was simple old-fashioned lust. On the day before the Democratic caucus, Madeline Croney had driven to her husband's campaign headquarters with a pile of freshly laundered shirts. Leaving her little yellow car idling in the courtyard, she had carried the shirts in the front door. Sixty seconds later she burst out the door again, flung the shirts into the bushes, jumped into her car, plunged down the driveway, swerved violently out onto Route 126, raced down Route 2 across the Charles River, and screeched to a halt beside the NO PARKING sign in front of the television studios of Channel 4 on Soldiers Field Road. Stalking past the startled receptionist, Madeline pushed through a door marked STOP DO NOT ENTER, tramped past a crew of stupefied cameramen, brushed aside the astounded meteorologist, presented herself to the cameras before a glorious satellite photograph of the northern hemisphere, and announced to the world that her husband was in bed with a Sunday school teacher.

"So if you were planning to vote for him," said Mrs. Croney, "don't. Take it from me, he's a jerk."

Croney's defeat was a disappointment to Putnam Farhang. The insurance portfolio of the Commonwealth of Massachusetts would continue to be distributed among a number of New England firms, only one of which was the Paul Revere Mutual Life Insurance Company. And Putnam's wife suffered her own moment of mortification. At the October competition of the Middlesex County Society of Flower Arrangers, Amelia Farhang failed, after all, to win the grand prize for creativity.

"She lost?" said Effie Fawcett, unable to believe her ears. "Those judges must have been out of their minds."

But it wasn't the judges' fault. And it certainly wasn't Amelia Farhang's. Amelia had spent an entire month in rapt concentration in her greenhouse, surrounded by masses of plant material and miscellaneous accessories. Her entry was a tropical fantasy, featuring a Venus flytrap and an assortment of elements flown in from Puerto Rico — a bunch of bananas, a gigantic frond of palm, and a spray of magenta orchids. But at the last moment, just as the judges were approaching her booth, Amelia reached out to adjust the palm leaf at the back of her composition. At that instant a large hairy mygalomorph spider was awakened by the heat from the bright light overhead. Coming out of hiding in the bananas, it ran briskly up her arm. With a wild shriek, Mrs. Farhang threw it across the room. Her hand struck the container. Slowly, fatally, the vase wobbled on its base, toppled, and fell to the floor with a crash. Amelia shrieked and shrieked. One of the judges slapped her face. The Venus flytrap caught a fly. The spider landed unhurt and crawled behind a chair.

But the barn spider on the door frame of the house at the bottom of Pine Hill was at the end of her days. John checked up on her whenever he came home from school, and kept a record. All through November and December she hung upsidedown beside her egg sac. Without a web she could catch nothing, and therefore she ate nothing. Even when John offered her a live moth, presenting it to her in a pair of tweezers, she showed **no** interest. She merely edged away and settled down on the other side of her egg sac. And when he looked for her in January after his first-semester exams, she was nowhere to be seen.

I wish I knew whether she froze to death or died of starvation, wrote John in his notebook.

Or maybe she just died of old age. Her egg sac looks great though, really fluffy and warm. All those little embryo spiders are well cushioned against the cold. Some nice warm day in spring they'll work their way out of the egg sac, and then there'll be barn spiders all over the place.

Spring was early that year. In the wilderness of the old orchard the cloudy blossoming tops of the apple trees were visible from Baker Bridge Road. Rabbits multiplied in the rabbit holes. Pheasants laid clutches of yellow-green eggs in the low tangle of catbrier. Sheetweb spiders spread their horizontal veils in every chink of the stone wall, and three newborn yellow jacket queens set up housekeeping under projecting boulders.

And as the days lengthened and the grass in front yards turned green, John's little brother Benny discovered baseball. His father bought him a ball and a bat and a tiny glove for his sixth birthday, and to everyone's surprise, Benny's entire personality underwent a dramatic change. He abandoned all intellectual pursuits. He joined the Peewee League and gave his heart to the game. But, alas for poor Benny! He was the worst hitter on the team and he just couldn't seem to catch the ball at all.

Neither could his Uncle Homer. Of course Homer had never claimed to be skillful at sports of any kind, being clumsy and butterfingered by birth and utterly lacking in natural physical grace. *But he was better at baseball than Benny.* With lordly condescension Homer took the boy under his wing on Saturday mornings, and taught him how to bunt to the infield and catch a pop fly and pitch a wild curve ball into the bushes.

The Spider as an Artist
Has never been employed —
Though his surpassing Merit
Is freely certified

By every broom and Bridget
Throughout a Christian Land —
Neglected Son of Genius
I take thee by the Hand —

Emily Dickinson

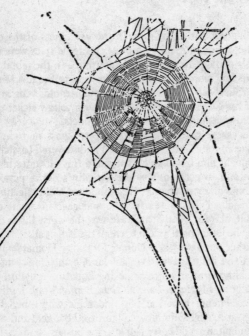

Afterword

ALEXANDER HIGGINSON'S HUNTING ESTATE IN LINCOLN WAS BROKEN up in 1939, and its subsequent history is of course different from the fictional account in this book. Less than two acres of land were sold with the eighteenth-century farmhouse at the foot of the hill. The pond and its adjacent field are now owned by a neighbor. The other fields, the woods, and the old orchard belong to the Lincoln Conservation Trust. Mrs. Bewley's house is imaginary. So is the Second Parish Church, which bears no relation whatever to Lincoln's estimable First Parish.

The characters are imaginary too. Even Jane Plankton has lost all resemblance to any living soul. Only her musical ineptitude in *The Memorial Hall Murder* was actually drawn from life.

A number of people have been friendly to this book. I am grateful to Chuck Howarth of Boston's Museum of Science and Chris Lahey of the Massachusetts Audubon Society. Laura Lougee of Parsonsfield, Maine, was generous with her knowledge of barn spiders. My indebtedness is especially great to Professor Herbert Levi of Harvard's Museum of Comparative Zoology and to his wife Lorna for their kindness in answering questions about spiders, and for helping me gather a small spider zoo of my own. John Hunter, curatorial assistant in the museum, found the New Hampshire barn spider whose eggs have now hatched above my laundry door.

My thanks go also to Ralph Macone, Dr. Gordon Winchell, Lincoln assessor Douglas Burckett, meteorologist Don Kent, and Anne McGrath, curator of the Thoreau Lyceum. The story couldn't have been written at all without the help of the Flints of Lincoln — Margaret and Warren Flint, Senior, and Warren Flint, Junior. Their good suggestions were drawn from a family history of several hundred years of land use in this Massachusetts town.